WARRIOR KING

BRITAIN: THE SEVENTH CENTURY

GODS AND KINGS
BOOK 3

MJ PORTER

MJ PUBLISHING

Copyright notice
Porter, M J
Warrior King (also published as Winwæd – a novel of 655)
Copyright ©2016, 2022, 2023 Porter, M.J,
All characters and events in this publication, other than those clearly in the public domain, are fictitious and any resemblance to actual persons, living or dead, is purely coincidental.

ALL RIGHTS RESERVED. No part of this publication may be reproduced, stored in a retrieval system or transmitted in any form or by any means without the prior written permission of the author, nor be otherwise circulated in any form of binding or cover other than that in which it is published and without a similar condition being imposed on the subsequent buyer.
ISBN: 9781914332203 (kindle)
ISBN: 9781796531510 (paperback)
ISBN: 9781914332227 (paperback)
ISBN: 9781914332517 (hardback)

❦ Created with Vellum

CONTENTS

Prologue	7
1. Penda, King of Mercia *Late Summer, AD651*	15
2. Penda, King of Mercia *Summer AD653*	23
3. Paeda of the Hwicce *Summer AD653*	29
4. Oswiu, King of Bernicia *Summer AD653*	37
5. Cynewise of Mercia *Summer AD653*	42
6. Æthelwald, King of Deira *Summer AD653*	52
7. Penda, King of Mercia *Early AD654*	56
8. Paeda of the Hwicce *Early AD654*	61
9. Oswiu, King of Bernicia *Summer AD654*	65
10. Alhflæd of Bernicia *Summer AD654*	76
11. Æthelwald of Deira *Summer AD654*	82
12. Penda, King of Mercia *Summer AD654*	86
13. Paeda of The Hwicce *Summer AD654*	92
14. Oswiu, King of Bernicia *Summer AD654*	99
15. Cynewise of Mercia *Winter AD654*	105
16. Æthelwald of Deira *Ad655*	108
17. Penda, King of Mercia *Ad655*	118
18. Paeda of the Hwicce *Ad655*	126

19. Oswiu, King of Bernicia *Ad655*	138
20. Talorcan, King of the Picts *Ad655*	141
21. Æthelwald of Deira *Summer AD655*	151
22. Penda, King of Mercia *Ad655*	160
23. Paeda of the Hwicce *Ad655*	164
24. Oswiu, King of Bernicia *Ad655*	169
25. Herebrod *Ad655*	175
26. Penda, King of Mercia *November AD655*	181
27. Paeda of the Hwicce *November AD655*	187
28. Oswiu, King of Bernicia *November AD655*	193
29. Æthelwald of Deira *November AD655*	196
30. Penda, King of Mercia *November 15th AD655*	198
31. Paeda of The Hwicce *November 15th AD655*	206
32. Oswiu, King of Bernicia *November 15th AD655*	213
33. Penda, King of Mercia *The Battle of Winwæd*	219
34. Paeda of the Hwicce *15th November AD655*	224
35. Oswiu, King of Bernicia *November 15th AD655*	236
36. Penda, King of Mercia *November 15th AD655*	244
37. Paeda of the Hwicce *November 15th AD655*	247
Epilogue	251

Cast of Characters	255
Historical notes	259
Primary Source Material	263
The Anglo-Saxon Chronicle	265
Or perhaps it happened like this???? (historical notes part 2)	267
About the Author	269
Books by M J Porter (in chronological order)	271

PROLOGUE
PENDA, KING OF MERCIA, AUGUST 5TH AD651, MASERFIELD

The site of the slaughter field is little changed. Every year I make this journey, and every time I expect the place to have altered beyond all recognition, to have finally wiped away the curse of the battle. Every year I'm disappointed and pleased to see so little altered.

My older brother lost his life here fighting King Oswald of Northumbria and, worse, at Oswald of Northumbria's hands. Yet somehow, and I find this the bitterest reminder of that battle, Oswald's death is honoured by the men of his kingdom and, further afield, by the men of their bloody Christianity.

But it was my brother who died here, my brother who deserves to be remembered, not Oswald. Oswald was a fool, buoyed by his belief in his Christianity and his God-given right to rule a kingdom, to rule all the Saxons' kingdoms.

I smirk angrily. The rage has never left me, even ten years later. My hatred for Oswald knows no end. Times have changed dramatically for my family, my wife, my sons and daughters, my nephew and niece, but the fury never diminishes. I doubt it ever will.

Oswald took my brother's life when he had no right to it. Oswald was merely a puppet dressed in the clothes he felt made him a warrior god. It was my brother who was truly the warrior. Eowa proved his worth and his ability in that final battle. I miss him every day and will continue to do so until I meet him again, feasting with our father and Woden.

If Oswald hadn't died on the edge of Herebrod's blade that day, I'd have spent the last ten years trying to seek vengeance against him. I'm grateful that Oswald found his death when he did, but the stories surrounding that death never fail to enrage me.

Oswald's religious men have managed to elaborate on how he died to make him into some sort of Christian martyr that their priests prattle on about in their long sermons. They revere Oswald. Pray for Oswald. I'm told there's even a lucrative trade in tiny splinters of wood alleged to have come from his holy wooden cross. He raised the very one against King Cadwallon at the Battle of Heavenfield, so named for Oswald's God-provided success and murder of Cadwallon. It's ludicrous to me. Cadwallon was a Christian. What power did Oswald have over a man of the same faith? Why would this God punish one of his followers and not the other?

If I weren't so angry, I might find the whole thing entertaining, but every year, on the anniversary of my brother's murder, I come here, and I mark the place where Oswald slew him. On that day, I find nothing humorous, failing to find any pride in my accomplishments since Eowa's death. On that day, I became what I'd always wanted to be, king of Mercia. But at my brother's expense. I never wanted that.

My brother and I were brothers first and only then allies or enemies. We played complex games with each other and even more so with our allies and enemies. Eowa shared my upbringing. Yet he thought in different ways. He didn't always see the answer lying in someone's death. I do believe that in the end, he realised that for our kingdom to be secure and for us to hold what our father had always desired, we needed to be ruthless and fair but also brutal in ensuring our successes.

Other kings, most notably Edwin and Oswald of Northumbria, tried to use the word of their God to gain what they wanted, subverting the wishes of their religion to their own; to rule every speaks to me here of things I've done and things he wanted to do that I must accomplish in his place.

I close my eyes, allowing the swirling memories of my past to form before my eyes. I see it all, as I did ten years ago, the long funnel that opened between the two warring sides and revealed the fierce personal battle between the uneasy allies and then bitter enemies, Eowa and Oswald. The two men had been grudging allies, but as soon as they became enemies, their true feelings toward each other played out before me on this battlefield.

I blame myself for my brother's death. I thought I'd taken reasonable care to ensure his survival. But I was wrong, so very, very wrong. This pilgrimage is as much to find comfort for me as it is to honour my brother.

Herebrod shares my pain. Of them all, he knows how much I tried to ensure my brother lived, and that the victory was ours and not just mine.

We're two foolish old men, each blaming the other for something almost beyond our control.

Together we walk the length and breadth of the old shield wall. As clear as though two thousand men stand before me in all their battle gear, grim-faced, cheering, or just downright scared, I can see it all. I torment myself with what might have been, comparing it to reality. But time is man's enemy, and with each year, a little more fades, and another small detail is forgotten. I fear that my brother will be overlooked, along with those small specifies; swept away from me like mist on a summer's day, and when I'm gone, they'll be few who remember, and even fewer who care about this battle, fought in the heat of a fiery summer.

I can't allow that to happen. His dynasty must endure. Our dynasty must last.

We were the warrior sons of Pybba, and we should still be.

Only we're not, and that grief has stayed my hand throughout the past ten years. I've not shied away from battle and war, but I've thought more before I acted, almost as though Eowa guides my steps, although no longer by my side. He was always the more cautious, the claims the kingdom, a man far more amenable toward me. A sort of peace exists between Oswine and me. For now. I know that Oswiu won't stay locked behind his borders forever. I understand that the curse of his family's honour runs in his blood. He still sees himself as a king of all his brother once claimed.

I disagree, and so does Oswine, and for now, we keep him at bay.

With the horse gone and Herebrod at my side, I'm too vividly reminded of the battle's outcome. It's known as Maserfeld, so now I have two great battles to my name, Hæðfeld and Maserfeld. One more must come. All great warriors face their enemies three times before they triumph once and for all. The skalds say as much in the old tales, and the British kingdoms agree on the power of three.

I've faced down Edwin and Oswald; there's only one more who can wish to attack me, Oswiu. He has his Christianity and his blood feud. They're a heady combination, so I keep Herebrod even closer to me than before, and his wife now lives amongst my people. Herebrod can no more travel to the home of the Picts than he can to Valhalla before his death occurs.

He misses his wife's home but understands my reasoning. He'd much rather be alive than dead. He'd much rather serve me than be hidden away in the land of the northern Picts.

Yet, my mind drifts. I've come to commemorate my brother. I must do so as I force my mind back to thoughts of Eowa.

His body doesn't lie here. I didn't wish it to, and neither did his warriors, instead returning him to his stronghold at Tamworth and the family barrow there. But for me, it's always the battlefield where Eowa lost his life where I feel closest to him. Here, in this place, I can hear the fleeting whispers of the battle as they once unfolded. I can still feel him in my arms as I embraced him that one last time, his body young and strong, melding with mine as we took on our Godlike qualities before beginning the battle we thought would make us the most famous kings on this island.

I can smell Eowa too. The stench of the battle on his skin after his death, the iron of blood and the leather of his clothes. I think Eowa aftermath with which to contend. He's like a child with no idea of the events that have influenced his parents' lives and cares even less for them.

Freki's a jarring reminder that the death I come to commemorate will one day mean nothing to anyone when we're all long dead and buried.

I forgive Freki, however. There are others here who were at the battle and know its impact on me.

Herebrod, resembling more and more the great angry bear I once thought him to be, and as grey as I am now, has returned to me from the northern lands of the Picts and stands at my side. His horse is more content to bend his head and pick at the grass beneath his hooves.

I consider if the grass still bears the tang of the blood of that battle. So many men died, so much blood was shed in the name of Woden and of this Christian God, that I imagine the grass grows so green here because the blood of those lost men and women nourishes it. The horses that at least pretend to stillness must know what happened here, just as surely as I do.

Herebrod is silent at my side, and so are my sons and daughters, niece and nephew, who accompany me on my vigil. Even my wife, Cynewise, rides with me, but she waits at the group's rear. This is the time for my pilgrimage, not hers, and she knows it.

She never disliked my brother, but they didn't know each other well. Her feelings at his death were ambiguous, but she raised his son and daughter as though they were her own following their mother's death. They love her as they should a mother. And me, well, they fear me, as they should a great warrior and leader of their tribe. But they also know that they can rely on me as their surrogate father and the leader of that self-same tribe.

They're my family. I'll never lose another member of it in battle, and certainly not on Northumbrian blades.

The idea makes me smirk, finally finding some humour in the day. Northumbria is no more, despite Oswiu's best efforts, Oswald's brother. Oswiu rules now only in Bernicia, and in Deira, another man kingdom on our island, and with the connivance of their priests. I was always far more blatant in my wishes. I wanted the kingdom of the Hwicce, and then I wanted Mercia. Now I have those two desires, but only at my brother's expense, and that was never the agreement I reached with my god, Woden. I asked only for what I felt was my due, gained through blood, sweat, effort and stealth.

I didn't want to win what my brother held unfairly, and in his death, I see something else at play. Be it the Spinners who guide our path or the treacherous ways of Oswald and his bloody Christianity, I don't know. I've never felt any malice in their religion from anyone but Oswald and his hated uncle, Edwin. Those two stepped straight from the hell of which their priests so often speak.

Men and women think Edwin and Oswald holy and not the great fiends I perceive them to have been. With their words and stories, these clerics somehow infiltrate the minds of men and women better than I do. They offer charming tales of holy martyrs. The images they paint inside the mind have a more lurid impact on men and women used to blood and death in their old faith, my faith.

It tires me, this constant battle as to who has the greatest God, the more prominent call on the loyalty of others. I know my feelings and belief. I know it to be correct. That's it—end of discussion.

Beneath me, my horse shifts, and I remember old Gunghir. He's gone now, the cantankerous old bastard. His death was difficult, just as his life was, but I miss him every day, grateful only that the beast beneath me shares some, if not all, of his grandsire's personality. He's named Freki, or Woden's wolf. I like the name, even if it doesn't quite match my horse's spirit.

One of my new beast's most significant failings is his inability to be still for even a moment. In this, he's like the prowling wolf for whom he's named. I take pity on him on this occasion. It's a hot day, and I'm weighing him down with my byrnie, battle armour, sword, shield and helm, worn to honour my brother.

I slide from Freki's back and smack his rump, a sign that I'm happy for him to meander off if he needs to, which he promptly does. He wasn't here for the battle; he wasn't born until there was only the more rational, my wife says with a wry smile when she speaks of him, or I vent my frustration at my more sedate ways.

I miss my brother.

Yet the time will come, and sooner rather than later, when I'll need to make war again, and on such a vast scale as I already have twice before. I'll need to ensure that Oswiu meets his death before I meet mine.

My sons, nephew, and younger brother are all warriors of great renown. But Oswiu is biding his time, waiting for the opportunity to claim what he thinks his brother lost at Maserfeld. I must ensure he not only fails to accomplish that but that he dies before he can set events in motion.

I've fought King Edwin and killed him.

I've fought King Oswald and killed him.

I'll fight Oswiu and ensure he meets the same fate.

The bloody Northumbrians must understand that the lands of the middle kingdom, the realm of the Mercians, is not theirs for the taking.

I'll ensure they learn that lesson well before I die and that the kingdom my son or nephew inherits is as secure as I can make it.

I stumble to the ground, landing where I know I cradled my brother's cooling body ten years ago. Tears fill my eyes and splash silently onto the ground that I still envisage is awash with my brother's life force, as though I weep tears of blood for his loss.

Ten years is a long time to be apart, but not long enough to have forgotten him or forgiven his murderer and the man who gained from the death of that self-same murderer.

Never that.

The passage of time is suddenly as nothing. I'm biding my time, just as surely as Oswiu is doing.

1

PENDA, KING OF MERCIA
LATE SUMMER, AD651

The news of King Oswiu's presumptuous actions reached me as I returned to Tamworth following my annual trip to Maserfeld. My smirk had been wry. How apt that one moment, I was contemplating my coming battle with Oswiu, and the next, he'd given me the perfect opening to attack him.

Hastily, my men had gathered. Some of my warriors were sent to the far reaches of my kingdom to protect it from any who chose to attack it in my absence. The rest had made ready to travel to Bernicia to punish Oswiu for his actions in killing my ally, Oswine, king of Deira, friend to Mercia, and more importantly, my personal friend.

Now, as I sit upon my horse, gazing at the coastal stronghold of Bamburgh, a place I've heard spoken of in hushed and awed tones, I can almost understand that respect. It truly looks as unreachable as men and women say. It speaks of a challenge just by its placement, but it is a contest that thrills me.

I've come to punish King Oswiu of Bernicia, and so far, he's put up almost no resistance, even though I'm deep within the kingdom he purports to rule. Where are his warriors? Where are his ealdormen protecting his people from the ferocity of my attack? It's almost as though Oswiu taunts me, so I've been careful in my advances. The year grows old, and the weather is chill, much colder than in my kingdom. It reminds me of when we attacked King Edwin of Northumbria at Hæðfeld all those years ago. Soon the rains and the freezing mists will form. But first, well, first, I must ensure that Oswiu is aware that he can't arrange the murder of those who stand in his way of claiming the kingdom his brother once ruled.

There must be rules of inheritance and eligibility, even in this unsettled time in which we live.

The fortress of Bamburgh, or Bebbanburg as some might say the name, is not as huge as I thought it would be. But I can't deny that its positioning is sound. It's almost impenetrable from land or sea. Yet, it must have a weakness, if not a flaw, then at least a way for me to bring Oswiu to justice for his actions.

Amongst my men, I already have a man who claims the kingdom of Deira in place of Oswine. I've ensured he'll hold his kingdom, despite Oswiu's wishes. Oswiu has no right to play kingmaker. Neither do I. Each realm must choose its king. All I can do is try and influence the loyalty of that king, with force if I must. I don't wish to rule anyone directly but my people, the Mercians, the people of the borders.

Even though we share our ancestry, the people of Kent, the West Saxons, and even the East Angles, each kingdom has nuances that I don't understand or even want to understand. To be the more dominant king takes knowing how to gain the loyalty of my adherents. It doesn't mean that I must directly rule men and women who would only resent my interference and see it as a malign involvement.

No, I believe in a light touch. I'd never meddle in the minds of men and women. Their beliefs are theirs to hold as they wish to do so. No king should have the power to enforce their views on their followers. It's only fitting that a ruler can entice them to war or induce them to rage, but not to a religion or a God that they don't wish to worship. What God would want men to revere them when they don't want to? Only a weak God, one who simply wants followers, whether their belief is genuine or not.

A feeble God will accomplish nothing with weak men to do his bidding.

I don't ride alone. I never do, and as I sit on my eager young horse, Freki, eyeing the fortress before me, I know that my sons and nephew ride beside me, and my brother as well.

Coenwahl, my younger brother, is closer in age to my oldest son than I am. He was born to my father late in life, his mother a small slip of a girl, and different to the woman who birthed Eowa and me. He's more like his mother than our shared father, yet he holds many similar ideals. Most notably, Coenwahl hates the pretensions of Oswiu, blaming him for our older brother's death. Just as I blame Oswald, Oswiu's brother. Coenwahl shares my passion and love of battle. He fights like one of Woden's warriors, with the desire and focus that I'd expect from a fighter blessed by our God.

While I attacked at Maserfeld, Coenwahl kept the kingdom of the Hwicce free from invaders to the south and assisted the king of Dumnonia in his ravaging of the West Saxons. Perhaps I should have taken Coenwahl to Maserfeld and allowed him to fight alongside Eowa and myself. If I'd known it would be the only opportunity we'd have, I'd have ensured he fought there. It would have helped our family's legend if the three warrior brothers, images of Woden made flesh, had defeated Oswald together. Men and women would have loved to be regaled with the tales of the three warrior pagan brothers.

But, Oswald's death, just as Edwin's before it, hasn't cowed the pretensions of the two warring families, the one from Deira and the other from Bernicia. Oswiu, while the king of Bernicia, believes he should rule the same kingdom his brother once did, that of Deira. I should be pleased that Oswine was such a strong king and held his own against Oswiu. But now, Oswine has been betrayed by his warriors and is dead. His men were bribed by Bernician silver to kill the Deiran king.

Æthelwald, the son of King Oswald, killed at Maserfeld, seeks to be king there now. Æthelwald looks to me, not his uncle Oswiu, to assist him in that quest.

I understand that Æthelwald and Oswiu have never been allies.

Oswiu resented his brother for wishing to make Æthelwald his successor. All these slights have made me, the man who brought about Oswald's death at Maserfeld, a more acceptable ally than the man who tried to prevent and then avenge Oswald's death. The irony of the situation isn't lost on me.

I hope my children and their cousins argue less than Bernicia and Deira's great families. I toil to make them allies, not enemies. Unlike my father before me, I've not allowed my sons and their cousin to grow up thinking that only one can rule after my death. No, my kingdom is vast. While my children and their cousin are excellent warriors, there's room for them all to lead. Even if one must be the over-king, the ultimate decision-maker, there's still enough for them all.

My family will be strong and will fight together, as no other Saxon family has done before. When I'm dead and gone to be with Woden in Valhalla, it'll be my sons and their cousin who rule our kingdom and make it strong. It'll be my daughters and my niece who birth the next generation.

I could smirk with satisfaction at the image I've created before my eyes, but I know my job will never be complete. There'll always be enemies with jealous eyes, who want the things that I've accomplished for themselves, and without the hard work involved. I've noticed that those men and women who seek power often only want it with half the effort it truly takes. Those with their position thrust upon them, often by an unexpected death, somehow grasp that power is a double-bladed weapon. That blade is balanced carefully in the middle by the hilt and constantly heated and re-forged to ensure the equilibrium remains. It takes skill to steady a weapon with two sharp edges without being injured in the process.

Many men could die at the hands of their blades if they prove inadequate for the task.

I don't believe that Oswiu ever learnt the lesson. That surprises me. But then, Oswiu's always thought he should be a king. Even when he was the third oldest brother and an exile, with his uncle in power within his father's kingdom, Oswiu wanted Bernicia's warrior helm to wear.

I muse on what Northumbria could have become if its royal family had been united, as mine is in Mercia, working toward a united goal. The priests and holy men speak of Northumbria as the very pinnacle of sophistication. They labour the point that the other Saxon kingdoms should be ashamed to be less than Northumbria. That the other Saxon kingdoms should strive to be as great as Northumbria. Yet, the words miss a very salient point. How great could Northumbria have been without Edwin, Eanfrith, Oswald and Oswiu? If I'd been its king? If unity and not disarray had ruled it?

No, forget that. I'd never have been the king of Northumbria, nor do I want to be. I've always craved only for the amalgamated kingdom of Mercia. Now it's mine to hold firm, but not too securely, and to rule as a wise man should, but one prepared to fight for the integrity of that kingdom and to ensure no outsider can claim it.

Oswald failed to understand this, and now Oswiu makes the same mistakes. They only see the horizons that bind them as temporary structures to be pushed and fought against until they buckle and allow them to ride roughshod over them. My borders are far more stubborn and physical, and I respect them. One man can only hold so much of this island and simultaneously ensure its inhabitants are happy, healthy and free from attack from other men. Those men who, as I say, eye what I have with longing but no understanding of the time and effort it's taken me to gain what I've accomplished.

'Father,' Paeda rides close to me, and I grin at him. I'm proud of my son. He's very different to the man I was at his age, but that makes him no less powerful. He has his band of warriors, his followers, and he rules them well, just as he leads the kingdom of the Hwicce, the land I first claimed. Paeda's built as I am. He rides his horse with the confidence of a man who trusts his mount implicitly. His war gear festoons him, although he doesn't carry a shield or war axe. He doesn't fear danger because he knows any enemy would have to fight their way through his men first, and that's not likely to happen.

'Paeda,' I respond, and he returns my grin. His men insist on calling him 'my lord.' I know he detests the formality. I think that even though we ride to war and have left a bloody trail in our path throughout Northumbria, Paeda sees our time together as being a reunion where he gets to be the son and me, the father.

'I've ridden to the north of the fortress. It's well-positioned. I can see no way of easily gaining entry,' he informs me.

I knew this before I began my quest to bring Oswiu to his senses. Yet it disappoints me to know there's about as much chance of making war against Oswiu in a shield wall as there is of his Christian God appearing before me in a parody of the visions their priests prattle on about at great length.

I know the plan here, but it's not the sort of work in which I exult. Some would say that my actions are those of a coward, and I'm not to be named as such. I'd rather that Oswiu was perceived as the coward, locked up tight within the fortress while his people suffer, as they have and must still.

That's why only so much blood has been shed. I don't believe in punishing those who aren't responsible for my anger. It's Oswiu and his warriors who should be brought to justice for their murder of Oswine, not the men and women who farm the land and have the misfortune to look to Oswiu as their king.

'Arrange for a contingent of the warriors to stay here,' I command. Paeda glances at me in surprise. 'I wish to visit this holy island of theirs. I want to see the place where Oswiu, and Oswald before him, allowed lies to be spread about my kingship.'

Paeda's face stills at those words. He's not as full-blooded a worshipper of Woden as I am, but neither does he believe the words of the Christian God. He's keen to listen. He wants to understand the mysteries that have made men and women commit strange acts in the name of their God. It's one of the reasons I insisted on coming so far north. I have a mind to see the place, and so does Paeda.

That it'll also worry Oswiu isn't without an advantage. He'll be desperate to know what we plan to do with his monks. I hope to make him fret. I don't think I'll kill the men. Why would I? Making men martyrs to some new religion and adding to its strange momentum isn't my intention. Not again.

Paeda rides away to carry out my wishes. I beckon Coenwahl closer to me. He comes with a quizzical expression on his weather-worn face that only clears as I tell him my intentions.

'We should take his bishop,' Coenwahl suggests. He's pragmatic in considering the options available to me. Coenwahl reminds me of Eowa's deviousness with his desire to use means other than battle and death to triumph.

'I don't much want his bishop. He'll just blather to me. Anyway, I thought the bishop had died. Do they get a new one straight away?'

Coenwahl utters a laugh at my feigned ignorance. He knows, that I know, that Oswiu is waiting for his new bishop to arrive from the holy island of Iona to the far north. My very presence here will place all those careful plans at risk. The monks on the island, just visible in the far distance as a smudge on the horizon in the darkened sky, will already be worried and unsure of their future. If I ride north a little and make myself at home there for a week or two, Oswiu will be frantic. Lindisfarne, or the holy island, as I've also heard it called, is a source of great political power for Oswiu. He believes, just as his brother did, that by being associated with the holy men of Iona, he's imbibed with extraordinary power. Oswiu supposes that Lindisfarne, an island community like Iona, only adds to that power.

It's laughable, yet I'd not thank people for taking away my close association with Woden. So, I try and understand it. After all, Oswiu's religious conviction is his greatest weakness. It's one I'll be able to exploit while he hides in his fortress, fretting about the future of his monks and bishop, who might or might not be on his way to meet Oswiu. I suppose I could send outriders and search for the new bishop. Perhaps.

'What do you hope to gain from all this?' Coenwahl takes the time to ask. I laugh at him through the coming gloom of night. As I say, he thinks about actions and their intentions.

'I want Oswiu to feel threatened, to realise he's not his brother and only lives because I allow it.'

'Not much then,' Coenwahl retorts quickly, not meeting my eyes as he gazes at Lindisfarne. I suppose he makes a good point. What is it that I genuinely hope to accomplish? What lies at the heart of my anger and hostility towards Oswiu? It can't just be that he lives while my brother lies dead and has done for ten long winters.

What is it that I want? I want back my buffer zone between Oswiu and Mercia. I want to remove any pretensions that Oswiu thinks he holds to the Deiran kingdom. I want Oswiu to know that my son will rule in my place when I die. Paeda is just as much of a warrior and man of politics as I am.

I want Oswiu to know how futile his hopes are. He's not the sort of warrior and leader that I am. Oswiu will never achieve the same recognition I have, no matter his adherence to his Christianity.

I think Paeda and his brothers have more extraordinary skills than I ever did. All I had was my sword and my shield. They have those attributes but also guile and understanding. When I'm gone, Paeda will make a great king, as will Wulfhere, my other son, and my nephew. And after them will come more of my descendants. Oswiu needs to appreciate that I'm breeding a dynasty, not some throwaway kingship to be ripped apart at my death as though I never existed.

I'd leave Mercia knowing that my family, who claim descent from Woden, are more potent than ever before and that none can endanger them.

What happens after that will be my son's legacy and my nephew's.

I can, after all, only foresee so far into the future.

2

PENDA, KING OF MERCIA
SUMMER AD653

I've never been a conceited man. I might expect to win my battles and outthink my opponents, but I've always known that a self-righteous man is almost as good as a dead man. As soon as a sense of satisfaction with a job well done infects a warrior, he might as well just hold his sword in his limping hand, ready for feasting in Valhalla.

No, I've never been superior, not like Oswald and Edwin before him. Both men were too sure of themselves and paid the price with their blood and deaths. They put too much faith in themselves and their Christian God. Both are actions I decry. In life and death, there's only one surety, and that is yourself. I know that lesson, and I hope my oldest son does too and that Wulfhere and Æthelred learn it well in the future.

I've been blessed with many sons and two daughters. My wife has fulfilled her duty to continue our family line. I'm grateful to her for that. That she's also equally fiery and loving only adds to the excitement of our marriage bed. She's a good wife. I struggle to be a good husband and father, but at heart, I'm a warrior, and my outlook on life is that of blood and sweat, iron and fire. There's nothing soft about me. I love fiercely and forever.

Like my father before me, I labour to make my sons and nephew men to be admired and feared in equal measure. Unlike my father, I respect them for who they are. None of the four boys will be a mirror image of myself. No, they all have their path to tread, and that's why I'm here today, looking neither smug nor self-satisfied with my accomplishments, for all that Oswiu glares at me in such a way that makes me think I should be looking pleased with myself.

Oswiu. For all that he looks like his older brother, Oswald, dead on Herebrod's sword for many a winter, doesn't have the same faults that Oswald did. Yes, he places far too much reliance on the Christian God and too little on the ways of men, but other than that, he's a more difficult man. He has his viewpoints, and they're hard to persuade him away from. He rules, and he thinks, just as Oswald and Edwin did, that men should share his viewpoint without any possible alternatives.

I rule, and yet this is perhaps one of the most important ways of earning the respect of others and keeping that support, I don't tell men what to think, and I appreciate the opinion of others. If I didn't, I'd never have been able to raise Paeda without rancor splitting our family, or Wulfhere, Æthelred or their cousin. My sons, even the young ones, have been taught to think and behave as they deem best and to become the men they want to be. I don't want copies of myself. I'm not the same man my father was, nor was Eowa. Coenwahl is his own man as well.

That's why I'm here today, chilly despite the season, watching my son being dunked under the great swirl of some far northern river. Finan, Bishop of Lindisfarne, has come to baptise the boy, take him into the bosom of their mother church, or so they call it, and all in the name of alliance and marriage.

The two sides of this alliance, Oswiu of Bernicia, and I, stand on opposite sides of the great swirling maelstrom within which my son steps. Yet I can hear the accented words of his bishop, and as soon as Paeda is baptised, a marriage will occur between my son and Oswiu's daughter. This should seal our decision to live in peace with each other.

I suppress an amused smirk as I watch my son coughing and spluttering his way as he resurfaces above the surging, grey-flecked river. It rained heavily two nights before, and now the distant hills, no more than an illusion in the distance, disperse their deluge all over my son and the bishop. I think this might be Woden and his tally of Old Gods taking revenge against Paeda for his perfidious ways.

Across the great river, Oswiu stands still, his son at his side, his daughter in her finery. I don't think she wants this marriage, nor does her young brother wish to become my hostage for their father's good behaviour, but that's exactly what the outcome of today will be.

Oswiu is different to his brother and his uncle before him because he's weak in the eyes of anyone who's not sworn their lives to him, given their oaths to fight for him in exchange for a place at his hearth come the winter season, and the chance of a farm to retire upon when those few lucky warriors are too old to swing their axes and swords anymore.

He's failed to keep his lands and borders safe. Now he must pay the ultimate price. As he stands, his brother's white-bladed sword prominent at his side, he must know that he's failed as entirely as his brother before him. Only this time, I've been lenient, perhaps mellowed by my age, and instead of war and death, I'm happy to accept him as an ally. To arrange not one but two marriages, and all for only the price of one hostage, his son and would-be-heir, Ecgfrith, a young boy of a similar age to my youngest son.

At my side, my wife stands and watches her eldest son closely. None would know of her great happiness at watching him convert to the faith that's almost identical to the one she grew up in, but she's delighted and also fearful. For all that she might still practice her faith, she's long realised that Woden, my ancestor, is the foundation of our dynasty. It's Woden who keeps us strong and allows my family to flourish, apart from my long-dead brother and his wife.

Paeda is taking a risk in his baptism to allow marriage to a girl who will resent him. But it was Paeda's decision, not mine. I demanded three hostages. Oswiu offered one hostage and two marriages. My son, smitten with Oswiu's daughter, allowed himself to be swayed to a union with her. And I, foolish old man that I've become, allowed him to have his way. Perhaps I have some softness to me after all.

I hope Paeda's experience with Christianity is better than Eowa's. Eowa allowed himself to be tortured with worries about what he'd done in abandoning Woden and the old ways, returning to them before his death. I told him it little mattered, but my words had no impact on him. I told him that Woden was within us, a part of our very being because he was our forefather, but even that knowledge worried him.

Paeda is more open-minded and less suspicious. Still, he assures me that he'll continue to worship Woden. This baptism is merely a balm to the soul of the princess he'll wed as soon as the baptism is concluded. Yet I think he wants to be swayed by Christianity. He's always been curious about it, and I'm reminded of that day when he spoke to me of Eowa and how he healed my long-dead horse, Gunghir. I miss the horse and see in that discussion the beginning of my son's change in perspective.

The man who stands with Eowa deep in the river is from Iona. He's Oswiu's new bishop and is called Finan. He's a younger man than I, but then, the majority of men here are. I'm old and grizzled and yet lean. This man from Iona, originally born either in Ireland or in Dal Riata, wears his hair in a strange way, the front half of his head shaved. Due to this, his eyes look as though they stare from an overly large face, looking too small and pinched. He appears animal-like, emerging from his winter hibernation into the bright light of early summer. I hold my amusement in place.

It doesn't do to ridicule the Christian priests, just as I don't mock the men and women who keep to the secret places and keep to my faith. There's power in the worship of Gods, although I feel there's much more in my worship of Woden.

As much as I try and pay attention to my son's baptism, I find the men and women who make up the Northumbrians who've come to witness this monumental occasion distract me. There have been pacts before, most notably between my brother and Oswald, but this is different. This is the result of my attack on Bamburgh, or rather, my not attack.

The bishop, Finan, hadn't yet arrived in Lindisfarne when I made my foray to the far north. In fact, Bishop Aidan was only just dead, and Oswiu was a vulnerable man because of it. And weaker because of his murder of the king of Deira. Feebler as well because I wasn't prepared to overlook his transgression. For too many years, since Maserfeld, the kingdom of Deira had kept Oswiu and me apart. By killing its king, Oswiu had been trying to undo that barrier between us.

Not only could I not let him come closer to my borders, I couldn't allow him any victory either. I needed to keep him locked up tight in Bernicia. His gaze needed to be drawn firmly northwards, not towards the south. Due to that, I've been using my contacts in the kingdom of the Picts once more. Eanfrith, Oswiu's brother, my ally at Hæðfeld, and dead on Cadwallon's sword, left behind a son, Talorcan, a member of the Pictish royal family. He's as prepared as I am to swipe at Oswiu. The situation helped immensely as Talorcan is now king of the Picts.

I wish his father had lived to see his success, but it's often the way that the son only succeeds once the father is dead. The same happened to Eowa and me. Our lives can be short and bloody. I'm lucky to have lived so many years, but I'm far from happy with my accomplishments. I have more to do, and most of it concerns the king of Bernicia, Oswiu. I can't blame him personally for my brother's death, but if he'd never come to reinforce Oswald, the victory would have been ours much sooner. Oswald wouldn't have had the capacity to face my brother in hand-to-hand combat. My brother wouldn't have died.

Many would think my decision to ally with Oswiu and his family is strange, but I work from a position of strength. My son will marry his daughter, and their children will have as much right to try and claim the kingdom of Bernicia as any others. That's why I've allowed this path to be trodden. I don't wish to wage war to gain Bernicia. If I add it to Mercia's reach through blood ties, my children and grandchildren can hold the much-enlarged kingdom. Or at least live in peace with each other.

Time will tell, and I'll not be there to see it.

By marrying my eldest son to Oswiu's eldest daughter, I set my family up for great things. By taking Oswiu's son as my hostage, I deny him the same freedom. This series of marriages and hostage-taking might look as though I'm working from a position of frailty, but I'm not. Those who understand the intricate relationships between our kingdoms will know as much.

I hope the marriage lasts longer than that between my sister and Ceonwahl of the West Saxons. Not that his repudiation of her has upset my careful plans. No, Ceonwahl was forced to flee his kingdom when he left my sister, and even now, he lives in fear of my revenge. I don't plan on taking it, but fear is a good thing and will keep him from meddling in affairs that are no longer to concern him.

But to the men and women who stand with Oswiu. I feel I should know them all, and yet I don't, only the presence of Æthelwald, king of Deira on my side, allows me to know who everyone is. He's making no secret of his support for me; after all, I helped him gain his kingdom after Oswine's murder on Oswiu's orders. Family connections in the northern lands are more of a hindrance than a help. Familial relations are stained with blood ever since King Edwin murdered King Æthelfrith, his brother by marriage.

That is why this marriage concerns me. I think the girl will be loyal to her father, not to my son. Yet, my son is happy and provided we watch her, I can't see how she'll have the opportunity to cause problems.

Or so I hope.

Still, the bishop praises his God, his face turned upwards, seemingly immune to the chill of the rushing waters around his feet and halfway up his body. I'm shivering just with the thought of it, but then, I don't need to get my feet wet today.

My son is drenched, his skin, even from this distance, parchment white. He's suffering for this marriage. I hope the girl is worth it.

3

PAEDA OF THE HWICCE
SUMMER AD653

The water is clear as it swirls around my middle, but I know my teeth are clenched to ward off the deep chill. My clothing is sure to take its time in drying. I'm pleased I was instructed to leave aside my fine clothes for the wedding. They would have been ruined before I'd even laid eyes on Alhflæd. Her haughty face would have flickered along my drenched length, and she'd have been displeased, even though I'm being baptised to please her.

I'm unsure if that would have amused me or worried me. I'm content to have avoided the necessity of dealing with any more of her ire.

I've spoken with her, of course, I have, on any number of occasions whilst Finan was 'educating' me in the ways of their faith. But tonight, when the marriage is complete, will be the first time we've ever been alone. Yet I already know her opinions of me. Fully. She's made no secret of her unhappiness and grudging acceptance of her father's wishes.

It doesn't seem to matter that I know I'm a good-looking man and that other women are keen to bed me. No, the only fact that matters to Alhflæd is that I'm Penda's son, and Penda killed her uncle, a man she barely remembers, but her uncle all the same. In Alhflæd, Oswiu has a fine advocate and loyal daughter, perhaps too loyal. I hope that with the correct persuasion and the right amount of time, I'll make her a devoted daughter for my father.

I know his opinion on my marriage. I also understand he respects me enough to allow the decision to have been mine. He'd rather have hostages, but a wife for his son and a new daughter are acceptable alternatives. I only hope that the beauty of Alhflæd hasn't allowed me to make a terrible decision.

From the moment that I saw her when my father surrounded Bamburgh with his warriors two summers ago, I knew that I desired her. She accompanied her father, standing on the exposed battlements, shrouded in a deep black fur cloak. Even that didn't mask her shining blue eyes and long auburn hair. I don't think anything could have.

She cast her haughty eyes over my father's encampment, and her gaze struck all the men. I don't believe there was one man within my father's force who didn't stop and stare at her. I know that Oswiu's move was carefully orchestrated, but it did not affect my father. His intention wasn't to gain a new wife for himself but to enforce his wishes on Oswiu, and ensure that he stayed firmly behind his borders.

My father assures me that my desire for the wedding hasn't undermined his military might. I hope he's right. I wouldn't want my marriage to allow Oswiu to gain undue influence within Mercia, or further south, where my father rules with his iron will. The kingdom of Kent stands alone but remains an ally. In the kingdom of the West Saxons, Ceonwahl remains an exile, too scared to return to rule his people ever since he repudiated my aunt and sent her back to Mercia, bruised and beaten, much to my father's disgust.

King Ceonwahl will remain in exile until his death. For now, the nobility of the West Saxons rule themselves almost autonomously, but only ever with my father's agreement. He's become something far more than the title of war leader implies, which was the only one he could claim when he was my age. He's become revered.

I'm proud he's my father and also terrified.

What will I be when he's gone? I'll never rule as he does. I'll never command the same respect or intimidate my enemy. No, I have my father and grandfather's heritage to call upon, but I'm no Penda of Mercia, the pagan, warrior king.

My thoughts make the ice of the water recede from my consciousness. As so many times before, I allow the bishop's words to wash over me, never through me. Alhflæd might have consented to the marriage provided I converted to her faith, but her faith means nothing to me. My father cautioned me repeatedly in this respect. He told me of my uncle's struggles with his faith. I remember my uncle fondly but as a distant figure. I always seem to have known that Eowa was conflicted in his faith. My father told me that if I chose to convert fully, the words streaming from his quick mouth without any rancour, I should ensure I did so completely. He said a half-hearted conversion would do me no good.

I listened to his advice and also the words of Bishop Finan and decided that it was better to pay lip service to the new faith only. I can see the power that my father's Gods claim. I never wish to stand aloft from Woden, my ancestor. I know that without him, I'll not be held in the same esteem as my father. I vowed, long ago, that if I were fortunate enough to outlive my father and lucky enough to become as great a force as he is, I'd rule after him, passing on the kingdom either to my children or to my brothers. There's no rule as to who should rule after my father, but I know that despite every piece of evidence to the contrary, my father will not live forever. I anyone is to rule after him, it should be me.

My eyes flicker between my father and my father-in-law-to-be, and I think about how similar the two men are and then how very different.

Oswiu is a warrior but also something of a monk. His clothes are rich, hung with jewels. His hair is thick and long, crowned with a circlet of something that sparkles in the bright daylight. He wears a ceremonial seax at his waist. There are many exposed foreheads in his entourage, a symbol of the Christianity his uncle and brother allowed into Northumbria. All this I can see from my place within the river.

My father's a warrior and nothing else. The way he moves, the way he breathes, the way he simply stands, they all mark him as a man who knows he's physically powerful and has men who will obey him. He commands respect for himself. He doesn't concern himself with ceremony or pomp. He stands as a warrior, only leaving off his shield and sword from his current costume. I know my mother forced him to leave his war axe behind, and this he grudgingly agreed to do, but he was adamant in his need for his seax and his other small weapons.

He said it was a baptism and a wedding, and that didn't mean it would be peaceful or free from attack. So he's adorned with his weapon belt prominently around his middle.

With that thought in mind, I know he also has a contingent of his most loyal warriors hidden away but within sight of the river. Should anything happen. Should Oswiu decide to attack, they'll come to my father's defense. Their instructions are clear. Kill the girl, and kill Oswiu if the opportunity presents itself.

I'm sure I should feel some outrage, but my father is correct in his fears. He humiliated Oswiu only two years ago when he tried to dictate events in Deira. This is his ultimate humbling, and any man would be keen to take their revenge when they thought their enemy was at their weakest. Why he would think my father would let his guard down now, I don't know, but my father never relaxes. He's always wary of enemies and the chance for any of them to take their vengeance against him. I don't even think he realises he's doing it most of the time.

I've endeavoured to learn the same level of alertness, for it's far too easy for men to think they're comfortable with what they have. It takes more effort and time to learn his level of vigilance.

But I digress. My father is a man of hard edges and a blackness that few understand unless they've learnt the true meaning of the fire that burns in the hearts of those few men who are born to lead. Or, as my father would say, imbibed by the power of his God. Oswiu is a man of the furnace as well, but he delights in the delicate patterns that can be cast onto the surface of weapons by a skilled man who's taken the time to learn how to craft the decoration. It doesn't make the weapon any stronger, just ornaments it, and that is why my father is the more able ruler. He doesn't waste his time with decoration. He uses iron for its true purpose, honing his edges and keeping them sharp.

He sees no need for unnecessary embellishment, and he interprets this baptism as just that. He believes that faith is too personal for such public shows of observance.

I must get used to more of this when my wife lives with me. She expects to bring her personal priest with her, and have services as often as once a week, just as in her father's household. I wish she could see the conversion for what it is, a political statement, but I believe that her faith is fervently held. I'll not be able to pull her away from it.

To know that I'll fail in that before I've even attempted to sway her back to the old Gods is a disappointment, and it does blot my enjoyment in becoming a husband. Her heart will always remain Northumbrian. She'll never become a Mercian, and I think she'll always maintain her conceited air.

I swallow thickly, the worries of my imminent marriage allowing a mouthful of the foaming river to leak down my parched throat. I cough and splutter, earning a surprised glance from Bishop Finan. He's a thin man, younger than my father, and so desiccated I can see his bones through the thin layer of his pale skin. Yet his voice booms from inside his frail body, and I know this is his power.

I've heard others speak of him reverentially. They believe the Christian God speaks through Finan, and who am I to argue with them? Yet I think much of it is an act, and tonight, he'll be hoarse from his endeavours.

But tonight, he'll be with Oswiu, and I'll be sharing the bed of my new wife on Mercian land. What he does after today may not be relevant to me, but I've been seen to be friendly with him. That will win me support in Northumbria, amongst the nobility, for it's not only their king who holds Bishop Finan in such high regard.

I've made myself some allies that Oswiu may not even know. Or, alternatively, I've made allies with exactly the people that Oswiu wants me to be connected with. The use of my learned alertness will keep me safe.

Finally, and by now, I'm sure my entire body is blue with cold, Bishop Finan utters his final exhortations and escorts me from the river to the Mercian side. My mother greets me there. A thick cloak envelops my shoulders, and she kisses my cheeks. This is her very public way of ensuring that my conversion is accorded the respect it deserves, for she's a Christian of the old ways. Whilst many might forget it, for once, it's an important distinction to make.

As the cloak settles around me, I hear the unmistakable sound of horses crossing the river. Now Finan has spoken his magic words to me, Oswiu is prepared to let his daughter near me. But I take my time getting warm and dressed. This is another of my father's tricks. He's the king; others can wait upon him. As his son and in the presence of King Oswiu, I must do the same.

My father also takes the time to stride toward me; for all that his eyes are watchful as Oswiu makes his way across the river. He's alert for any kind of treachery, and now could be the time that it comes. Oswiu must come before my father, renew his homage to him as his overlord, and then consent to the marriage. As I know only too well, it's one thing to agree to the terms my father imposed on Oswiu, it's quite another to go through with those terms.

My father has had spies at Oswiu's court since his submission. Not that Oswiu necessarily knows as much. The news they've been sending south has been a mixture of good and bad. Much of what they report is the idle musings of bored and drunken warriors, but perhaps there's truth to it. We'll know soon enough.

The horses that Oswiu and his daughter ride, along with the fifty warriors who accompany them, are good stock. They walk through the water without hesitation, even though it must be cold and a shock. Their harnesses are polished to a high shine and in good condition. Oswiu has spared no expense in coming to this meeting. I know he's failed to recover all of his losses from two years ago and that his followers still speak of my father's invasion with unhappiness and unease. Yet Oswiu seems serene.

Has he, after all, and despite everything I've heard to the contrary, decided to accept his position with as much good grace as possible?

I doubt it. Yet, I don't know what he does have planned unless it's something to do with his daughter and her marriage to me. I don't know, and I wish I did.

However, my eyes rest fully on Alhflæd, and all thoughts of her father's politicking leave me.

She's a beautiful woman. I feel my desire rising. Whatever else happens, I will at least enjoy my time bedding her.

I doubt I'll ever make her love me, but the hope that I will do so drives me to walk across the ground that divides us and offer her my hand so she can slide from the horse she rides confidently.

She flinches when I hold my hand up to her. I swallow my unhappiness. I do so want her to desire me at least, but if she can't even hold my hand, then how will she feel when she's naked and in bed beside me?

The thought worries me until some action from her father has her holding her small hand out to me. I clasp it with my cold one. Her hand is too warm, and her face is a little flushed. Is it fear that grips her or a little excitement of her own? I wish I knew.

'Lady Alhflæd?' I offer softly as she slides from the back of her horse, and her eyes finally meet mine. I'm none the wiser to her true emotions as the smell of her wafts past my nostrils as she walks to meet my mother and father.

To all intents and purposes, it seems that she's forgotten all about her father's presence. But my father hasn't. I watch with interest and see Oswiu's reaction shadowed on my father's stern face. Oswiu is playing the part of the bride's father well, behaving himself, and that, as my father would say, is the surest sign that some mischief is being plotted against him.

My mother, always aware of her position as Penda's wife, greets turn away from his frozen stare and focus on my daughter and her coming marriage.

I think she might just have found a flaw in her plan.

There's no possibility that Penda will allow her to cause disharmony within Mercia. I might just be sentencing her to a life of unhappiness, and there's nothing I can do about it. Not now.

Penda has my son as a token of my desire to hold to the agreement made at Bamburgh, and now he has my daughter. My family is splintered and broken. A father can't hope to keep his children loyal to him when they are so far apart and, more than likely, made to listen to the views of those who now support and nurture them. How could they do anything but begin to hold the same views? Yet, for my daughter, I had held out a small hope but Penda has just extinguished it. Whether he wants to rule Bernicia or not, it's clear that he doesn't expect me to keep the land for long.

When I return to the north, as I will after this ceremony, I must make more alliances and bring people to see Penda for the true menace he is. Just as he's done in the past, I must make an effort to ensure that my nobility, and those in the kingdoms that neighbour Penda, the West Saxons and the East Angles, and perhaps even the men of Powys and Gwynedd, begin to understand that Penda will never stop in his ambitions to have some form of say in the way each kingdom is ruled. I need to think as he and Cadwallon once did when they turned so many against the rule of my bastard uncle, Edwin, and reset the kingdoms.

I must do more than sit and plot, hamstrung by Penda's reach.

I also need to kill Herebrod, and finally, bring my brother's killer to justice. Somehow.

The Mercian nobility has drawn near to listen to the words of Finan and to witness this marriage. I already know that it's going to fail. My daughter is merely a piece in a much larger game.

Yet it's then that I finally catch sight of my son for the first time in over a year. Ecgfrith. He was no more than a child when he left my kingdom in Penda's entourage, and I've grieved for him every day since then. I failed him, as no father ever should, and was left with no choice but to face a full-out attack from Penda, or let him take my boy to guarantee my good behaviour. He was resentful and angry when he left, and now he won't meet my eyes.

Today I lose my daughter, and it seems my son is also lost to me.

He's grown a little. His hair has lightened under the milder climate, and I see muscle under his tunic where in the past, there was only the long stringiness of boyhood. Penda is training my son to battle, as every father should, and I swallow thickly.

Is he training him to fight for or against his brothers and sister in Bernicia?

Against his father?

Only time will tell, and as I watch him, standing confidently amongst men and women who are total strangers to me, I see a hand snake over the boy's shoulder and squeeze it in comfort.

My heart almost stops beating when I follow that hand higher and see it belongs to a man I vowed to kill even before he murdered my brother.

Herebrod.

Penda has allowed my son to become close to the very man who took my brother's life and, in doing so, ruined my family's power base in Bernicia.

Fuck, I hate him.

Herebrod, aware of my scrutiny, watches me closely and only turns away when he knows he's gained my attention. He does so with contempt. He knows his hold over my son and me.

Penda is as calculated in his actions as ever.

He'll not allow my daughter and her new husband or my son to wreak havoc on his kingdom.

No, Penda is completely in control of this situation, and I can see no way of ever gaining the upper hand.

Not unless he died.

And how would I bring that about? Not when I've squandered any chance of surprise I might have had by commanding the murder of Oswine?

5

CYNEWISE OF MERCIA
SUMMER AD653

I watch Alhflæd with interest, beginning to understand my son's fascination and desire to make a marriage pact with her. I once felt the same about Penda. The thought of marrying a man who didn't share my father's views and was one of the hated enemies of the British had filled me with fear and loathing in equal measure. Yet, my father and my brother had gone ahead and agreed to the arrangement, almost without consulting me. But the first time I saw Penda, I knew I wanted him as my husband, no matter my fears about his reputation and faith.

Penda, a youth I'd only heard spoken of in awed tones by those who'd fought with him, had won over my firm resolve with just a flick of his interested yet disinterested eyes and the ambition I'd seen reflected there.

I'd known then why my brother had been so keen for the marriage to go ahead and why he'd not listened to my complaints or tried to win me over to the idea. The smirk on his face as he'd witnessed my first meeting with Penda has stayed with me ever since. He'd known how much I'd desire the man once I met him.

He'd not been wrong, and although I'll never thank him for ensuring I had such a good marriage, he knows it was the right thing to force my hand and that of my father's, as I've since learned he also had to do.

Clydog did me a huge favour that day, in ensuring I was the adored queen of a man who was always going to extend his reach far beyond the land that he could legitimately lay any claim to through the happenstance of his birth. Clydog must have foreseen that my husband would respect me as much as he does and would accord me more power than most women in my position can ever hope to achieve.

I run his household for him and provide him with healthy and robust children, but more, I ensure his ambitions stay firmly under control and achievable. I've tempered his violent streak a little and increased his ability to see far into the future to know how actions taken now will resolve themselves in five or ten winter's time.

This marriage is the only variable that he and I have disagreed openly about, but now I see, as my brother once insisted, why my son wants this young girl as his bride.

He sees the spark of intelligence in her eyes, and although it shows distaste for her coming marriage, her demeanour is much as mine was. He thinks he's found himself a woman who'll rule as I have.

I only hope that she turns that fervour to the benefit of Mercia and not Northumbria. If not? Well, if not, I've no problem ensuring that her life ends abruptly and quickly, no matter my son's desire for her.

The girl, her eyes cast demurely downward as the bishop speaks the words of the marriage, must feel the heat of my gaze as she raises her head to look at me with no hint of fear or worry. She knows what she is and what she wants to achieve. Her beauty and cleverness surprise me.

I'll need to watch this girl carefully. I doubt she'll be as easy to convert to our way of thinking as I was.

She breaks my gaze at a touch from the bishop on her arm, but I continue to watch her. She's a slight girl, not really yet a woman, with a delicate face and hard eyes, and a small pointed chin. I imagine she's been much pampered by her father and kept away from the searching eyes of the men of his war band. A good father should protect his daughter from the unwanted attention of men who drink too much and think with their cock and never their heads. I wish her mother were here so that I could see what she might look like when she's older. But I've met Kentish princesses before, I know they have the same nature as this little minx who's just been dropped into our ordered and caring family.

She's also pale, almost too pale, as though she's made of mist and clouds and not flesh and blood. But I know she'll bleed just as much as anyone else, and it better be for the sake of my family and my son and not for her father.

Oswiu isn't a bitter man, but he almost is. My husband allied with his older brother and was responsible for the death of his next brother. He now holds the complete island of Britain under his sway. His alliance with Talorcan, Eanfrith of Bernicia's son, shows that he can convince any to his cause, even men and youths who should, by rights, hold Penda to account for the deaths of their fathers.

Being thwarted in his ultimate ambition to take command of Deira has soured Oswiu, I can already tell in both his stance and his attitude to events taking place before him.

Bitter men make poor enemies and even worse allies. I don't know how Penda plans on healing the rift with him. But I know it would have been quicker, and no doubt less painful, if Penda had simply killed him there and then. I can't help thinking that his efforts at a less bloodthirsty conclusion to their discord will only result in more bloodshed when it becomes impossible to ignore Oswiu any further.

Penda knows my views, and so does my oldest son. Being men, they both choose to ignore it whilst fully expecting me to right any wrongs that should arise, should my viewpoint be correct. In the meantime, I must do all I can to prevent the necessity for further war, and that will involve me befriending the young woman and bringing her into my confidence.

Already I don't wish to do so. She appears as vaporous, but I see signs that she's been forged from fine iron and that, I think, will make it impossible for us ever to act together. Yet the possibility of forcing her to my will is an enticing one. My sons and my daughters are growing quickly. I'll need something to occupy my thoughts and mind whilst Penda and Paeda congratulate each other and enjoy their peace and their hard-won victories.

The girl meets my eyes again. I allow a slow smile to form there. I want her to think I'm friendly toward her, that I've not judged her so soon. I must lure her to my side, just as surely as Paeda must entice her to his bed.

Her eyes look troubled and unfocused. I see that she's thought about this day as often as I have. She knows who I am without introduction. I imagine she knows who everyone is within Penda's court, especially the great noblemen Immin, Eafa, Eadberht and Herebrod, alongside their wives and children. She'll try and win them to her side by affecting some sort of innocence. I'll need to warn them all, especially Herebrod, the man who killed her uncle.

Oswiu has long despised Herebrod, trying to plot his death in the past, forcing Herebrod to travel by circuitous routes to reach his wife in the land of the Picts during the winter. And Herebrod must live, for he's Penda's oldest friend and his contact with Talorcan, the son of Eanfrith of Bernicia. Penda supported Talorcan's bid for the kingship, and now Talorcan supports his hobbling of Oswiu. Oswiu is squeezed tight between two enemies and barely seems to notice.

Immin is a man from my kingdom who accompanied me when I married Penda, just as Alhflæd has permission to bring an advisor with her. Penda hopes it won't be some prattling monk and makes me smile when he complains. But it will be a jabbering monk who stays behind with her. We both know that. It's not as if one of Oswiu's warriors would be allowed to remain, certainly not one of the skilled men who lived in exile with him. No, it'll be a monk, and Penda will complain whenever he sees his bald head, but that's for Paeda to concern himself with, not myself.

Immin is a commanding man because of his allegiance to Penda's children and me. He also made a stunning marriage to a woman from the Magonsaete. Her father's powerful in his own right, and when he dies, as he must soon, for he's a shrivelled grape of a man, Immin will claim his followers as his and will grow in power twofold.

Eafa and Eadberht are brothers and younger than Penda, yet Eowa held them in high regard. Their powerbase is centered near Tamworth. They tried to ensure Eowa's wife and children stayed safe during the campaign that ended with the tragedy at Maserfeld. Penda esteems them because of their fervent loyalty to his dead brother. I find the brothers too fond of reminding Penda of their support of Eowa, and in this one regard only, Penda cannot see past their words and actions. The two brothers are selfish men, keen only to emulate Eowa and Penda, and yet neither man has an inkling of the true cost of Penda's position. Neither would be able to work together if Penda were dead and gone. They would spend too much time trying to outdo the other.

I don't dislike the brothers, but neither do I respect them as much as Herebrod and Immin. But they do assist Penda in ruling such a huge kingdom, and so I tolerate them.

The other real man of power within Mercia is Penda's brother, Coenwahl. Until today he held much of the kingdom of the Hwicce under his command. But Penda has bestowed that position upon Paeda. In return, Coenwahl has been given more difficult lands to hold in the disputed territory between Penda and his one-time ally, Cynddylan. Coenwahl is more conciliatory than Penda has ever been because, despite himself, Penda harbours a grudge against Cynddylan for not returning to the battle site at Maserfeld quickly enough.

Although he never speaks of it, I know that he feels that Cynddylan must share in the blame for Eowa's death.

I know it, and I think Cynddylan realises it too. But if I asked Penda about it, he'd deny it vehemently. He thinks he blames only himself, but he accuses Cynddylan in equal measure, although never Herebrod. Herebrod is his oldest friend, and he could never blame him for failing to protect Eowa when he needed it most.

These aren't the only men within the kingdom who hold great power and sway with Penda, but they're the most important ones that even I try hard to placate and get along with. I know that Alhflæd will try the same; she might even try and undermine me to gain the patronage of my followers.

I doubt she'll succeed.

I take the time to look at the way she holds herself. She's dressed in beautiful clothing. It's impossible to doubt the wealth of Oswiu when I glance at her. She has amber in her silver hairclips, and delicate embroidery along her soft blue overdress that might even be silk. It flashes with rubies in the toggles, where a thick gold necklace touches her neck, festooned with a cross of her new God, also made from gold. She already wears two rings on her fingers, one set with a blue stone, perhaps from Dal Riata or the lands across the sea, and the other, no doubt from her mother, a princess of Kent, who would have grown up used to the trinkets and show of the kingdoms on the Continent.

Alhflæd might prove to be expensive to dress if she expects to look this immaculately attired every day of her life. No doubt she has many bone combs and even more jewellery from her father that she can wear.

I find it all a little gaudy. I prefer to wear my wealth in small ways. The great iron key that hangs around my girdle is my main embellishment, a reminder to all that I'm the wife of Penda and that I hold the key to his grain houses as well as his great hall. Immin is the only man, other than Penda, permitted to be less than respectful to me. I expect everyone else to remember that whilst Penda fights with his war axe, shield and sword, I protect his kingdom through my alliance with my brother in Ceredigion and by ensuring his bloodline continues.

Penda's ancestor was Woden. His father was Pybba. His sons and daughters will live on after his death, which I pray will not come for many, many years to come. I enjoy my position and wouldn't wish to relinquish it to another, especially not my son's new bride. Then I smirk, enjoying the thought of the challenge to come. I almost hope that she'll try and take away some of my loyal supporters and turn the head of Eafa and Eadberht, for Immin and Herebrod will have no time for her.

I've always known I'm like my husband, but now I think I may be even more similar, relishing the idea of an enemy who, I hope, will be as skilled as I am.

The ceremony finally concluded, my son, his face bright with joy, walks sedately to introduce his wife to me. I watch the interplay between the two of them intently. Alhflæd takes a deep, deep breath, steadying her nerves and her resolve. Although she doesn't look to her father for guidance, as she steps close to him, she does falter. Quickly, she regains her core of confidence and curtsies respectfully to me. I almost feel a twinge of guilt for my earlier thoughts as I realise how truly young she is, how dainty, how small in a world built on the reputations of men who think themselves giants.

Almost, I say, for the eyes, she drags to my face are defiant and daring, blazing with the intensity of her unhappiness and determination to do whatever it is her father has tasked her with.

I know a challenge when I see one. I see stubbornness and resolve in equal measure pouring from the girl.

She's not come as a peacekeeper or a weaver of the threads that can guide a man to a life of happiness and contentment. No, she comes to cause trouble, and she means to start immediately.

'Cynewise,' she mutters as Paeda introduces her, the lack of my title causing even Paeda to wince. Her voice is as soft and wispy as the rest of her bearing, deceptively so, because she speaks loudly enough for all to hear so that it falls to her father to correct her.

'The Lady Cynewise,' he says more loudly than Alhflæd, his rough voice starkly contrasting with her own, quieter one. She bobs her head as though in apology and makes her body language subservient. I glance at her father, my eyes sparkling with annoyance. He too doesn't falter under my gaze.

Yet, they've forgotten an important fact. I'm Penda's queen. I hold the hearts of many of the men and boys in his entourage, and it's at that moment that one of the most important makes his appearance. Ecgfrith stumbles into view, accompanied by Wulfhere. I hear the sharp intake of breath from Oswiu as Ecgfrith ducks his head and almost shouts, 'Lady Cynewise,' as he rushes past me, intent on his games and his play.

He's a good child, a boy I'm proud to foster, or so I excuse it to myself. It feels better than saying the boy is here as little more than a slave to my wishes.

He's also grown quickly under my guidance. He's happy and delightful in the company of Wulfhere. He understands why he's in Mercia and not with his father, but he doesn't understand all the distinctions of the arrangement. Who would burden a child with such things?

'Sister,' he stutters in surprise at seeing Alhflæd, abruptly coming to a stop. He's forgotten all about the reason for our grand endeavour today. His eyes swivel to his father, and he grins at him, much to his father's delight, and then much to his disgust, turns and asks for my permission to go to him.

This reunion couldn't have gone better if I'd planned it and had the boy act in this way. His enthusiasm and respect for me is clear for everyone to see, and as I nod to show he can rush to his father, flinging his arms widely around him, it's his sister that I watch. Her displeasure is easy to see. No doubt, she hoped to find her brother still loyal to her father.

Her inexperience will be her undoing. Why would a boy of no more than ten winters understand that his loyalty should be to a man who lives many days ride away and who he never sees? No, it was inevitable that Ecgfrith would come to love me.

Paeda, aware that his introduction of his wife hasn't gone to plan, closes the space between us and kisses me on the cheek. He's a tall boy, much like his father, and as his lips brush mine, he's already apologising for his wife's behaviour. I don't like that.

'It's not your place to apologise,' I mutter, my tone neutral. I walk away from the girl without allowing her to say anything else. It's Oswiu I wish to speak to, and Wulfhere accompanies me as I meet my foster son's father for the first time.

I can feel Penda watching me, but he doesn't move to interfere.

Instead, he talks with Bishop Finan, enquiring how matters are on Lindisfarne and how the building work progresses. He doesn't let Oswiu forget how complete his invasion of Bernicia could have been.

Bishop Finan stumbles his way through his answers, but Oswiu fascinates me. I'm pleased to see that he greets his son well. It's evident that he cares for the boy and hasn't forgotten about him now that he resides within Mercia.

'Father, this is Lady Cynewise,' Ecgfrith introduces us, his voice high with excitement. 'I live with her and with Wulfhere.' He points at my son as he speaks, and Oswiu perhaps despite himself, grins widely at the boyhood delight and friendship between them.

'Lady Cynewise,' Oswiu repeats, and I reach out to grasp his arm in friendship. The movement momentarily stumps Oswiu, but he recovers quickly. We greet each other at last. I can feel the strength in his arm and the firmness of his grip. I hope he feels the same in me. I might be a woman, but I'm as equal as I can be amongst Penda's men and his warriors. Should men ever attack my home, I'd be able to defend my children and my women well should the men fail in their duty.

'Lord Oswiu,' I offer him his title, as he has mine. There's to be no acknowledgement here of who is seen as a king and who isn't.

'My thanks for your care of my son,' he manages to say, although his eyes are back on his son. I see the longing and the need there. He's failed to keep his son 'safe', as he would see it. I don't wish him to ever fully understand how much love and care we all bestow on his son in the absence of his father.

'As agreed, we care for him and ensure he receives the training he needs.'

'He's grown so much....' he says, voice trailing off as Ecgfrith races to be with his foster brothers. I feel an inkling of pity for the man. Penda extracted a heavy price from him that day. Oswiu must feel the loss of his son, especially when discussions have taken place regarding the marriage of his elder son, the one from his first marriage, with one of my daughters. And still, there's no guarantee that peace will be settled between Mercia and Bernicia, not when

Deira sits so firmly in the way and is more an ally of Mercia than Bernicia.

The strained family relationships between the two kingdoms of Deira and Bernicia stem only from the wishes of over-ambitious men. It seems that if they were less single-minded, they'd accomplish more, much more.

Yet I know I can feel no pity for this man.

'Boys are likely to grow,' I offer sedately and then begin to turn away, 'just as kingdoms are.'

His sharp intake of breath at my words makes me smile as I cover the short distance to stand with my husband. I nod once to show I've accomplished the task he set me. He reaches over and plants a small kiss on my cheek, his beard brushing against my skin, reminding me of my wedding night.

What a night that was!

6

ÆTHELWALD, KING OF DEIRA
SUMMER AD653

I watch Oswiu and his men from a safe distance. I don't wish to be forced to confront my uncle, not now that Penda has stripped him of his son and daughter and his ability to force his way into my kingdom.

I claim Deira instead of Bernicia, which by rights should be mine if only my uncle hadn't moved more quickly than I could after the death of my father. He had the remnants of the defeated army at his command, and I didn't. I didn't travel with my father to Mercia because he insisted I remain behind to protect his sterile wife and to stand in his place should the unimaginable happen.

My uncle didn't even send word of my father's murder, instead riding to Bamburgh with all haste to claim the kingdom in his name. It was the summer, so my father's remaining nobility had been at Ad Gefrin, where we often spent the long dry summers. I'd not even known of my uncle's return until men had ridden to me and told me that a hostile force occupied Bamburgh. Only when I'd travelled from Ad Gefrin to Bamburgh had I been made aware of the horrifying truth. By then, it had been too late for me to do anything but accept my uncle's usurpation of the kingdom.

He had my father's warriors. He had the remnants of his war band from his exile in Dal Riata. Little caring for my father's wife, but knowing that my uncle wouldn't welcome my father's wife within the kingdom, I ensured that we escaped together, not to the east or the north, but instead to the west, where I managed to convince my uncle's cast-off wife to offer us support. She did so willingly, anything to thwart her husband, who'd left her with no plans to return.

It's taken me years of plotting to place myself in a position of strength. It's been Oswiu's presumptive attempt to take back Deira that's made what at times has felt like a hopeless endeavour a reality. I don't like to think of having any similarities with the dead king Edwin, but it seems that just as he had to take advantage of an emerging situation when he could, so have I.

Oher men, most notably Penda, have provided much of my good fortune, and although I like the old warrior, I'd rather count all of my work as mine. I've been forced to pray for days to seek forgiveness from my Christian God for allowing the less-than-Christian Penda to be my saviour.

I've spent good coin on having a religious foundation raised in his honour. I'm grateful to Penda and resentful all at the same time.

My consolation is that at least he didn't make the stroke that killed my father; neither did he take my birthright. No, that was the work of my uncle, and the killing stroke came from Herebrod, a man who hated my father for allowing his brother, Eanfrith, to be killed at Cadwallon's instigation.

The conflicted loyalties I hold are baffling.

I must be loyal to my Lord God, my father, my cousins, my over-lord Penda, and to any others who somehow have a family relationship with me or can call on my religious affiliations.

After the meeting at the River *Ad Murum*, where Paeda gained baptism for his soul and a wife for his bed, I feared that Oswiu would try to take advantage of his closeness to my borders to reclaim what he believes is his to rule.

Twice in the last two years, he's tried to make overtures of friendship to me, but I can't forgive him for his lies and deviousness when my father died. He knows it as well. He should have ensured I became king and that he was my most valued advisor. He should have tried to bridge the rifts that divided our family rather than widen them.

I sent his holy men away, even Bishop Finan. I've no intention of reconciling with him, and I've ensured that my borders are well-defended. I can't stop assassins from plying their trade, but that doesn't stop me from attempting to do so. My household warriors are ever vigilant. None may come into my presence unless I know them or another man confirms their identity.

My home is almost as well defended as Bamburgh, albeit on a much smaller scale. I don't plan on taking any chances with my uncle. He'll tire of his peace with me and will once more turn his eyes towards Deira. He's too ambitious not to.

I didn't attend the meeting at *Ad Murum*. There was no need for me to do so. Penda and I are allies. I owe my hold on Deira to Penda's determination that Oswiu shouldn't profit from the murder of my predecessor.

That I also owe it to my birth, and the anger of those incensed by Oswiu's actions following the battle of Maserfeld isn't forgotten either. But it's Penda who can make or break kingdoms as he wishes.

It's Penda and not my uncle, who's the power within our close-knit collection of kingdoms. To Penda goes my respect, and I confess, I fear him more than my uncle. But my uncle will try and take what's mine, and so I watch him closely, as do my warriors. I have a party shadowing their every step and more warriors, both in front of them and behind, checking that they don't leave behind any hidden reinforcements or encounter them along the way.

I know my uncle of old. He's a warrior, and he acts before he thinks. However, on this occasion, he's had nearly a year to plan his meeting with Penda. During that time, he'll have come to terms with my kingship. He might have decided that this is the perfect opportunity for him to assert his will once more.

Penda must share my fears, for he's sent a contingent of his warriors to reinforce mine. I'm grateful and angered that he thinks I can't mount a successful attack against Oswiu. I've sent Penda's men to the north to wait for Oswiu to travel past the reaches of Deira. Luckily, their leader, Glæðwine, was happy to comply with my request. No doubt Penda has asked for details of the kingdom of Bernicia, and Glæðwine will be able to provide them. He'll also see how my kingdom fares and whether I do enough to protect it from Oswiu. He'll see that my precautions are many and varied.

In the distance, I see the riders stop close to a small brook, and my heart jumps when more men ride toward them. What is this? Is this what I've been fearful of? It's too far away to make out details, but the riders seem to come from the north. Perhaps something has befallen the kingdom of Bernicia in Oswiu's absence? My optimism flares when the majority of the men kick their horses to greater speed, leaving behind what I must assume are the slower members of the party.

I almost wish I'd forced myself closer now, but in time I'll know what has befallen Oswiu. I know that whatever it is, his misfortune will please me.

He shouldn't have claimed my kingdom, not if he didn't want a lifelong enemy.

Satisfied that everyone from Oswiu's kingdom is focused on returning to Bernicia, I turn my horse and head for my home at Goodmanham.

I have a kingdom to run now that I'm assured its enemy has left it.

7

PENDA, KING OF MERCIA
EARLY AD654

I pace my hall. I'm angry, but it's not that which forces me to my feet. No, I find the chill of the winter has permeated to the core of my body, and I'm just plain damn cold. I don't know how Herebrod could stand to spend his winters with his wife amongst the Picts. To the north, the weather is far too harsh for my old bones, worn down by my years of fighting, practicing to fight and riding, my horses and my wife.

My anger stems from the intelligence I've received that Oswiu isn't content with our current arrangement. He moves to incite others to war against me. If the information is correct, and I imagine it is because my informant at Onna's East Anglian court has sent me news of his fears, I'll need to move against Onna. At the same time, I'll have to ensure that Oswiu's son and my hostage is punished for his father's rash actions.

I care greatly for the boy, as does Cynewise, and my younger sons. They'll resent me if I discipline Ecgfrith for his father's transgressions. But I don't think I'll be left with any choice.

Perhaps I should have made war against Oswiu when I had the chance and burnt his fortress of Bamburgh. I could have watched remained his smoking bones and been assured that he would cause me no more problems. But I chose peace, not war, and I'll regret that decision, just as Cynewise warned I would.

As to Oswiu's daughter, she works hard to cause problems for my son as he rules the kingdom of the Hwicce on my behalf. She's not an easy woman to please. She tests my son with daily demands for religious artefacts. She has no support from the Hwiccan nobility and none whatsoever from the brothers who assist me in ruling the Mercian heartlands around Tamworth. Herebrod will go nowhere near her, and Immin has never responded to her demands.

She's alone in our kingdom. She doesn't seem to understand that she only her husband will protect her. No one else will come to her aid. Never.

I could punish the girl instead of the boy, but she's my son's wife. I don't wish to interfere in their relationship. It's strained as it is, and my son, for all he professes to love Alhflæd, ensures he rides with his men as often as possible. His absences only add to her unhappiness and unease.

I should have denied him when he asked to marry her. I knew it wouldn't be a happy union, and it's not and never will be. She denies him in the only place she can, in their marriage bed. No children have yet come of their union, and so she can find no happiness in the joy of becoming a mother.

She'll become embittered if their relationship doesn't heal. Already I search for another bride for my son, a woman who'll be a more convivial partner and more importantly, who'll allow him to bed her so that he'll know the happiness of being a father.

The same isn't true of the other marriage between my family and Oswiu's. No, my oldest daughter and his first-born son are happy together. They already have a child on the way. They'll make me a grandfather first. That makes me feel old and no doubt explains my rancour with the news from Æthelhere of East Anglia, the brother of Onna, and someone who calls himself my ally.

King Onna plans an uprising, ostensibly to return the displaced king of the West Saxons to his kingdom, the man who married and then spurned my sister. I have no intention of allowing Ceonwahl to reclaim his kingdom. I have a close relationship with his noblemen, who are more than able to rule without the meddling of their king. Provided they never act against the interests of my Mercian kingdom, I am content to allow the situation to continue.

I'll need to meet Onna on the slaughter field when I know his true intentions. To halt Oswiu and his plans for the future, I'll kill Onna and install his brother as the king there. It'll distance Oswiu from his allies and the relatives of his wife in Kent. It will provide a true border between my kingdom and his. Unless he attacks along the River Trent, he'll have no easy access to Mercia as the British kingdoms, remembering his father all too well, will not deal with him. They allow no access to their kingdoms.

I'll also need to send word to Talorcan in the Pictish lands and have him attack Oswiu from the north. I already know he intends to move against the kingdom of Dal Riata, and this will allow him to extend his ambitions. If our attacks are coordinated, Oswiu will quickly realise he has no friends, only enemies to harm him. Talorcan has become a good ally of mine. Between us, I'm sure we can squeeze Oswiu so that his kingdom declines rather than expands.

But that is for the future. For now, I need to concentrate on the decision of Onna to rise against me, whether or not it's been initiated by Oswiu. Eight years ago, when Onna took my sister's husband under his protection, I ravaged his borders, but quickly stopped. I didn't think the man was worth any more effort. Certainly, my sister was pleased to be rid of him. She's married now to a man from Cynddylan's kingdom and far happier. Eight years of peace for a few fires was worth the small price I paid. I wonder what little I'll need to do this time to chastise Onna and keep the borders free for many more years to come.

Yet my men are restless, as am I. We've not fought a true battle in many long years. We did little more than burn Bernicia whilst Oswiu cowered behind his walls and then turned our attention to Lindisfarne, his holy island. It might be time for a proper battle.

I consider that as I pace. Where could I choose to march against

Onna? I would want it to be a good site, with my victory as assured as it's ever possible to be.

I should discuss it with Eafa and Eadberht. They know the borderlands well. My decision made, I call for the brothers to be summoned before me. They'll come quickly from their mead hall, and between us, we can plot a battle or a war, whatever I decide to make.

Still cold, I call for my winter cloak and venture outside. The deep black of the winter season has been and gone, yet the frosts persist. I know that the beginning of summer is still many chill nights and days away. The slow turning of the year frustrates me, adding to my hatred of the cold. I could almost wish my life away, hoping for the sun's warmth to seep into my old bones. Instead, I do the next best thing and call for my horse, Freki, to be saddled. I'll ride across my land and perhaps visit my childhood haunt with Eowa in the small forest to the east of Tamworth.

My younger sons race to join me. I smile good-naturedly and tell them they can ride with me. They're as cold and fed-up with the persistent winter as I am, but the presence of Ecgfrith reminds me of the problems his father is causing me and the revenge I'd vowed to take against him.

His voice is high with excitement, just like my sons'. I know, in that moment, as I watch him greet his horse with affection, that I'll never be able to punish him for his father's actions. No, I'd rather keep the boy as one of my own and never return him to his father than disfigure or take his life.

He's been in my household for nearly two full winters, and I look at him as no different than my sons. I know they see no difference, either. They treat him as well, or not as brothers will do, as they do each other. They'd hate me if I did anything to Ecgfrith. It's different with Oswiu. My sons think nothing of him. They know him only as the brother of the man who killed their uncle, a man they don't even remember. Yet, they understand the importance of family honour. The conflicts of their friendship with Ecgfrith are years in the future, and I regret that I've made it a necessity.

I frown at the thought. My father would never have been so soft-hearted as to worry about conflicts in my future. He gave me a beast of a horse and ensured that Eowa and I would always struggle with our family ties and duplicate desires for our future. Perhaps my decision has been a good one after all. If Ecgfrith is ever returned to his father, my sons will learn a valuable lesson in loyalty. I don't know what type of man Ecgfrith will be when he's older. I hope he's less ambitious than his father.

But that's if Ecgfrith is ever reunited with his father. At the moment, I can't see that in his future. No, Oswiu must have decided that his son could be a victim of his expansionist plans, and so Ecgfrith may well spend all of his life in Mercia. At least he'll have his older half-brother as his constant friend, although perhaps not his sister. I may have to demand she's sent to one of the nunneries that Paeda has been asked to build within the Hwiccan lands. My wife tells me it would be an admirable place for her to go if she can't reconcile with her husband. Certainly, she'll not be allowed to return to her father.

None of his children will. Not now.

My horse stamps his hoof with impatience as I sit atop him, considering my options. His bad temper reminds me of mine. Without further thought, I command him to pick his way through the neat and tidy stables outside to where my warriors wait to escort me, my younger sons, and their foster brother.

We'll all ride together to the place of my childhood games. When we're there, and despite the cold, I plan on allowing them to run riot through the woodland countryside. The chill air will have lingered amongst the tall trees, the small stream will probably be frozen, and it will be as though a mythical creature has stalked through the land.

I'll tell them stories of the Old Gods, of Woden in particular. I'll wait to see how long it takes Ecgfrith to mention his Christian God or whether he might forget in the moment of childish exuberance that there's even a conflict for him to worry about in his future.

8

PAEDA OF THE HWICCE
EARLY AD654

Alhflæd stalks from our bedroom as she does every morning. I once thought there was the possibility that she'd grow to love me, but that was a misguided hope. That first night, when she allowed me to consummate our marriage when I knew joy and happiness, and I made her scream with delight under my hot touch, I thought she'd allow us to become lovers and marriage partners.

But the next night, she was cold to my touch and has been ever since. She seeks redress for the enjoyment of our lovemaking and its failure to produce a child. She tells me a child would have made her unacceptable delight in the sorry state of affairs, at least allowable.

I wish I'd never married her, but now I'm stuck with her. Not only does she shy away from my touch within the marriage bed, but she also seeks to cause problems amongst my men and the great families of the Hwicce.

I'm lucky that almost no one heeds her words or follows her attempts to set long-time allies against each other. But I know that one day that luck will run out, and she'll find someone to help her in her meddling.

My father allowed me the marriage because I asked him to, but he was uneasy about it. As always, he knew more than I did. I should have listened to him and allowed him to claim another of Oswiu's sons as a hostage, rather than his daughter as my wife. If I'd refused her charms, then there'd be no need for me to listen to the sermons that her priest insists on giving every day. I'd be under no compunction to build a church or a nunnery or a monastery, as she demands.

Leaning against the soft pillows that cushion my head, only the scent of her hanging in the air, I allow my mind to wander back to that first night together. To remember the excitement I'd felt in finally bedding the beautiful woman I'd first glimpsed on the wooden ramparts of the fortress at Bamburgh.

She's been pliant under my touch, almost daring me to do whatever I wanted to make her desire me. Her skin had been soft and warm beneath the heated furs, and her mouth had been open and inviting beneath mine. She'd even gasped when she first saw me naked, a sign I'd taken as a good one, although now I think it was inadvertent and that if she could recall it, she would.

Our lovemaking had been slow and leisurely. She'd not been the first woman I'd ever taken to bed. Some of the older women, keen to say that they'd had Penda's son if not Penda himself, had taught me the true way to love a woman and to make her scream with pleasure and hum with delight. I'd used all those small touches and tweaks on Alhflæd thinking I was doing the right thing.

Now I wish I'd shown her far less of myself, made our lovemaking more perfunctory. That way, I'd miss it less, and it might even have brought her back to my bed, for despite what she'd said, Alhflæd was no untried woman herself. No, she knew enough to let me know that she's been ridden before, and although that should have angered me, it hadn't. Not until she refused to sleep with me again and has done so ever since.

I'll never have a child with her, and whilst Oswiu holds to his agreement with my father, there's little I can do about it. Should Oswiu move against my father, it will be acceptable for me to cast her aside and have another woman as my wife. I can't wait, and indeed, I find myself listening avidly for messengers from the north or from my father, who tells me that I've been punished enough for my ill-conceived marriage.

I hoped we'd find joy in our shared faith, even if I were only a superficial convert to Christianity. But not even that isn't enough for the woman who said she'd only marry me if I converted to her faith.

No, the sooner she's gone from my side, the better it'll be for my kingdom and future.

The noise of a commotion in the hall sees me leaping from my bed and pulling a thick cloak around my naked body. Alhflæd has only just left our shared room. I wrack my mind to think what she might have accomplished in her short absence. But it is indeed Alhflæd who stands within my hall and shrieks, although whether in fear or joy, I can't yet determine.

Quickly I take in the scene before me. Alhflæd is on her knees, her head resting on a wooden stool as she wails and shrieks and I look around for someone who can tell me why she acts as she does. It falls to Immin, my mother's greatest supporter, to stride toward me.

'There is news, my lord,' he offers quickly, 'from the east.'

'The east?' I ask, still trying to determine why this affects Alhflæd as it does.

'Onna, King of the East Angles, makes ready to ride to war against your father. I've come to command you and your men to make themselves ready for war and to ensure that the Hwiccan kingdom is secure in your absence.'

Ah, it's all starting to make sense to me, and suddenly Alhflæd is before me, her face tear-streaked, although still beautiful. She reaches for my head, so much further above hers. Although I try and remove her hands, they stay firmly in place, pulling her lips to meet mine in a gesture that's so unfamiliar it takes me long, long moments to realise what she's trying to do.

She's fully dressed and yet, as she kisses me, grinding her way through my cloak so that she touches my chill skin, I feel her reach out and grab me. Despite myself, and even though I know this is all a ploy to stop me from casting her out, here and now, I feel myself stiffen at her touch. Above her head, Immin looks first shocked and then amused. He knows as well as I do the game she's playing.

Yet, I've been lying in my bed thinking of the touch of her skin against mine, of her hot breath on my cheek as I lay above her, and her open body beneath mine. Although I wish I didn't because I've finally got the excuse I need to get myself a new wife, I lift her in my arms as she continues to kiss me, surprised again by how light she is, and I turn and make my way back to my bedroom.

I'm about to ride to war. When I get back, and the truth of her father's involvement is well known, I'll be able to set her aside and get a new wife, but in the meantime, I'm but a man with a man's needs. So I take my wife back to our bed-chamber, and I pleasure her and myself as I've not been allowed to do since our marriage night.

I can hear Immin laughing in the next room. As Alhflæd's enjoyment climbs ever higher, and her gasps of joy and delight begin to escape from the room, I hear more and more people laughing at her blatant attempt at keeping safe whilst her father makes rash moves and risks her life.

Damn, she's a fine woman, her legs long and shapely, her breasts just a handful and between her legs, I find a comfort I'd hoped to enjoy ever since we married.

If our union makes a child, I'll acknowledge it. If it doesn't, I'll have enjoyed myself with a beautiful woman one last time.

I laugh as I kiss her, enjoying her touch and her urgent need to have me fill her with my seed. I banish all thoughts of what the future might hold.

For now, I'm getting exactly what I want.

9

OSWIU, KING OF BERNICIA
SUMMER AD654

To the north, Talorcan, my nephew and King of the Picts is doing most of my work for me, invading Dal Riata and ensuring that the Dal Riatans have no interest in challenging my borders. The kingdom of the Gododdin is nothing more than a name, a whisper of the past. These occurrences mean I'm free to concentrate on causing problems for Penda and his Mercian kingdom.

Throughout the long dark winter, when I was bereft of my daughter, Alhflæd, as well as my young son Ecgfrith, my men moaned and complained, told me I'd given too much away when Penda invaded my kingdom. I growled and shouted back, telling them they have short memories, I told them they had forgotten about the very real menace that Penda had exerted when he'd come as far north as Bamburgh and, worse, much worse, had taken it upon himself to visit Lindisfarne and hold my monks and my holy house to ransom.

They complained and whined even more, telling me I should have faced Penda there and then, not allowed him to burn my surrounding land, leaving only Bamburgh standing. I asked them if they would have fought for me. If they would have given their lives to ensure the safety of my dynasty and my kingdom. They'd subsided into men who knew the truth of my words. Only in giving them that truth, my unhappiness had resurfaced, and I'd sought the advice of my God and Bishop Finan.

What right did a pagan king have to lay claim to anything? What power did the oaths I'd given have over me when they'd been given to a pagan king. Bishop Finan, understanding my need for redemption and for hope for the future, had gifted me with the knowledge that no Christian man should be accountable to a man who had no faith in his God.

So released from my oath, I only had one more problem to overcome; that of my young son and my married daughter. I knew my older son would be happy no matter what. His marriage was a good one, a happy one, or so he'd told me. The same couldn't be said of my daughter, but it was my young son who worried me the most. What would Penda do to him if I attacked? What would his wife do?

To this Bishop Finan and my God. had no real answer. They could offer no reassurance, for what would a pagan lord do to a hostage who was no longer guaranteeing any peace? It was an unexpected visit from one of Onna's messengers, deep in the winter, which gave me the hint of an idea. What if I didn't attack directly but used a proxy?

King Onna has long been uneasy with Penda on his borders and even unhappier that he must still shelter the deposed king of the West Saxons, Ceonwahl. Ceonwahl came to me, his eyes brooding, his expression hooded. He'd been a convert under my brother to the Christian God. Although I know he'd done so unhappily, he'd accepted the conversion more than his marriage to Penda's pagan sister. It'd taken a brave man to cast his wife aside. And an even more stupid one to do it when Penda was able to drive him from his kingdom, and banish him.

Now Ceonwahl wonders through those kingdoms that are not averse to earning the wrath of Penda, the kingdom of Kent, of East Anglia and mine. There's no one else who would even want to stand against Penda. Too many of the other kingdoms have been his allies, either at Hæðfeld or at Maserfeld, leaving Ceonwahl with none or few options.

Yet he presented me with one I'd have been a fool to walk away from. He said he and Onna would attack Penda, hopefully, force him to battle, and then I could attack from the north as well.

It was an idea that initially held no charm for me, but slowly, and with the unhappy voices of my nobles in my head, I grew to like the idea. All Ceonwahl needed was money and an assurance of my support. Both I willingly gave, and when Ceonwahl left with the warmer weather, travelling by sea back to East Anglia so that Penda would never know he'd ever visited, he did so with forty of my warriors. Those warriors were keen to engage in battle against Penda and knew they did so with my full support, although it couldn't be acknowledged until victory was achieved or they spoke of it on their deathbeds. Whichever came first.

With my men gone, I began to dream of a future without Penda and with my son back at my side. My remaining warriors calmed under my touch, more eager to listen to me than they had been for the past year.

But now, I wait anxiously, on the borderlands with Æthelwald of Deira, for the news that will let me know that Penda has suffered an unexpected defeat at the hands of Onna, Ceonwahl and my warriors.

Ælfwine, my next oldest son, is sheltered deep within my fortress at Bamburgh. Should the worse befall us, he'll rise and rule after me. But I'm not alone. I have my warriors from my youth in Dal Riata. I have more than fifty noblemen with me, men who were once warriors and have been gifted with land for their endeavours to assist me. I don't stand alone, and these are the very men who wanted me to take action.

They'll stand with me should we get the opportunity to attack Mercia whilst Penda is engaged in East Anglia. We all share a breathless anticipation of the moment when we hear of his defeat and not one of us will even consider the possibility that this hastily thrown together plan won't work.

My wife is angry with me for risking so much, but I know the sort of king Penda has become. His reputation precedes him, and if I don't force his hand through the attack from Onna and Ceonwahl, I'll never have the opportunity I need to take advantage of his distractions.

No, as soon as I receive word that Penda has engaged in battle against Onna, my men and I will ride to Goodmanham and stake our claim to the kingdom of Deira. Without Penda's support, I doubt that Æthelwald will be able to mount any sort of defense or counter-attack. If I'm blessed by my God, as Finan assures me I am, I'll do more than just that. I'll restore Æthelwald to his position as my nephew and atone for my sins. That way, I'll gain an ally just as quickly as I lose my alliance with Penda.

If everything goes as I dream it will, that is.

For now, I must play a waiting game, and for a man of my age and ambition, it's not the easiest way to pass my time. I want nothing more than to confront Æthelwald, and demand he becomes my oath-sworn man, just as he should always have been, although he sees the past very differently. He believes I should have made him king in the place of his father. Even now, he tells any who'll listen, including Penda, that I kept his father's death a secret until I was able to call Bamburgh my own. Whether that's true or not, is for me to know and not for Æthelwald. He's my nephew and should stand with his family, not with the enemy who brought about his father's death.

If he'd allowed me to claim Deira in his name upon the death of Oswine, then Penda would have never taken my two sons and my daughter from me. No, Æthelwald has much to be blamed for. I intend to exact my vengeance on him just as soon as I've turned him to my alliance and gained the dominant position against Penda.

Until then, I must linger impatiently and watch Æthelwald and his men as they try to determine why there's a small contingent of Bernician men waiting to ride through or around the kingdom he rules. I'd hoped to keep my presence secret, but it's impossible to keep so many horses out of sight. I only hope that Onna is making his move in the East Anglian lands, and that soon Æthelwald will be called upon by Penda to go to his aid.

Unless, well, unless Penda has seen through my ruse and knows exactly what I'm planning. I haven't ruled out that possibility, but I'm hoping that it's not why Æthelwald is shadowing my every move.

Willyn, one of my longest-serving warriors, went with Ceonwahl on the ship, but he promised me that he'd personally return with news as soon as possible. I've not seen him for nearly three months, and in that time, I've learnt to worry, which angers me.

I'm a great warrior, the king of my tribe, and a father with many children. Yet the loss of my friend Willyn would make my endeavours pale into insignificance. He's always believed in me, even when I was an exile with not one but two older brothers holding a better claim to the kingdom of Bernicia than I. Yet he always supported my ambitions. I only hope I've not overreached this time.

I'm prepared to sacrifice my sons and daughters, not my friend. My friend has known me for longer than all of my children combined. I'll need him to help me rule when I become king of Northumbria, not just Bernicia.

Ealdorman Alduini disturbs my less-than-palatable thoughts. His face is troubled and unhappy. He didn't wish to come with me to the borderlands, but as he would have spoken against my plans if I'd left him behind in Bernicia, I left him with little choice but to escort me. He once served my brother and my older half-brother, the short-lived king of Bernicia. But Ealdorman Alduini's never been keen to affiliate himself with my plans and wishes.

'My lord king,' he manages to stumble. I turn angry eyes onto the old face, white hair, beard, white and wispy, and his legs feeble on either side of his horse.

'What is it?' I snap. He grimaces at my tone. He knows I don't like him just as much as he doesn't like me.

'King Æthelwald would like to speak with you.' He speaks so blandly that it takes long moments for me to understand what he's saying.

'What have you said to him, you old fool?' I retort with annoyance and a surge of fear, but Alduini simply shrugs and goes to ride away.

'He rode out to meet with me when I was scouting for you. He asked to speak with you. Over there.' He points through a straggle of trees I'd been using as camouflage and through which I can see a man on his horse waiting for me. He's slightly uphill and can no doubt see this exchange even through the trees. I grunt with annoyance. I don't wish to speak with Æthelwald. I've not seen him for years and would happily wait for many more. Only when I'm in a position of power can I entice him back to my alliance.

Seeing as he rides alone, I kick my bored animal through the budding undergrowth and make my way out into the open expanse. I don't know what Æthelwald hopes to accomplish today, but if he's after an apology, he's come a long way for something I will never give him.

My head swivels from side to side as I check to ensure I'm not riding into a trap. I ignore the hiss of anger from some of my men as they realise what I'm doing. But it seems that he's truly alone, and as I come within sight of him, I startle with surprise.

I've not seen my nephew for some time, years, not just months. In that time, he's become the man his father was at his death. I've often heard people speak of someone sharing their image, but until now, I've never experienced it before. Now that I have, I understand just how strange an experience it truly is.

Then I notice his sneering expression, and a quiver of unease rushes through me. Æthelwald hasn't come here for an apology. He knows something that I don't. I almost wish I didn't need to know what it was. It can't be good. He wouldn't have come alone if he'd known he'd face my warriors.

No, Æthelwald's bold move in coming to me alone speaks of a victory for Penda and a defeat for Onna and the rest of my men.

I swallow, and he notices my movement, a flicker of amusement passing through his eyes at the conclusions I've already drawn.

In that movement, I see his father again, my brother, the man whose kingdom I tried to usurp whilst banishing his son, who now stands before me. In a moment of fear, I can at least be man enough to admit my failings to myself, if not to anyone else.

I almost wish I'd not spent that last ten years ruling Bernicia. I almost wish I'd given it to this snarling beast of a man who has no love for me and never will.

'Uncle,' he says, his voice low and growling to match the look on his face.

He wears a long beard and moustache, his hair the same colour as his father's, and his eyes just as perceptive. I wonder if he sees his father when he looks at me. I certainly see him when he looks at me.

'Nephew,' I respond. There's no need for titles such as king.

'You're wasting your time,' he says without preamble. I almost thought he would make me beg for the news he holds, but he's seen my face and realises there's no point.

I imagine that all my hopes and dreams have fled from my previously animated face, and now I sit with nothing but lost faith.

'Explain?'

'King Penda was aware of king Onna's intentions and Ceonwahl's. He attacked them before they could strike him. Onna's dead.'

The news is shocking. Numbness creeps through my body, where only moments ago, confidence had filled me and flooded me with righteousness. And Æthelwald isn't done with me yet.

'Your daughter has lost her marriage. Your young son is imprisoned. Only your oldest son retains his freedom, and he's converted to paganism and proved his loyalty to his new father by ensuring that Alhflæd is always watched.'

I want to know how Æthelwald knows all this. How he can come to me with such outrageous stories, but there's a deep vein of truth in what he says. If I were Penda, I'd have done the same, although perhaps not been quite so kind to my older son, born of my union with the princess of Rheged.

'You were at the battle?' I ask, just because I do truly want to know on what basis he tells me all he knows.

'No, I wasn't, but King Penda sent word and a warning for you.'

He signals to someone behind him, and I realise that he's not come alone after all. I almost don't want to know what he has with him. It's bound to be a grizzly reminder of my continued disloyalty. For a terrifying moment, I fear it might be the body of my dead son Ecgfrith, murdered by Penda because of my disloyalty. But the horse that ambles toward me is one I recognise, and so too is the man upon the horse.

It's clear then how Penda knew of my involvement, how he knew to punish Ecgfrith and Alhflæd, for on that horse sits Willyn. He's beaten and bloody, and I fear that worse will have been done to him, and so it proves as he comes into clear view.

Penda has blinded my oldest ally, my greatest warrior. He'll never raise a sword or fight for me again.

I look at Æthelwald with anger, and he meets my blazing eyes fully.

'Uncle, you've made a firm enemy of king Penda now. He says he'll make good on his earlier promises to you. He sends Willyn back to you as a reminder of how men blinded by ambition can see little of the future.'

The words make horrifying sense to me. They surprise me by their Christian nature, for Penda is the pagan king, the man that all the priests from Iona caution against. The one that all the priests from Kent abhor. Yet he seems to have a true understanding of the main guiding principle of my religion.

'Willyn,' I call to the horse plodding toward me, its head down low, being guided only by its recognition of my beast.

'My lord,' Willyn sobs, and in that moment, I appreciate how wounded he is, how bereft and just how much Penda has taken from him.

His next words rob me of the ability to speak as tears stream down my face.

'All the men are dead, my lord king. My apologies for my failure. I should have led them better. I shouldn't have been captured.'

His words are a raw wound, just as his sightless eye sockets gaze at me. Whoever blinded him ensured the task was carried out well. He'll have scars but nothing too terrible, other than his lack of eyes. It's almost as though the person responsible for stealing his eyes has lavished loving care on him. It certainly wasn't an act committed in the horror of the shield wall but a cold and calculated move after the battle, when my warrior would have been hoping for an honourable death.

I feel anger begin to replace my initial fear.

'What does he plan to do?' I ask, but Æthelwald is looking at Willyn with such pity he doesn't hear my words.

'You know, he didn't escort him to me. He was left to wonder as he might, taking whatever path his poor old horse could find. He didn't know what he was eating or where he was going. He could have died on his journey, and all you care about are Penda's plans.'

I jolt at those words. I'd assumed, wrongly, or half-wrongly, that Penda had sent Willyn to Æthelwald, to ensure he made it home to me, to ensure that I saw the terrible ravages done to him.

'Someone found him drowning in a river, the both of them, and recognised the colours of his shield. He was just a farmer, but I rewarded him handsomely, and Willyn told me all he knew.'

I take the time to really look at Willyn then, to determine the extreme conditions he's endured. It feels as though little time has passed since I last saw him, and yet he's shrunken. He's also trying to speak over Æthelwald.

'It was my choice, my lord king, my choice.'

I don't know what he's talking about and look to Æthelwald as though he might be able to answer the question on my face that Willyn will never see again.

Æthelwald shrugs.

'You should hear his story, not ask me. My work here is done. I didn't need to escort him here, but I thought it was as fine a way as any other of giving you due warning. Penda will come for you. Everyone in the south knows it. I suggest you get off my borders and worry more about your own.'

'Nephew, you should stand with me, fight against Penda,' the words rip from my mouth without thought. I wish I could take them back when I see the distaste and anger on Æthelwald's face. Why did I speak so?

'We'll never stand together, uncle,' he spits, 'the time for that is long past. The time for family unity died with my father on the battlefield at Maserfeld.'

He turns to ride away, and I shout once more, 'Wait.'

He turns back slowly, and his preparedness to listen to my words, as angry as he is, makes me think there might be the smallest possibility that his hatred isn't as full-blown as he thinks it is.

His eyes are cold and dark, though, as I hastily reach for a few pieces of gold and silver stored in a small sack on the side of my saddle for when we're deep in enemy lands and need to bribe farmers for food.

'I don't want your silver,' he barks. I shake my head.

'For the farmer who saved Willyn's life. Please, will you see that he gets it?'

My nephew drops his head to one side, as though weighing the words I've spoken.

'I've already rewarded him, but yes, I'll see he gets this as well. And I'll tell him that King Oswiu of Bernicia rewards those who follow him blindly with gold they can't hope to eat. I pray it will turn him away from any false allegiance he might hold to you for such generosity.'

His words sting, as they're meant to, but I have nothing else I can give a farmer, nothing at all, other than my horse, and I need him to get me back to Bamburgh. But he's gone before I can think of any reply, the purse in his hand. I know he'll gift it to the farmer. He was always a boy of his word.

As Æthewald rides off, more of my men slide from our pathetic camouflage and mill around in confusion and horror, at the state that Willyn is in and the knowledge that the other men are all dead and gone.

'Tell me,' I say to Willyn, 'about the choice you were given.'

Willyn turns his sightless face to look at my face, still unused to his missing eyes, and sighs deeply.

'He told me I could stay and live with your older son or return to you. He gave me food but offered me no guide other than my horse.

He put much faith in my horse's ability to get me safely back to Bernicia.'

I've heard this said of Penda before. He prizes his horses highly, none more so than the beast he rides to war.

'So, he gave you food and a horse and set you on your way?'

'No, he gave me food and nothing else. I was lucky that he left me by one of the old roads. The horse kept to the flat surface, and other than that, I relied on the kindness of men and women I met on the way.'

I'm not sure I believe the tale. I feel sure that other than when he almost drowned, someone working for Penda must have shadowed Willyn. There's no way a blind man, in full battle gear, on such a magnificent horse could make his way blindly through the countryside without someone robbing him and taking all he had, even if it was just his bag of stale bread and cheese.

The men all listen intently, some of them, but not all of them, appreciating the message that Penda is sending to me.

Bernicia might be a wild land, but Mercia is peaceful and calm under her king. And more than that, it's prosperous enough that no one would want to rob an old warrior along its roadways.

Fuck.

It's a very powerful message.

10

ALHFLÆD OF BERNICIA
SUMMER AD654

My husband doesn't even come to me to tell me of his victory. I don't send for him either. There's little point.

My father has abandoned me, left me to the wiles of the Mercian king and his prince. I can't even fill my womb with his seed to make my marriage a more palatable experience for either of us and to be restored to my previous position. When my husband rode away to make war with his father, I prayed for my womb to fill with the embers of a new child. I wept bitterly when it didn't happen. Since then, I've not even seen my husband, let alone had the opportunity to entice him back to my bed.

I could curse myself for being a fool, for being the instrument of my downfall and unhappiness, but I know I'm not. It's all my father's fault; a Christian king who said he loved his children, all of us, and then allowed Ecgfrith, myself and my older half-brother to become victims of Mercian aggression.

I look back on our final conversation with each other when he assured me of his love and his plans for the future. Of how he'd disentangle me from this unwanted marriage. I see he lied just as surely as every other king or prince I've met or heard of. He gave his word to me, to Penda, to just about everyone, and has satisfied none of his oaths or promises. He's a weak man, made weaker in the light of Penda's continual success against him.

I should have made myself more amenable to Paeda, but at the time, I'd thought I would only be with him for a short amount of time. How could my father, a man of such military might, with the power of persuasion at his fingertips, not find a way for me to cast aside the marriage and serve my God instead?

Ever since I heard the words of Bishop Aidan as a small child, I've wanted nothing more than to become a nun, to labour only for the good of my God. I had no plans to be a wife or even a mother. I certainly had no intention of allowing myself to enjoy the act of making a child. That I did, and would still do, is a terrible sin, I must pray even harder to have absolved.

Not that my husband has been cruel to me. In fact, the very opposite, but neither of us is happy with this marriage. Now that my father has made it known he'll support anyone who rises against Penda, even those who've failed to beat him in the past, there seems no point in even continuing with the façade. So, I have my wish anyway. My older half-brother, Ealhfrith, has been made responsible for the only kind of imprisonment that Paeda is prepared to inflict on me, sending me to be cared for by the fledgling church in the territory of the Middle Angles. I'm far enough away from any border with East Anglia or Bernicia that no one would attempt to rescue me.

I'm a prisoner. I don't think I mind at all because I'm safe and away from my lying father. There are enough warriors outside the door to prevent any from trying to attack this small stronghold that belongs to Penda's daughter and her husband.

Well, apart from the fact that I know that Paeda is looking for a new wife, one who'll be far keener to lie in his bed and carry his children for him. I wish it were me, but my father demanded I was as difficult as possible and cause as many problems for Paeda and Penda as I could. Whilst my father has been unable to keep to his promises, I've succeeded in every way possible.

My father is a failure. He's taken the name of my Lord God and subverted it to his ends. I can only pray for his soul and hope that my exhortations on his behalf will ensure he retains the ear of his God. Not that he deserves to. He's earned nothing for his labours and shouldn't benefit from any special favour, no matter what Bishop Finan tells him.

Ealhfrith is the proud father of a son, a small child he often brings to see me and pray with me. He's just as religious as I am. I know we share many traits. We may be the children of a king who has pretensions to be Christian, but our faith is a deeper conviction. We believed the words of Bishop Aidan and then Bishop Finan. If we can show Paeda and Ealhfrith's wife that being pious isn't a bad thing, that it can mean something in and of itself, we'll have accomplished a great thing, far more than my father and his warriors have ever managed to do. Faith shouldn't be the result of a superior military power but one that stems from a quietly held inner belief. Faith is a personal matter. Those who shout the loudest, so I've learnt, tend to have the smallest genuine belief.

The child is no more than a babe, yet Ealhfrith sits with him on his lap. The three of us listen willingly to the priest from Iona, Cedd, who teaches us the true faith, not the faith of kings who want to contort it to their ends.

I'm not so much a prisoner as allowed free rein to meander through the small but well-maintained hall that Ealhfrith and his wife live within. It includes a small section within the great hall that's curtained off and been made into our place of worship, complete with a wooden altar and a space for the priest to keep his holy instruments within.

I feel more content here than I have done for many, many years, even when I lived with my father. I could be happy here, I think, unless my father infuriates Penda more than he already has, and Penda is left with no choice but to have me killed. It's not a comforting thought, but at least in death, I'd be freed from the bonds that tie me to this world where I can only be one of two things: a wife or a nun. There's no other option available for me. Although I want to be a nun, the fact that I also wanted to be the mother of Paeda's child when he rode away to war makes me think that I'm not as content to be just a holy woman as I once was.

I worry for my younger brother, and so does Ealhfrith. Ealhfrith, who's won the respect of Penda and his wife, another Christian for all that her faith is self-contained, worries incessantly at the effects that Ecgfrith's murder would have on Penda's soul. When he first spoke of it, his face earnest and young in the dim light from our candle, sitting cross-legged on the furs placed over the wooden floorboards as he rocked his son to sleep in his arms, I thought he was doing no more than trying to tempt me to speak ill of Penda. I thought he wanted me to say something that would be seen as treasonous, a pretext for my murder, but it seems I was wrong.

Penda, the pagan king, according to Ealhfrith, must have a soul. It must be protected if our island isn't to descend into the chaos of constant warfare that runs rife through the British kingdoms that our ancestors conquered so easily because of their unease with each other. If no one would help another, then how could they provide a concerted defense against the warriors who came in their ships, with their sharpened weapons and the thought of conquest on their minds?

Ealhfrith, raised at his mother's court and not my father's, has a different view of the Saxon kingdoms than I do, which intrigues me.

He sees Penda as a unifying force, almost benign now that he's achieved so much, killing not one but two pretentious Northumbrian kings. He might have been a brutal man in the past, but now that he has achieved so much, he can be more conciliatory. Men know he'll carry out his dire threats, but he's more deadly with his tongue than with his sword and spear these days.

I think that Ealhfrith is too much in awe of Penda, too desperate to ensure his own survival, to understand what Penda truly is. He's a man of blackness and iron from the very stories of our God's struggles. But Ealhfrith is my brother and my only ally. I don't wish to lose his support.

His wife, Cyneburh, doesn't exactly hate me, but she's never overly friendly. Neither does she resent the time her husband spends with me. She sweeps in and out of the room to claim her child whenever he needs feeding, and other than that leaves Ealhfrith and me to talk and use our time as we see fit, provided we both spend some time outside and walk around the enclosed stronghold as often as we can.

I could almost like her, but she's her mother's daughter and her father's daughter both. I've heard her making decisions, and speaking with her warriors, for they're hers and not her husband's. She enforces her will upon her household. She's fair and judicious, but once she's made her mind up about something, there's no swaying her. I wish my father had allowed me to rule as she does, even if it is only within her household, within the kingdom of the Middle Angles. The people who look to her as their local lord respect her and fear her equally.

I'd have liked to rule as she does.

Sometimes she's kind to me, giving me fabric to make new clothes or telling me how my young brother fares. She tolerates me as many others wouldn't, especially within Paeda's household. But then, I know I can cause no problems here. Her household is fiercely loyal to her and her husband. I have no one other than my half-brother even to try and convert to my thinking.

I never much liked Ecgfrith. I didn't exactly miss him when he was taken by Penda as surety for my father's oath of allegiance. But now I worry for him, and see the possibility of a way to undermine Penda. I think Penda is too fond of Ecgfrith. I think he'll speak of his murder for his father's crimes or his blinding or maiming, but he'll never do it. His God, so I hear, doesn't think highly of blood sacrifices of children, or so Penda says when he justifies why Ecgfrith still lives. I think he sees Ecgfrith as more than just a hostage. He would call him his own son if he could do so without upsetting his warriors and ealdormen.

I half believe him, but in my heart I hope that Penda sees a child, not Oswiu's son whenever he looks at Ecgfrith. I think that will keep Ecgfrith safe no matter what my foolish father does. Ecgfrith, I realise, might be the only way I ever gain my freedom, should I want it. When he's the king of Bernicia, as must soon happen if Penda takes his revenge against my father, he'll free me, and will do so with Penda's good wishes, knowing that I never desire to have any part to play in court politics again.

Yet, for all that I live with the king's daughter, I know much of the events outside these walls are kept from me. They see no need to do any more than treat me as the princess I should have been, albeit one incapable of providing her husband with heirs.

I don't know if it's my fault, or a punishment for lying with a man who's only half a Christian for Paeda doesn't profess my faith as I do. No, he, like his father, understands our religion only in terms of its potential political advantages. He is still, at heart, a follower of Woden despite his baptism and eagerness to hear the words of Bishop Finan.

For now, I'm content. I'll live my life in my nun-like way, with my brother and my priest and my distant husband. I'll pray that my father sees sense for the first time in his life and understands that Penda is not a man to strive to overthrow.

Perhaps Ealhfrith is correct in his view.

With Penda as the guiding power within our kingdoms, there might just be peace. If only men would let him rule as he must.

11

ÆTHELWALD OF DEIRA
SUMMER AD654

S eeing my uncle once more, in person, has shocked me and reawakened all of my conflicting feelings toward him.

I hate him and despise him for stealing my kingdom from me. At the same time, he looks so like my father that I find it difficult to reconcile my memories of my loving father with this hauntingly familiar face of a man who betrayed me.

I almost wish I'd not taken it upon myself to return his blinded warrior to him, but then, what sort of man would I be if I couldn't even gaze upon the face of the man I hate so much?

I know God preaches forgiveness, but there can be no forgiveness where deceit has been used against me. It's Oswiu who sinned, not me. I don't see why he should receive my forgiveness.

But, well, he's my uncle, and I have little enough family left other than my wife and my young sons.

I shouldn't have come. I don't want to second-guess myself where Oswiu and Penda are concerned. Penda didn't kill my father, although he died in battle against him, a clean battle, or so I've heard, where my father died protecting his faith, or so he thought.

I see no sign that Penda means any harm to the spread of the Christian faith. He simply doesn't share those beliefs. I respect him more for having the courage to follow his path, for believing in his gods as fiercely as I do in mine than for playing false to himself in the hope that he might gain more support.

My father died for a cause he thought up, nothing else. Penda had no intention of attacking Christianity, either in Iona or in Kent.

My uncle, though, he's a different matter entirely. His movements might have been impulsive, but they were still well thought out. He knew what he needed to do in order to become king in my place, and he took those steps. His hand wasn't forced. He didn't have to do it or face death. No, my uncle is the more despicable man, not Penda.

Yet.

No, I banish the thoughts from my mind. I think only of the possible retaliation Penda will take, for I can't imagine him allowing my uncle to keep his life, not now. Penda has acted as peacefully as any man could. He permitted my uncle to speak oaths instead of war cries. My uncle has repaid that faith with blood and the forge's heat.

My uncle should have chosen a better enemy, perhaps my cousin in the Pictish lands, Talorcan, but not Penda.

Penda has a multitude of alliances. Every time my uncle attacks him, or indeed any king from the north attacks him, it's Penda who grows in stature and power.

King Onna of the East Angles is dead. In his place, his brother, King Æthelhere of the East Angles, rules with the support of Penda. If Penda decides to march north again, to meet Oswiu in battle as he should have done three years ago, Æthelhere will support him, and so will I. So too, will his son, his brother and the king of Gwynedd. They've long been allies.

And more men will flock to his banners as well. Men from Dumnonia, from Ceredigion, where his wife hails from, and even more besides, including my cousin, king Talorcan of the Pictish lands. I've only met Talorcan on a handful of occasions, but he's a scheming man, long allied with Penda in honour of his arrangement with his father before the battle of Hæðfeld. I imagine even the men of the West Saxons will march with Penda. Ceonwahl, once more in exile, only this time on the continent, will try and reclaim his kingdom from them and will fail.

The kingdom of Dal Riata may well join with Penda, anything to ensure that Oswiu is hobbled in the north and penned in to his retracting kingdom of Bernicia. I doubt men will speak of him with the same awe they do my father.

No, my uncle has enemies everywhere, and Penda has only allies or men who don't wish to become his enemies. My uncle has hideously exposed himself with his contingent of warriors sent to support Ceonwahl and Onna. He'll not be allowed to slink back to the north and forget it occurred.

Penda can't allow that to happen, not now. That means I'll have to firm up my resolve toward my uncle. Penda will expect my support, as he gave his to me when my uncle murdered Oswine, and left the kingdom open for me. I want to give it to him, provided he has no view to claiming control of my kingdom. Not that I think he will. He's not my uncle or even my father. His oversight is different. He's taken the time to learn what makes men loyal and what makes them turn at the earliest opportunity.

But he's underestimated my uncle's rage, and that might cause him problems in the future.

I rein my horse in from its slow plod and turn to look once more at my uncle and his warriors. They've not moved from their place in the open field, close to the small-forested area they'd been hiding within, and the flash of metal in the sun is almost blinding.

My uncle's a warrior. He was taught to fight in Dal Riata, just as my father was, and he's even had the time and the position to expand on his skills. Even so, when I look at him, with his handful of warriors, and I think of Penda, with his mass of warriors and the allegiance of the great men of his kingdom. And from other kingdoms. I know that my uncle has no possibility of withstanding the attack. I can't see that Penda would allow himself to be swayed by the offer of yet more oaths. Not even for his son and his wife, who now live apart.

No, my uncle is a small man who thinks too much of himself. I appreciate that it's a similar position to the one that Penda and his brother once found themselves in, but it's different. Penda spoke with his sword and his shield, not with his God, and that has made his reputation grow and expand. There are more fantastical stories about Penda that are untrue than there are fantastical stories about my Lord God, which may well be true.

At some point, someone will have to write down the stories. Perhaps that's what Penda planned when he allowed one of the Ionan priests to escort Alhflæd upon her marriage. If not, I'll need to think about asking one of my priests to do the work. I don't believe a man with Penda's renown should suffer from a lack of someone to record his exploits and his great deeds.

He's a pagan, but that's not what makes him such a larger-than-life character. It's his very viewpoint on his place in this land and what he must do to ensure that he lives up to those expectations.

No, if I turn to the south, I imagine I can see a shield wall so long it stretches along the border of our kingdoms and onwards into the disputed land between Gwynedd and Northumbria of which my grandfather once tried to lay claim. Penda commands men as others order sheep, only with a far better-trained dog than any man can lay claim to.

I see a shining wall of moving steel and iron. It advances, gaining traction, going faster and faster until it meets a small thing of wood and flesh, with a sudden burst of brightest red. And then nothing, as the shining wall advances going ever onwards, onwards, until it meets the remains of the ancient wall to the far, far north, that rushes through both Dal Riata and the remains of the kingdom of Gododdin.

Penda is a force that will never be stopped. My uncle will be crushed beneath the weight of his success and his allies.

My uncle will die.

A long and painful death. I hope. And he'll have no one to blame but himself.

And I couldn't give a shit.

12

PENDA, KING OF MERCIA
SUMMER AD654

My bed is warm and soft, my wife sleeping softly at my side, but I find my thoughts too confused for sleep to worm its way into my consciousness.

Our preemptive attack against King Onna was easily accomplished. He was barely ready for the attack and certainly wasn't expecting such a concerted mustering of my forces against him.

Paeda took Onna on his sword, whilst Herebrod and his men attacked those loyal to Oswiu and left only one man alive. I could have watched from the sidelines, but I didn't. I fought with my men as I always have done, especially as my younger sons were with me. They watched the way men fight and attack, the way men piss themselves with fear and run before the battle has even begun, just as Ceonwahl, previously king of the West Saxons did.

I can't believe I ever thought he was a worthwhile match for my half-sister. No, she's much more happily wed with a man from Cynddylan's lands. She'll birth many warriors, provided she lives through the experience as she should. She's a stubborn mule of a woman, and I would expect her to look upon childbirth as her equivalent of a battle.

She shares my father but not my mother, and she's not Coenwahl's full sister. As he felt his life ebbing away from him, my father perhaps enjoyed women a little too much and a little too often, with no thought for the result of his union and the effect it might have had on his sons' wishes to gain control of the Mercian kingdom.

I'm lucky that my younger brother and sister are so loyal to my cause. They could have meddled and brought me nothing but problems, just as in the Bernician kingdom. The family loyalties there are so split and intermingled, that it's no wonder Oswiu is unable to bring together a force capable of even threatening me.

And Oswiu is the cause of my sleeplessness.

Well, not Oswiu, but his young son, Ecgfrith, a boy I'm not afraid to say of which I've grown very fond. I don't wish to harm for his father's failings, no matter that was the intention behind him coming to live within my household.

Yet, I can't be seen to be weak. Already I've allowed his sister, Alhflæd, to retire from her marriage and live as she wishes, because she's no good to Paeda as a wife. Paeda must have sons to train and teach so that they can rule upon his death. Alhflæd won't even let the boy bed her, let alone carry his child. And her half-brother is more than happily married to my daughter. It seems Oswiu is infecting my kingdom more by stealth than by iron, and it's all of my own doing.

But the boy? What should I do with him?

My younger sons are far too fond of him for me to seriously consider having him killed. I've clarified that I intend to do so, but I simply can't. While he stays here, I look weak, and I can't afford to appear weak, not when Oswiu is determined to threaten my carefully constructed alliances.

I won this kingdom through war. I'm happy to don my war gear and ride to battle upon my warhorse, but not if it's unnecessary. I have allies everywhere and only one enemy. Is it worth my while to attempt to attack him again? To meet him in battle and bring about his death, just as I did his brother and uncle before him? Or should I allow him to have his peace and liberty, never being sure whether or not I plan to attack him?

Is it better to have him uneasy than roundly defeated?

If I attacked him and killed him in battle, as I imagine would happen, who'd rule after him? Would it be his nephew who already reins in Deira, or would I be confident enough that the nobility would follow Ecgfrith that I could install him there as my king by proxy? Would it be worth the effort?

One day I'll die and leave behind three sons and a nephew who are all capable of holding a kingdom together, but would they be able to hold together the alliances that I've personally forged and that stretch from the kingdom of Dumnonia in the south to the land of the Picts in the north?

They don't have my reputation to assist them. I mean them no disrespect in saying that. Our kingdoms are too young, too weak, to stand without a strong leader. Look at the West Saxons. They find it easier to rule themselves with their king in exile. Look at Oswiu. It's been over ten years since he became king of Bernicia, and still, he fails to make any advances and regain the kingdom his brother once ruled. His attempts to retake Deira have failed, partly because of my interference but also because other men want him to fail.

People want me to succeed, but will they want the same for my sons and nephew?

And what of Ecgfrith?

The men who once had as much influence as my family did within Mercia before my brother and I both took far firmer control of the kingdom, all shout for blood and war. I harbour the thought that they hope I might die in battle and they might regain their little plot of land. But I think that more than anything, they wish to fight. They grow tired of our settled way of life, of being members of the most powerful kingdom. Who am I to deny them the opportunity?

When I die, the whole island of Britain will undergo a monumental shift as men seek new alliances and enemies. I must ensure that my kingdom can defend itself, and to do that, there must always be war.

But do I want war? And does it even matter if I don't?

My eye must always be on the future, not on the past. I must act in such a way that I ensure the survival of Mercia as it now stands. I can't even consider the thought that it might crumble upon itself and revert to its constituent parts. Become subject to whoever is the king of Northumbria, East Anglia, Kent or even the bloody West Saxons.

The Mercian people, the men and women on the borders of everywhere, have fought hard, have lost those they love and have spilt more blood and sweat than any of the other kingdoms to carve out this piece of land that has no set boundaries or borders. It has no rivers demarcating where one kingdom ends, and another begins. They deserve the opportunity to make war, to make a new generation of men into proud warriors who will fight and die in the name of their king and their legendary founder, Woden. Who am I to deny that when I have so much influence amongst my fellow kings?

And so to Ecgfrith. I think I must keep him, as I want to, and turn him to do my bidding. I will make him an ally of Mercia, not an enemy, and so make him a king in the place of his father. That means I must once more call on my allies, and make firm my boundaries and think of marching north.

I should have fucking done it three years ago when I reached the fortress of Bamburgh. I should have burnt Oswiu out of his home and his mead hall. I should never have made peace with him.

Perhaps in old age, all I've relearnt is what I already knew in my youth. The words of men mean nothing when they're uttered under threat. Men will always wriggle out of oaths and alliances they made when weak as soon as they become strong again.

Fuck. I should have killed Oswiu at Maserfeld, chased him from the battlefield and mounted his head on a stake next to his damn brother's.

So resolved, I finally sleep, for I know that in the morning, I'll need to start planning and plotting, alerting my allies to my plans and deciding the best place to attack and the best time.

Hæðfeld was a winter battle, Maserfeld a summer one, I've just fought Onna in the summer sun, and I've fought him in the past in the early winter gloom. All I know for sure is that this time I'll not be working to tempt Oswiu to come onto Mercian soil. No, this time, I'll attack deep into his heartland and give him the same sort of fear and worry I experienced when I thought Maserfeld would end with a defeat as opposed to the death of my brother and Oswald.

I'll have to send Herebrod and his men to find a convenient location and perhaps ask Æthelwald as well, and even Ecgfrith. But he left home when he was so young I doubt he's done more than travel between Oswiu's royal residences, from Bamburgh to Yeavering, to the monastery on Lindisfarne to the other royal estates in Islandshire and beyond. No, it'll be Æthelwald I can talk to, but to be on the safe side, I might ask Ealhfrith. Of all of Oswiu's children, it's Ealhfrith I find to be the most loyal and content with his life.

But then, he was a prince in his native Rheged, and he's still a prince in Mercia. He's lost little through his marriage to my daughter. I've gained myself a grandson, who I find I almost like. He reminds me of my age, and that I don't like, but he represents the future that I'm striving to secure for my family. For that reason, he's a very real reminder that life will continue without me and that all I can do is prepare as best I can for that time.

I'll also need to make provisions to ensure that Mercia is protected without me. In this, I'll need to rely on the support of Immin, Eafa and Eadberht. Immin will protect my wife and my younger sons, whilst Eafa and Eadberht will decide who remains behind in Mercia and who ventures to the north with me.

My warriors, even the ones who now seem to me to be the same age that Aldfrith was when I was making my mark at Hæðfeld, will wish to ride with me. Be it one last adventure, or just the start of another new one, they'll not remain at home, even if I command them with fire and blood to do so.

Old men with iron in their make-up can never stop being warriors and harbingers of death, nor should they want to. Certainly, I don't. Well, so I tell myself.

The weight of the tasks I've set myself temporarily stuns me. So many people to cajole and speak to, so many small details to arrange if I'm to leave my kingdom for any length of time. Yet it will be worth it.

I've decided. My ambition is to set Ecgfrith up in his father's place as king of Bernicia, albeit under the firm and watchful gaze of his older half-brother, a man who's more loyal to me than his father. On the southern border, Æthelwald will keep Eahlfrith loyal, and to the north, Talorcan will watch like a hawk, waiting for any misstep so that he sweep in and claim his other birthright, that of the kingdom of Bernicia.

In the morning, I'll call my loyal followers and warriors before me to tell them of my intentions. We'll see how much time it takes for Oswiu to hear word of my intentions.

It won't be long of that I can be assured.

13

PAEDA OF THE HWICCE
SUMMER AD654

Ceredigion

I've been to my mother's place of birth before. It's a land of sea and wind, rain and sheep, a description that always makes her cry a little with its blandness because she knows it's correct. Oh, and small little churches filled with men who think they'll be saints one day because of the abject deprivation they chose to live in.

I find the whole conflict between the two Christianity's to be an unsettling one. It reveals how convoluted and constructed the whole thing is. The old Gods, Woden my ancestor and his ilk, offer no narrative that I must abide by, other than they might appreciate the occasional battle and blood sacrifice. find it to be much more to my taste.

Whenever I asked the Ionan priest who lived with me when I was married about the constraints of his faith compared to my mother's, he could only shrug and tell me that his ways were the ancient ones, the correct ones. He said my mother's faith was far more similar than dissimilar. But then I encountered Bishop Birinus from the Continent, and the differences were once more far more pronounced than the similarities.

I think I care little for a doctrine that appears so rigid and inherently changeable and dependent on the interpretations of men no more qualified to tell me how to live my life than I am.

My uncle lives in a fine hall, not far from the crashing coastline. It's to him that my father has sent me. I could almost take it as an insult. My father and my uncle have been allies for so long that it seems almost ludicrous to make the journey and speak with him of our plans. But then, I assume that this is why the pair have been allies for so long. My father is not only married to his sister. He also accords my uncle a great deal of respect and gives the time and effort needed to remain on good terms.

My father and me, I think ruefully, know only too well how fleetingly marriage alliances can remain in place.

After the battle at Maserfeld, my father permitted my mother to travel to her homeland and visit with her still-living family. It was a sign of two things, my father's confidence in his success and his utter faith in my uncle. It means that I vaguely know my way to my uncle's main residence and whom I'll encounter on my travels.

I think it's my father's way of releasing me from my burdensome marriage. I wonder vaguely if he and uncle Clydog are plotting a new marriage for me or if I see a conspiracy where none exists. Time will tell.

My uncle rides to greet me when I see his home. His warriors have long been trailing me, but they think I didn't know they were there, which is something I'll have to warn my uncle of without humiliating him. His borders are as wide open as those of Mercia. He must protect them as fully as my father does his own. If not, he'll lose his kingdom, although I doubt that'll happen. He's been king here for longer than my father has been in Mercia, and they could have been firm enemies, only they chose to become allies instead.

Clydog is a huge man who's spent much of his time fighting off the ambitions of those who share his borders to the north, if not the south. Sliding from my horse and striding out to greet him, I'm taken by the similarities I see in him to myself. I always thought I looked like my father, but it seems I have just as much of my mother's family in me as well. That should make this easy.

Clydog's gasp of surprise as he envelops me in a hug makes me realise he's seen the resemblance as well. It's amusing that whilst other kings and would-be kings have tried to assert their difference from those they try to rule, my father has completely merged with his own. He embraces those of the old tribes who wish to return to their homelands and marries into the royal family of one of the surviving kingdoms. It's another mark of my father's forethought, conscious or unconscious. He's never tried to present himself as anything other than he is.

He knows his family, with the help of Woden, rode through the lands of what became Mercia, claiming what they could and killing when they couldn't coerce others with their swords or words. He's never denied that nor that he gained much of his kingdom through the shedding of blood. Yet it was only ever done so that he could become the man he'd been born to be. There was no real malice but firm intent.

'Uncle,' I say, although his embrace muffles my words, and he laughs at me.

'Fuck, you look like my father,' he offers as he steps away from me to continue glancing up and down my length. 'Fuck, fuck,' he continues, laughing as he does so. 'I thought the old bastard had come back to try his luck with me again.'

I don't think I know much about my mother's father, but I laugh along. It wouldn't do to upset my uncle with my ignorance.

'Your mother is well?' he thinks to ask as we make our way inside his great hall, where the smell of cooking mutton is pouring through the open doorway. A warm wind blows along the coastline, and in its wake, I can hear the crashing of an angry sea on the cliff edges.

'Yes, thank you. She sent you gifts.'

'I'm sure she did,' he mutters a little darkly. I almost ask him what he means, but my father, mother and uncle have a far longer history together than I do. There are events about which children should always be ignorant.

'And your father?' he asks more brightly. 'Is it true that we'll be riding to war again.'

Clydog, just like my father, is a man who made his name in blood, death and fire within the shield walls on a battlefield. They live for war.

'Yes, to the north this time.'

My father has decided that there's no time for secrecy. He wants Oswiu to know his intentions and that his kingdom has never been less secure than it is now.

'And what will he do when he gets there?' my uncle asks, beckoning to his servants for food and mead.

I've not come alone. A party of twenty men escorts me. I see that my uncle is ensuring they're fed and cared for as well. Clydog does so without thought. It's become his second nature to accept that warriors glittering from head to toe with iron will walk in and out of his hall without thought.

'That remains to be seen,' I say with a shrug, swigging deeply from the drinking horn. But Clydog is a sharp man, just as my mother is a clever woman. I already know, as my father did, that the answer I gave him will be unsatisfactory. Neither is it to be the only one. My father made it clear that Clydog was to know all of his plans. There are to be no secrets between the pair of them.

'For some, yes, but not for me, surely?' there's the hint of a challenge in Clydog's deep voice. I'm almost tempted to delay the inevitable a little longer, but he's my uncle, and he deserves my respect.

'He plans on killing Oswiu and placing the boy in his place.' Clydog, drinking as I spoke, splutters at my quietly spoken words and looks at me in surprise.

'It's true then, your father has gone soft in his old age?'

That wounds, as Clydog knows it will. I look away angrily. It doesn't matter that my father said he'd react this way. I don't like to see my father's plans occasioning such laughter.

'No,' I say slowly, trying not to snap my reply but Clydog grins at me again.

'I mean no disrespect. It's just that I've heard others say as much and it worries me. Your father has fought for too long to be seen as old and decrepit.'

'My father should have killed Oswiu last time. I was instrumental in begging him not to do so, and all for a woman who doesn't love or desire me.'

Now Clydog looks sympathetic to my plight, and I wish he didn't.

'Women should not affect our battle decisions,' a howl of annoyance greets those words from Clydog's wife. He winks at me as he continues. 'But they bloody do. You shouldn't blame yourself. It's a shame her father is a lying piece of scum.'

'It is, yes,' I mutter, thinking of my first sight of Alhflæd again and wondering what magic had bewitched me to fight for a marriage, not a kingdom. I could have been the king of Bernicia, or so my father teased me, but I settled for a marriage that has been anything but pleasant and fulfilling.

'Come, let's talk of battle tactics, not women,' my uncle continues to joke as he toasts me, and I relax. My father has sent me here so that I can hear other men's opinions on my decisions and understand that there's no one to blame for the current debacle but bloody Oswiu and his ambitions. It's Oswiu who's made what must now happen inevitable. It's Oswiu, not myself who's to blame for the coming battle after so many years of near tranquility.

'I have a small matter to tend to anyway, along the northern borders. You could ride with me. Perhaps we'll find another ally.'

Gwynedd lies to the north of Clydog's kingdom, and Powys to the east. My father has always maintained good relationships with both kings, well apart from Cynddylan, who my father refused to communicate with for years after the battle of Maserfeld, blaming him for coming so late to the battle that Eowa lost his life. But Clydog has never shared the same good relations. My mother tells me it's similar to the Saxon kingdoms. We fall out amongst ourselves and constantly try to be better than our neighbours. I know that Clydog will use my presence as a means of gaining a favourable outcome with Gwynedd, but that's also as my father thought.

His first ally was Cadwallon of Gwynedd, a king in exile because of Edwin of Northumbria's pretensions. He knows that Cadwallon's dynasty will be easily swayed into joining the new alliance against Northumbria. If, in the meantime, we can gain some cessation of the constant border warfare between Ceredigion and Gwynedd, that's all for the good.

My father also chuckled when speaking of the matter and told me to ensure that only the best warriors, those who routinely argued with their swords and war axes, were allowed to join the attacking force. The constant discord will work in his favour for it will mean that both Clydog and Cadafel will bring well-tested and trained warriors with them.

My father hopes to have at least twenty allies when he rides north. Clydog is number six, after myself, the king of Dumnonia, Æthelwald of Deira and Æthelhere of East Anglia. Some men will bring smaller contingents with them, amongst them Immin's war leader, Herebrod and his war band and Eafa of Tamworth, who will represent him and his brother's interests in the north.

I also think my father will allow Eahlfrith to travel with my sister's warriors. If not, they'll be offended and feel slighted.

And, of course, Ecgfrith of Bernicia will also journey with us, but he won't have men to command. Rather, he'll be with either his brother or my father.

The noble families of the West Saxons will also send representatives. My father hazards a hope that even the aloof ruling family of the Kentish kingdom might join with him. Their daughter is married to Oswiu, but it seems they're unhappy with his ruling abilities and his failure to make good on his intentions to convert all of his kingdom to the Christian faith. And to the north? Well of course Talorcan, king of the Pictish lands, will join my father.

Cadafel isn't quite as reliable as an ally as Cadwallon, but he provided a small contingent of warriors for the battle of Maserfeld and has remained on more or less good terms with my father ever since.

It'll be interesting to see what he makes of my presence on his borders alongside my uncle.

And then, even though my uncle says he wants to talk of war, I notice that the hall has been swelled by the arrival of at least ten young women, all enticing as they walk amongst the warriors and all looking my way.

My uncle chuckles at my sides, and my aunt rolls her eyes with annoyance, but even I feel the tug of desire and begin to think that my father had this arranged long before he even told me I was to meet with my uncle.

It's as though he's allowing me to enjoy myself and come home when I've fought a few more battles and bedded a few more women. My father is allowing me to gain more of a reputation for myself than that of a thwarted lover and Christian convert.

I could thank him for his forethought, but as one of the women sashays closer to me, all thoughts of my father flee from my mind. There's a time for battle and a time for lovers, and this is a time for the latter.

14

OSWIU, KING OF BERNICIA
SUMMER AD654

My journey northwards is sluggish, hampered by Willyn's slow progress and my men's unhappiness. They've won no battles, and they're returning home empty-handed. I've failed those who still live just as surely as those who've lost their lives fighting for Onna and Ceonwahl.

I've failed as a giver of rings and a gifter of treasure and land.

And worse, I've infuriated our enemy, and I know that he'll be coming for me. My options are limited.

My sons are lost to me now, and my daughter is as well. Although I've more sons and daughters, what I lack more than anything else is an ally who'll join me and fight against Penda.

I don't even know where to begin looking. Whom should I approach? If I'd not attacked the Gododdin, they might have joined me. If I'd not attacked the Dal Riatans, they might have joined with me, but it seems that my only hope of allies lies over the sea to the east, on the island the Dal Riatans share with the other tribes, and where the holy men of Iona stem from.

But my brother almost severed all of our ties with those kings with his violence and determination to win renown. I can't even call upon my first wife's family because they vowed I'd never be forgiven for leaving her. Neither will my current wife's family support me, for they are far to the south. Between them and I lies the massive kingdom of Mercia, over which Penda presides as king, unbeatable and chillingly efficient in exerting his power.

I need to consider my options carefully and be cold-hearted in my attempts at circumventing the retribution that will be coming my way.

I need to be as devious as Penda has been in the past. I must take his allies from him without him realising, and to do that, I need to start with my family first. My nephews hate me, but I might be able to convince Talorcan that Penda is as much a threat to him as he is to me. Likewise, I might be able to convince Æthelwald of Deira that Penda is his enemy.

But ideally, I need to know both of my nephews better, and I've been remiss in that regard. If I reach out to them now, will they see through my attempts at friendliness?

I feel hopeless and lost, and not even seeing my fortress at Bamburgh, high on the coastline in the distance, lifts my spirits. I believe Penda will come and burn my home, even if I'm within it. It's nothing short of a miracle that he didn't do so before.

Those of my warriors I left to protect my family ride out to greet me when I'm less than a day's journey from Bamburgh. Their expressions are perplexed. I shouldn't have returned yet. They know my appearance isn't a good sign. Even my wife joins them, as does Bishop Finan of Lindisfarne.

It's a bright summer day, yet my mood is black, and the outlook is bleak. I know that when my explanation is given, the looks between them, will mirror mine.

The outlook is hopeless. The possibilities for the future are limited.

'Perhaps it would be better to simply leave?' my wife asks, in her first moments of fear, but even Bishop Finan shushes her.

'We'll pray,' he offers, indicating the holy island of Lindisfarne. I almost wish it could be that easy. But if a few prayers to my God could resolve my predicament, I wouldn't be in it in the first place.

'We must consult the blessed relics,' Finan continues. It feels strange to hear once more my brother's bones being spoken about as though he's a saint. This is what drives Finan. For he believes my brother is a saint. That he was a man tested in his holy conviction to his God and a man who died to honour that belief.

It angers me that even in death, my brother is deemed somehow more able, holier than I can ever be. Yet, if there's even the smallest possibility that my brother is truly holy, I'll need his help to defeat Penda and keep the kingdom within our family line.

I nod quickly, content to allow someone else to decide for me. Instead of turning for my fortress, I wind my way toward Lindisfarne, allowing only my wife, a handful of my household warriors, and poor Willyn to travel to Bamburgh instead.

Willyn is weak and sick. He needs to be nursed back to health, and then he's begged me to allow him to live with the monks on Lindisfarne. He doesn't wish to be a burden to me, or so he says, but I know the truth of it. He doesn't want me to be constantly reminded of his failure and what it means for the future.

I'll give him his wishes when he's well. I'm grateful he desires to be out of my sight each day. I think he's right. His presence would annoy me and anger me both. I don't need to be reminded anymore of how badly I've miscalculated.

The route to Lindisfarne takes me beyond Bamburgh, and it's there that I kiss my wife goodbye, a more solemn kiss than before I left to tackle Penda. In that touch, I feel my wife's horror and unease. She's a very devout woman, but even she understands the task I've set myself is monumental.

It might mean my death. While that won't portend her death, it might well mean that she has to watch all of her sons and daughters lose their own lives, for they're the next generation of my family. They'll all have equally good claims on the loyalties of the warriors who once served me. These men will want to make them their leader, their king.

Bamburgh is as regal and unapproachable as ever. It was built by my father for his first wife. Throughout the years since, it's been variously repaired, and minor adjustments have been made to the placement of the great hall. The workshops that line the walkway, from the great wooden gated palisade to the interior, have changed as well, but it's still very similar to how I've known it since my childhood. The walls have remained, most importantly.

It's my home, and I was deprived of it for many years when I was in exile, and I don't plan on being so denied again.

My only consolation is that Penda has nothing as stunning as my home, at least not that I've ever seen. His kingdom is landlocked, and unless he uses one of the great rivers that thread his kingdom, I don't see how he could ever build something to the same specifications. It's the coastline that makes it so indomitable, so difficult to get inside of, and yet at the same time, it's the sea that makes life inside the fortress manageable. We live off the fish marooned inside the small sea lake to the rear of the fortress when the tide is exceptionally high. The sea makes it almost impossible to enter for anyone untried in trying to gain access.

I love this fortress, although I do regret its confined spaces. I much prefer the open expanse of Yeavering, but deep in the hills, on one of the few flat pieces of land in my hilly land, it's not as easy to defend. The ramparts that enclose Yeavering are in constant need of replacement as the wood rots in the wet and torrid winter rains and snows.

In the distance, I can see the other islands that dot the coastline, hazy in the summer sunshine, but it's toward Lindisfarne that I turn my gaze.

The island is tidal, often cut off from the mainland for long periods, surrounded by glistening golden sand, and with the enticing belief for those who follow my God that if they can just reach the monks and the bishop there, they'll find salvation and forever be freed from their earthly worries and constraints.

When Penda marched almost straight past Bamburgh, making his way to Lindisfarne, I knew he had me at an immediate disadvantage. I was surprised that he understood the patent allure of the place.

Penda is a pagan. He's never been shown the error of his faith. Yet he instinctively understood the importance of Lindisfarne to mine. Fear had swept through the fortress as all eyes had turned to Lindisfarne, with no thought for the safety of the men and women within Bamburgh, but instead fear for the monks, without their bishop, as Aidan had only just died.

My warriors, including my wife, had demanded I take action and take my men to protect the monks. But I'd been powerless to do anything. I couldn't allow my men out of the fortress without them having to engage with the force that Penda had left behind under the joint command of his son and his brother. No, Penda had well and truly surrounded me, making any action I'd chosen a failure before I could even think about it.

I'd berated myself. I should have thought of the monks, but I'd not appreciated that Penda understood their importance to my faith and kingship.

For five long days, I'd worried and wondered exactly what Penda had been doing on Lindisfarne. Five long days through which I'd barely slept and hardly eaten, my wife distressed beyond belief, and my thoughts running wild with stories I'd heard whispered of Penda's brutality and hatred of the monks of the new God.

It seems I needn't have worried. But I only discovered that *after* I'd made my peace with Penda and the monks had been released from their slight confinement. They'd assured me that Penda had simply wanted to look around their fledgling church. That he wanted to learn about their faith and understand how they thought they served their God with their constant praying. He'd not stopped them from continuing their duties, although he'd placed a guard so that no one could leave or enter the island.

Even now, I wish I knew what Penda had thought as he ran his hand over the precious treasures of the Holy Church as he gazed at the casket that contained the body of Bishop Aidan, recently entombed beneath the church. What must he have thought, because it's obvious to me now that he wasn't swayed to abandon his pagan God, Woden, by observing the Christian monks?

The monks, too relieved to have escaped without even a scratch on them, had gabbled about Penda's interest and open-mindedness to their faith. In that, he'd won a greater victory than if he'd taken blades into the church and its attendant buildings. I found myself not only the victim of an almost impossible treaty with him, one where the only concession was that his son would convert to the Christian faith to marry my daughter but also with a religious community that had always worked entirely for my endeavours. And which had been subverted by Penda's gentle treatment of them.

Even now, with Bishop Finan demanding that I visit the monks again, I know that their experience of Penda will temper anything they suggest. They might even blame me for my current predicament and agree with my wife that I should simply leave Northumbria for good.

I shiver at the thought.

My future looks bleak, but I hope that something will present itself to me and make it possible that I'll survive Penda's coming attack.

What that might be, I don't know. Still, as my horse's hooves connect with the long causeway that leads to Lindisfarne and my bishop and monks, I know that it'll take some almighty intervention to prevent the inevitable, to stop my death. For the first time since my conversion, I'm starting to doubt that's it even a possibility.

15

CYNEWISE OF MERCIA
WINTER AD654

The kingdom is peaceful, but my husband is not. Not once since the engagement with Onna in the summer have I felt my husband sleep softly. All day he masks his true feelings, but during the night, his sleeplessness is riddled with his anger toward Oswiu and the knowledge that he can't allow Oswiu's interference to go unanswered, even if he'd like to.

And I? My thoughts are ambiguous. My husband ages, and his death might well stalk him at any time now. But for over ten winters, he's been the strongest king within the Saxon kingdoms. No other has been able to match him in terms of prestige and reputation. Yet still, Oswiu, despite Penda's conciliatory actions, continues to work actively against him and to question his authority.

For once, Penda finds himself in an unusual position. He chose words, not war, three years ago. He regrets it. What he chooses to do now might well be how he's remembered in the future. Should he attack again? Should he opt for the more sly approach of having Oswiu assassinated? And yet that's not Penda's way, not at all.

He'll kill men, but he'll do it with his hands. He wouldn't ask another to kill on his behalf.

That means he has only one option, to amass his allies and ride north.

My thoughts on the matter are little different. Yet I feel unease and I've never experienced that before.

Penda should send our son, not go himself. But Penda will not listen to my logic. He'll say that as the king, he must face Oswiu.

I agree with him, but I also don't.

If only Oswiu would accept his defeat and slink off to his fortress and stay there until he meets his death. With his love of infuriating his enemies and allies alike, I can't see how Oswiu will survive much longer. He's a younger man than Penda but only just. His death must come soon.

Penda has sent our oldest son to gain the support of my brother in Ceredigion, and he'll stay throughout the long winter. In his time away, Penda uses his title of king to gather his other allies. There's no need for stealth, unlike in the past when he was forced to move in the shadows, ensuring his actions were unknown by his enemy. Oswiu will already know that he's miss-stepped and that retribution will be swift.

Indeed, it'll be Oswiu who'll need to move carefully. Yet I can't calculate whom he'll turn to. To the north, Talorcan has sent word that he's met and killed the king of Dal Riata in battle. While Dal Riata still has another king, he'll be wounded and more intent on attacking Talorcan in revenge than offering to help Oswiu against Penda. I'm not even aware that the new king of Dal Riata has any sort of connection with Oswiu. It seems that with the death of Domnall Brecc, the son of the man who assisted Oswiu and his brother when they were exiles from Northumbria, the family line has been broken. There might not be anyone in Dal Riata who feels any sort of tie to Oswiu and that will work to Penda's advantage.

As much as Domnall came to hate Oswald and conspired against him, that was more because of Oswald's flagrant disregard for their shared childhood experiences than anything else. Their shared childhood should have made them allies that it didn't is of itself a worry. So often, these children born to their parents hate each other and then hate those fostered with them. If each parent could only have one child and be assured that they'll prosper and rule after them, much of the blood lust that riddles the kingdom would be eliminated.

None of the kings in the Saxon kingdoms will ally with Oswiu, not even his wife's kingdom of Kent. They know what Penda can do in battle when he rides to war with his trained warriors, with their herd of powerful horses beneath them. The horses are just as deadly as the men. I'm pleased that I've never had to live in fear of Penda coming to attack my home or that of my brother.

The alliance that my brother brokered might not have been to my liking at the time, but I'm grateful for it now and hope to continue to be so.

I reach over for my husband. He doesn't know that I lie awake with him each night, waiting for his breathing to still in snatched moments of sleep. He doesn't know that of everyone here, I understand why he frets, for he speaks in his sleep and in those moments, I've learned of his father's prophecy all those years ago. And of his additional prophecy. The one he gave just before he died. The one that Penda has tried even harder to forget.

It's that prophecy that deprives him of sleep, that worries him in the dead of night. That prophecy worries me, thinking of a future when I won't have a husband as powerful as Penda.

It's also that prophecy that's forced me to seek out the old Gods, to question them and their ways and to find some assurance from Woden, my husband's ancestor, that the foretelling was little more than the dying words of a sick man.

Once I have that proof, I'll be able to assure my husband of his victory, but until then, I share his fears and his worries and know that they'll be the cause of his undoing. Not Oswiu, never Oswiu.

16

ÆTHELWALD OF DEIRA
AD655

My men and I are ready, and now we simply wait for Penda at our muster point. We ride for the north to seek out and attack Oswiu, the man who'll not be cowed by Penda and who refuses to acknowledge that he's the weaker man. And that he has nowhere near the number of resources at his disposal that he'd like to think he does.

Whether he thinks his Christianity will help him or not, I little care. I'm a man of the new faith, my father would have had it no other way. I accept that my God has far more important matters to attend to than ensuring a sly, manipulative man retains his kingdom.

If my God is to prove to be as all-seeing and all-understanding as I've been led to believe, then by rights, he should revel in the opportunity to cast Oswiu aside. Yet the thought makes me smile. My God is not one of the Old Gods. He doesn't walk beside me. He doesn't care about the actions of men, provided they honour him, as they should. He certainly wouldn't concern himself with my alliance with Penda. He'd not cast me out just because I've chosen to stand with the man responsible for my father's death against the man who stole my kingdom.

My new kingdom is rich and wide, and my borders, apart from to the north, the one I share with my uncle, are quiet and calm. This attack on Oswiu isn't a secret. It couldn't be. Since Oswiu's interference in East Anglia last year, the men and women who rule have been waiting for Penda to call on their alliances, to demand that they gather their warriors and ride to war. That's exactly what I'm doing. I'm more than pleased to do so.

I don't know exactly what Penda has planned for Bernicia should Oswiu fall. I know the simple knowledge that my uncle is dead will be enough for me. His death will go some way to assuaging my guilt over my father's death, a death I think I could have prevented if I'd been sent to help him instead of my lying and deceitful uncle.

Rumour has it that he didn't even try and stop my father from being murdered. Men who fought beside my father, and were lucky enough to escape with their lives, tell me that all Oswiu did was issue commands from the rear of the shield wall. He didn't raise his sword against the might of Penda, Eowa and the men from Powys and Ceredigion, preferring to wait for my father to die so that he could claim his kingdom.

Only a year later did he even slink back and try and regain my father's dismembered body, and to be honest, I don't for one moment believe that the bones he brought back were truly my father's. I think he grabbed any from the battlefield, and the bishop of Lindisfarne, so keen to have a martyr, simply accepted them.

No, my uncle is the instrument of his downfall. I hope, no, I pray, that this time he truly does meet his death.

I have over seventy-five warriors, all of whom I would trust implicitly. I also have a further thirty or so, but I do doubt their loyalty. They allowed my predecessor to be murdered on Oswiu's orders, and so, although I'm taking them with me, I won't be fighting near them. No, I'll thrust them to the front line, where they're more likely to meet their death. Not that I think Oswiu will have anywhere near the number of men that Penda will have with him.

Oswiu has no allies other than the monks and bishop of Lindisfarne. If his force numbers over two hundred men, it will be a miracle. I would imagine that many of them will be no more than farmers, enticed by stories of wealth and glory to stand with their lord when they should be at home tending their crops and their animals.

My outrider, the man who's been following Penda and the progress he and his allies have made, assures me that between them, they bring almost a thousand men. Certainly, he said, too many for him to count. He continued, and here he was a little fanciful, but I appreciated it all the same that from his position high on a hill, they looked to be ants crawling over a rotten piece of fruit.

Although he apologised for his description, I rather like it, provided that it's Oswiu who's the rotten piece of fruit.

'How many banners did you see?' I query him further. His name is Wealdhere. He's lived in Deira all his life and served both my cousin and my uncle before me, but I trust him and he knows it.

'At least twenty-five,' he offers, his brow wrinkling as he tries to remember.

Twenty-five? That's a huge number of men to have brought. I'm relieved that I fight with Penda and not against him. In the past, he's been a part of alliances with half that number. Although he comes with fewer men than I expected, it all makes sense. Oswiu stands alone, and as I said, he has few men, if any, to call upon as his allies. Penda has perhaps too many allies, and they must all be involved, but that doesn't mean they have to bring all of their warriors with them.

I anticipate that only the most experienced, or conversely, the least experienced, have been drafted into service on this occasion.

'How long?' I ask.

'By the end of the day.' He sounds firm as he speaks. He knows how quickly so many men can journey through the landscape. I'm pleased as well. My men and I only arrived late last night. I'm happy that I won't be keeping Penda waiting. It's late in the season, the nights are already starting to draw in. Although I approve of waiting to begin our attack until after the harvest has been brought in, I also worry that the weather might change too soon, plunging us into the dreary rain and mist that can afflict the country before the snows begin.

I shiver at the thought, even though the day is beautifully warm under the gentle sun. The men of the south often forget how quickly the weather can change in the northern lands and how it can go from summer to winter overnight with the first crisp frost.

True to Wealdhere's word, it's early evening when I finally see Penda and his men riding toward me. We've set a small camp close to the River Swale, just a temporary encampment, for we'll be moving on tomorrow or the next day at the latest. I've ordered many fires be built or set so that the warriors coming my way will be comfortable as they eat and sleep. I hope they appreciate the thought but then dismiss that. These men are warriors. They could sleep on a tree branch in a howling storm, snow up to their waists below them, and not think of the discomfort. They train for war and the privations that it might bring.

Yet when Penda rides into the first comforting circle of light, his face is creased with amusement. He leaps from his horse and rushes to greet me, enveloping me in a huge hug.

'My thanks for your forethought,' he booms, indicating the fires and the cooking pots suspended over many of them. 'The men and I are hungry, the horses too. Riding is voracious work.'

He roars his words so that as many men can hear him welcoming me as possible. I know some still question my allegiance to Penda, much to my annoyance. This is Penda's way of acknowledging that and trying to prevent any bickering between the groups of men. Warriors always want to fight, and even the smallest upset can result in a full-scale assault, even on allies.

'The journey has been good?' I think to ask, turning to beckon for food and drink to be brought for Penda, his son and the rest of his allies. As full dark has fallen, the shapes of men flickering in and out of the firelight make it difficult to determine how many join my war band. Still, the increase in conversation and the way the wind seems to be holding its breath makes me believe that Wealdhere counted well. Penda has brought a vast amount of men with him.

'Very good. The days are warm, the nights a little too chill, but other than that, everyone is keen to engage with Oswiu. Do you have news of his whereabouts?'

This was my part of the alliance. As the most northerly of the Saxon kingdoms, Penda tasked me with watching Oswiu, and with trying to determine what his plans were and where he decided to stage his defense. I've had spies and merchants plying their trade between the two kingdoms, but it's been one of my monks who's been able to provide the most information.

Brother Wilfred came to me on the wishes of Oswiu, to try and tempt me back to his allegiance. But he'd only been spoken to me on several occasions when he made it clear that he felt no loyalty to Oswiu, only to my father. Oswiu should have spent more time determining whom he sent to speak to me. It showed me just how cavalier his approach was. He still thinks that as I'm his nephew, I should stand with him. He doesn't understand that his disloyalty has made that impossible.

Wilfred, at first hesitant but gaining in confidence as his actions were unnoticed, has been able to keep me, and therefore Penda, fully appraised of everything that Oswiu has tried.

'Oswiu doesn't plan on allowing you to attack Bamburgh again. Instead, he's left his family there and has plans to entice you ever further north.'

'Why, what's to the north?' Penda asks, eagerly eating the food provided for him. I watch Penda carefully. There have been rumbles that he's too old, that he's no longer the warrior he once was, and yet I see none of that in the man who sits before me.

He's filled with vigour, his questions clever and insightful. I believe someone is trying to undermine him. That must be the work of Oswiu and his monks. No, Penda is the king I've always imagined him to be. Even when he sits and eats, I can feel the force of his power. He's a great warrior, a noble king, and if anyone needed more of an illustration, he need only look at the men who sit or stand to eat with him and do as he commands.

I recognise many men and others I'll need to introduce myself to when the meal is done. I've appraised Penda of the situation. Still, as I talk, my eyes roam the rough grouping of men, my eyes almost blinded by the dazzle of the fire over so much highly polished iron and silver. The men have removed their helms and set them by their feet. As the fire flickers along the cuts and shallows of the helms, it's almost as though another twenty men have joined Penda's alliance, but these are the ghosts and shades of men who stood with him in the past, who've since met their death, such as Cadwallon of Gwynedd, Clemen of Dumnonia and Domnall Brecc of Dal Riata.

I swallow convulsively. I truly pity my uncle now. His death will not be long in coming.

But even though those dead men stare at me across the fire, it's the living that I examine carefully, assuring myself of their loyalty.

Firstly Paeda, Penda's son, meets my eyes. He's younger than I, but not by much, and he's been saddled with my cousin for a wife. I hear the marriage is unhappy and unfruitful. I know I'd not have wanted to marry her, despite the stories of her beauty. Alhflæd wants nothing more than to spend her time on her knees praying to her God. When Oswiu's dead, Paeda will be able to remarry without fear of any retribution from him or his bishop and monks.

Paeda shares his father's build and also his pent-up energy. It's almost as though sitting for any length of time is a punishment for him. I hear he also shares his father's skills with weapons and that although Paeda was once more open to sharing my faith, he's since firmly recommitted to following Woden. Woden was the ancestor of his family line, and he fights with the strength of his God at his side. I wish I could watch him in the coming battle, as opposed to being a part of it, but I'd only be able to observe if I were his enemy and that I don't wish to be.

Beside Paeda sits another man who also shares many of Paeda's features. This, I assume, must be Clydog, his uncle on his mother's side. He's the same age as Penda, and I can remember being told that if the two of them hadn't been allies, they'd have been firm enemies. They don't look alike, but their actions and speech are similar. And as I say, for all that Paeda looks like his father, in the flickering campfire light, I can see where Clydog's heritage has been passed onto Paeda. He's truly the result of an intermarriage between the Saxons and the ancient British, who once claimed this island solely for themselves.

Clydog is a fierce warrior but a Christian as well. That means I can like him without any fear of recrimination. It also highlights Oswiu's lies in pretending to make this battle about the new God and the old. Penda is a tolerant king. He allows any to worship whom they want to, even his wife and older son.

It's with a start that I next recognise Ealhfrith, my uncle's older son. I'd forgotten he might be a part of this engagement. He's married to Penda's daughter. They have a young son together. He's turned against his father, discontent that he reneged on his alliance with his father-in-law and put him in an unwinnable situation. He must either lose his wife and son or his father. I know which one I'd choose. It's not even something I'd need to think about.

Ealhfrith and I have never been anything but wary companions. We spent some time together when we were younger, but obviously, he became the son of a king on my father's death and I became merely a nephew. I've never given much thought to my true feelings about him. I hope that I don't need to now. Ealhfrith is the son-in-law of my staunchest ally. I must be friendly with him for that reason alone.

Perhaps it would be best if I forgot we were even related.

The next man I notice, staggering into the fire-light, a wide grin on his face, looks so much like Penda that I feel my eyes swiveling from where I know Penda already sits, back to the new man. And then I remember his name, Coenwahl. He's Penda's much younger brother, who could almost be his son. He shares the family resemblance and Penda's innate belief in himself. Of course, he'd be with his brother. He'll have been with him in the kingdom of the East Angles as well. He has just as much of a reputation to build for himself as Paeda does. Penda would have to be blind not to see it.

A further man stoops to speak with Clydog. I consider which kingdom he represents. He must be one of the British for he speaks in a different language to Clydog, no doubt sharing some secret or other. Clydog feels the weight of my stare and turns, his hand extended to introduce me to Cadafael.

I remember then that Cadafel succeeded Cadwallon in Gwynedd.

He's not his son, and in fact, Cadwallon's son probably shares many of my own opinions about my usurping uncle about this man. He took the kingdom because Cadwallon died so far away from home. Yet he seems to have ruled well. Or at least, I've not heard others complain about him. Not so my uncle and his meddling ways in the minds of men.

I take all this in quickly and then re-focus on Penda. He's not noticed my speculative eyes.

'To the north?' I remember his question about what lies to the north. 'Very little, but it's ground he knows well. I understand he spent much of his youth just sitting and watching the borders, trying to determine what Edwin was doing and why he was doing it.'

Penda nods quickly at my assessment of the situation.

'He has no ally there then?'

'None at all, Lord Penda. The Bishop of Lindisfarne told him that he'd find allies but has failed to do so. Not one man will stand with Oswiu. They know he'll lose everything. They also understand that he shouldn't even try and retain it.'

There are grunts of agreement from the other men. I imagine it makes them feel better to know they're not the only people to appreciate that by allying with Penda, they're making the right decision.

Penda's reach far surpasses anything Edwin or my father was able to gain. That he's also managed to hold onto it for well over ten winters is an important point to note.

'So, he'll travel far into the north and hope what? I'll tire of looking for him?'

'No, I think he'll be hoping for the first snows to come so that your men become miserable and disheartened and that your food runs out.'

There are cries of outrage at my words. Penda holds my gaze for a long moment and nods his appreciation. He must see some truth in them. I've done the right thing in speaking my mind.

'We should move more quickly then,' Penda says when his allies have calmed down, although I still feel the odd disgruntled look turned my way. How many of these men think I'm not to be trusted? Time will tell.

'Tell the men we won't rest tomorrow but when we get to the old wall. It should only take us another day, perhaps two. Then we can send scouting parties out to track down Oswiu.'

One man groans at Penda's words, but the rest accept them readily enough. Penda has ultimate control. Is there no one who will speak against him?

And then one voice does, and surprisingly, it's his son, Paeda.

'I think we should rest first. That way, we can sprint into Bernicia, perhaps split the force, and encircle Oswiu before he can get too far north.'

Penda raises his hand to hide his mouth before he replies, but I think he smirks at his son. I certainly see a raised eyebrow from Coenwahl. Penda wants to be questioned and is pleased that his son does so.

'The terrain makes it hard to move fast once we're in Bernicia,' Penda offers, and Paeda nods.

'I remember from our attack on Bamburgh. But equally, it makes it difficult for Oswiu to race away from us.'

'He might take a ship?' Penda continues to press, but Paeda shakes his head. I'm thinking the same. Oswiu has no problem with using boats, but if he does so now, he'll be giving up his kingdom without even fighting for it, and that goes against everything I know about my uncle.

'No, he won't. He'll stay and fight for all that he'd rather not. He thinks that he can beat you no matter what.'

'Why?' Penda asks me, his eyes blazing fiercely in the firelight, and I regret the answer I need to give, but it's a truthful one, and it's one that everyone here needs to be aware of.

'Because his bloody bishop has told him he will, on the authority of his God.'

'Fuck,' Penda says, and in that one word, I hear his annoyance at Oswiu. To have a man who thinks he's powerful as your enemy when he's not is one thing, but to have a man who thinks he's powerful because of his God is quite another.

Penda understands the significance of my words and also their innate power. Men who believe that Gods are on their side are deadly and dangerous both. Penda knows because he has the power of his ancestor, Woden, standing at his side.

He doesn't so much sigh deeply as take an extra moment to digest what I'm saying and then smirks again.

'Fucking Oswiu. I'll have to get my Christians to attack him rather than my Woden worshippers. That'll teach the little prick the truth of the matter.'

His words are met with the good-natured laughter and shouts of men keen to fight and prove their worth. I don't miss the intent behind those words.

Penda will do anything to prove to Oswiu that his God, my God, has no power whatsoever.

I hope he's right and also wrong, all at the same time.

I raise my drinking horn to him as the other men are doing.

Time will tell.

17

PENDA, KING OF MERCIA
AD655

The men still cheer my words, perhaps not appreciating their truth. If it's true that Oswiu believes his God will provide his victory, and his small force will triumph over mine, then I must take some action to put an end to his ambitions.

Whilst I might not like the idea of directing this battle from the rear, I also know that if I send my son in my place, the men will follow him with just as much enthusiasm and respect. I'll also be able to say that my son is a Christian who comes to kill another Christian.

I'll play the mind games of which Oswiu is so fond. Just like Edwin and Oswald before him, these Christian kings think too little of strategy and too much of prayer.

I have one small concern, and it's a small one because I can't see it having any effect on my campaign to defeat Oswiu unless, well, unless it seems to be about to come true.

My life was mapped out for me long before I had any say over who or what I might be. My father told me of his prophecy regarding my brother and then whispered another to me on his death bed of how I'd meet my death.

The image he painted of where I'd die has always been writ large in my mind, but to date, I've not found the place or even considered where it might be. Now, as I ride through land I've not visited before, I find myself searching along every valley from the viewpoint of every peak. However, as of yet, I've still not found the place, and I'm confident that we'll soon come upon Oswiu. That means my victory will once more be assured.

No one knows of this prophecy, although I think my wife might suspect it. I don't want others to know. It would make me look weak and foolish, just as weak and foolish as Oswiu now appears.

I walk with Woden beside me, directing my arm and my decision-making. He doesn't excuse what I do or even assure me of a victory, not in the way that Oswiu seems to believe his God does.

'We'll rest tomorrow,' I finally mutter, remembering the discussion my son and Æthelwald were having. The men acknowledge my decision. This is a pleasant place to rest the men and the horses. We're still within Deira, war isn't yet set in stone. Oswiu has no right to come into Æthelwald's kingdom. We will, as I suggested, do better to rest up here, firm up our plans, and then on the following day, I'll begin sending men to search for Oswiu. I'll send an equal number of Christians and pagans to show my disregard for Oswiu's beliefs. None of the men who've allied with me uses their religion as a be-all and end-all. They don't use it to offer excuses or justify their actions.

I don't know what the bishop of Lindisfarne has been telling Oswiu, but I'll be more than pleased to show him that he's wrong.

My kingdom is calm. Fuck it, the majority of this island is calm under my over-kingship. Oswiu can go fuck himself if he thinks to undermine what I've achieved through my sword and words.

As I settle myself to sleep before the high fire built by Æthelwald's men, a messenger forces his way to my side. He's sweaty and gasping for a drink, but before he has either, he bows before me and delivers his message.

'King Penda, Talorcan of the Picts, sends his regards and hopes your combined endeavour will succeed.'

I like the man already. He's often ridden between Talorcan and me ever since I told Herebrod he was too damn old to do it to cover my fears that Oswiu would murder him given half the chance. Herebrod took the comment badly and still sulks whenever I hear from the Picts. In his heart he knows I was right to restrict him, but that doesn't seem to matter when stubbornness has a say.

'My thanks,' I mutter, 'is Talorcan ready?'

'He is my lord, yes. He can't wait to encounter his uncle in battle.'

The messenger sounds as enthusiastic as the rest of my men. I can't help the grin that slides across my face. We've taken our time in deciding the best line of attack and it seems that careful planning, and not some bloody Christian God, will dictate the outcome of the coming engagement.

'Are you to stay with us or ride back?' I ask, knowing I have a less than stern expression, but he's not watching me but rather Æthelwald. Perhaps he's not met him, or maybe he knew his father. The resemblance between Æthelwald and Oswald can't be denied. He might feel he sees a ghost from his past and wonder why he's here. Or perhaps it's the fact that he looks like his own king. Talorcan and he are, after all, cousins, and some family resemblances can't be hidden.

The messenger looks at me and then back at Æthelwald, his mouth slightly slack as he considers his next words and tries to mask his surprise.

Æthelwald has noticed the scrutiny he's under, and he stands and walks around the campfire. As he does so, I watch Talorcan's messenger for any sign that he may react badly to seeing my ally. The flickering flames cast shadows along Æthelwald's face, and even I'm reminded of his father and uncle. There's something about these men of the Bernician royal line, and it's not easy to determine exactly what makes them all appear so alike, for it's no one thing. Few of them share a nose or a chin or even the same lips or hair colour, but all of them carry themselves as though they were born to be listened to, to be admired, and to direct men as they see fit.

It's a pity that whilst they have the aptitude for it, they can't do so.

Æthelwald's curious about the man gazing at him. I introduce them, ensuring that Æthelwald understands why he's being scrutinised as much as he is. The two men are hesitant around each other, none seeming to want to speak the first words. In the end, I pass them my drinking horn, ensuring that they have to share a drink of mead, and the tension in the air passes.

As the two talk, I consider the past and the events that have brought me to this. I realise too many men in my alliance all claim descent from fathers, uncles or grandfathers who are more likely to hate me than not. I'm pleased that my strength and power surpass family lines. That's as it should be. Family loyalty is incredibly important, but so is understanding that some men make better lords than fathers, uncles or grandfathers. I learnt it when I was young, and my father couldn't fully attain his gains.

I've also realised much of my current predicament stems from events that happened almost before I was born, when Æthelfrith of Bernicia decided to claim Deira as his, in the process, cementing the alliance by claiming a Deiran bride for his second wife. It was she, not Bebba, the woman for whom Bamburgh is named, who gave Æthelfrith his herd of sons. He should have stayed content with Bebba and her one surviving son, Eanfrith. That way, much of the last twenty winters of my life need not have happened.

If Æthelfrith hadn't stolen Deira for himself, Edwin wouldn't have been forced into exile. Edwin wouldn't have found support at the court of Cadwallon's father. Edwin wouldn't have found a bride from the Mercian king and wouldn't have been able to use the power of his alliance with Raedwald of the East Angles to attack and kill Æthelfrith.

Æthelfrith was as grasping as his sons are now, and his ambitions were even more vast than mine. He ruled all of the northern kingdoms down to and including some of the Powysian kingdom. In doing that, he made firm enemies of the old British kingdoms, and that meant Edwin, when he sought sanctuary there, was welcomed with open arms. The need for revenge was too great to be ignored.

It's taken me years to decipher events that occurred before I was old enough to ride my faithful horse Gunghir and to determine what I wanted from my life. Yet even now, it's Æthelfrith's ambitions that drive events within our island.

If Æthelfrith had been less ambitious, he wouldn't have birthed an entire generation of boys and men who wanted nothing more than to rule all of this island and to do it no matter how. It would have meant that this new Christianity would have had no way of finding a footing in the northern kingdoms, not until the men from Rome had come to spread their word. And they're a fearful lot. I don't think they'd have made the trip to the northern kingdoms. That would have meant these battles I've fought, and the one I must still fight, wouldn't have taken on any religious overtones.

I'd have fought them with Woden by my side. The enemy would have clashed with their own God, be it Woden, Thunnor or Freya. It would have been as chaotic as the old Gods like it. No one would have spoken out against it or tried to make it into a war of religion rather than a war of men.

Beside me, Herebrod shuffles into place. He's foul-tempered and grumpy for all that the weather is fine, and we've not yet encountered any problems. As I say, he grows old under my eye. I'm sure I do under his.

'A fine mess we're in once more,' he groans with a wry turn of his mouth.

'Always,' I offer as a reply. I can't deny that this isn't how I expected to end my year.

'You should have just killed the shit,' he continues, his eye glinting in the reflected light of the fire. He's come to goad and test my resolve. Of all the men here, there's probably only he who would even dare to speak to me in such a way. Although I like to have my opinions and actions questioned, most do it in a more politic manner.

'Can't you just grow old like ... like, well, I can't think of an example, but can't you just do it?'

'What, and miss out on all the action?' I retort quickly. I've heard these arguments from my wife. I don't wish to hear them from my friend.

'Well, if you didn't piss everyone off so much, maybe there'd be no need for action.' I look at him sharply, wondering how much he's saying reflects his true feelings. His straight face suddenly creases into laughter at meeting my eyes. He reaches out to grasp my arm and snatch my drinking horn away.

'You bloody thought I meant it?' he says, tears of laughter streaming down his face at my melting outrage. I 'accidentally' spill my drinking horn as I pass it to him.

He continues to laugh and slop the liquid into his mouth. It's my turn to growl at him now, but that only makes him laugh more. By now, all the men who sit around the campfire are watching us.

'Ignore him,' I shout, 'he's drunk too much, and he's a bit God-touched the daft old sod.' My words have everyone laughing at his antics. It's his turn to look annoyed.

'Bastard,' he mutters, straightening himself and taking a full swig of the drinking horn. 'These men are supposed to fucking well respect me, and they won't if you tell them I'm half mad.'

'Then you shouldn't try your games on me,' I retort, revelling in the familiar tone of his voice and the camaraderie I've always felt with him.

'I only came for a damn drink,' he mutters, his eyes continuing to hold a trace of resentment.

I pass him my drinking horn once more, and he grunts. He's still unhappy.

'I'm too bloody old,' he mutters after taking another swig of mead and wincing as he does so. 'I ache all bloody over, and it's still the damn summer.'

'It's only just summer,' I console, but he's having none of it.

'Why are we doing this?' he demands instead. His voice has dipped very low so I have to lean close to hear him.

I consider his words carefully. He's questioned me before but never with such earnestness in his voice, and I feel he deserves a truthful answer.

'Oswiu and I are enemies. We hate each other because we want the same thing. I have it, and he doesn't, and he's desperate for it, but desperation shouldn't allow him to take it. I have to prove that to him. Otherwise, my family and, more importantly, Mercia will suffer on my death.'

It's the first time I've truly considered my motivation. In the past, I thought it was my superiority, my right to attack Oswiu, but sudden clarity has made me realise who and what I am. I doubt Oswiu has ever considered his actions in quite the same way.

'The Christian faith teaches that it's wrong to hate,' Herebrod surprises me by saying. I bark a laugh at him. I'm surprised he knows as much as he does about Christianity.

'I think you might be telling the wrong person,' I complain. Herebrod raises our shared drinking horn to that.

'It shows that his faith is a cloak he wears, a mask even. He no more believes in his faith than Paeda did. It's a weapon.'

'Yes, it is,' Herebrod agrees, a smirk on his face. I begin to understand why he speaks to me.

'We should use it against him?' I question, and he nods.

'We should and not just by sending Christians against him. We should find ourselves a few bishops and respected monks whom we can ally with.'

'Where would we find them here?' I ask, liking his idea but despairing about being able to do anything about it now.

'The men to the north of the mountains share the old faith, the people of Rheged, of Gododdin. We could go anywhere and find a few bishops and monks.'

'It'll just delay our attack?' I gripe.

'It might prevent the need for an attack at all. Oswiu has no allies other than his Church. Undermine his faith, and you undermine even those allies. They won't be able to stand with him if you can show that he's not truly a Christian.'

I turn to stare at Herebrod, pleased he's sought me out. I should have spoken to him at length about my coming attack before.

'How would we even do that?' I question. He looks across the fire to where Æthelwald and Talorcan's messenger still speak.

'His faith is genuine,' he offers. 'And he hates his uncle. I imagine he'd help you.' I watch Æthelwald carefully for a long moment. I trust him. I gave him his kingdom, but he's his son's father. I didn't want to allow him to undermine my campaign. Herebrod is suggesting just that. I'll have to think about it.

He senses my hesitation.

'Or his son. He doesn't much like him either.'

'I like it,' I speak slowly, 'It would be good to have won the battle without the fight, but, well, after last time, I think I might need the fight, or my reputation will suffer.'

He's already thought about that possibility, and he doesn't bother to respond, instead lapsing into silence so I can think about his words.

I've never yet shied away from a battle, even when I went as far north as Bamburgh fortress, I knew I was prepared to burn it to the ground and kill everyone within it. Only, as a warrior of great renown, I preferred to at least allow the women and children to leave with their lives.

It was my son who convinced me not to kill all the men, to take the offered treaty. I don't blame him for his desire to marry, but I blame myself. I shouldn't have listened to him. I should have done what I went to do.

'Fucking Oswiu,' I mutter angrily. Herebrod barks a laugh at my frustration and anger. He knows it means that I'm more than halfway to agreeing to his plan.

18

PAEDA OF THE HWICCE
AD655

I watch my father and Herebrod carefully. They have many, many secrets. Herebrod is my father's most loyal friend and his longest-serving commander.

Herebrod knows more about my father than I've ever been allowed to know. I'm desperate to know what he's talking to him about, but I know better than to intervene. My father has always been open with me about everything, apart from the discussions that he and Herebrod have. Sometimes I feel a tinge of jealously. Other times I see them as two old friends, too caught up in themselves to realise they exclude others.

Herebrod has a family in the Pictish kingdom. He's never sought treasure or land in Mercia for his sons. However, I'm sure my father would give it to him without hesitation. Herebrod prefers to live two separate lives. One with his wife and family to the north, where his wife holds all the power. And this one, with my father. I've considered his decisions to live the way he does. I don't think I'd want to follow his example, but I can also appreciate it.

Better to fight for a warrior away from the prying eyes of a wife and sons who might disagree with you than argue about it. Or so I tell myself. When Oswiu is dead, Herebrod will be able to return to the north again, something denied him for the last few years, when worry has stalked my father about Oswiu's intentions toward him.

I'm not the only one watching my father, either. I turn and catch the eye of my uncle. He could make himself a part of the group, but he doesn't, instead making his way to sit beside me.

'Nephew,' he calls loudly, crashing to the ground beside me, making so much noise I look at him in surprise.

He raises his eyebrow and winks at me.

'It always helps to remind every bugger here that you're related to Penda and his son. It gives me a bit more respect from the rest of the Saxon scum.'

My uncle speaks as he does on purpose, hoping to raise the ire of some of my father's nearby warriors. I'm so used to his derogatory remarks that I ignore him. I've learned through the last winter spent in his company that he likes to raise a man to anger just to see how easy it is. He tells me it's a good way of knowing how a man will react in battle, but I've yet to see any evidence.

'Uncle Clydog,' I say overly loudly, and he chuckles at my involvement in his petty show of power.

'What are those two fuckers talking about?' he asks, bending his head toward where my father and Herebrod talk. I shrug.

'I don't know, but I'd like to.'

'They've always been close. I don't see it myself. Herebrod's an ugly little duck and I'd rather never look at him.'

I almost choke on my mead at that statement. I can't see any resemblance between the dark and mean-looking Herebrod and a little duck. He's not even ugly.

'You need an ally such as Herebrod,' he offers then, his eyes busily taking in the activity in our large camp. There are men everywhere, carrying food or polishing weapons or simply sleeping, worn out by the day's exertions.

'What?' I ask abruptly, surprised by his change of tact. Clydog is often like this. His thoughts jump all over the place, although he normally offers very good advice when I've managed to decipher what he's trying to tell me, which can take a while.

'No man, no matter how closely he walks with his God at his side, can truly rule alone. He needs someone to tell him he's a total cock sometimes, and it's best if that news comes from a friend.'

'You think my father's being a total cock?' I ask in surprise. Clydog chuckles at me, his face old and lined in the firelight. It reminds me that I'm a youth to these old men despite the fact I've already lived the lives of two men, what with the saga of my wedding and wife and my conversion to Christianity.

'No, I didn't say that. But well, you might have a point,' he continues, humour making his face a mask of shadows and lines. 'No, I was saying you distance yourself from your men. You should have an ally amongst them. Someone you can always trust to tell you the truth.'

'Why, whom do you trust?' I ask him. He grins.

'I'm a total cock, you know that!' His laughter is so violent that I almost think he's choking. When he finally stops chortling, he looks at me, his eyes intent and bright in the sparking light of logs dying on the fire.

'You're a clever man, a quick learner. You think before you speak and before you act. Your father's proud of you. He might never say it, but he wishes he were as much like you as you wish you were like him. Find yourself a bloodthirsty brute to stand at your side. I think you're going to need it.'

My uncle's never spoken to me in such a way, not even through the long dark winter nights when he could have said anything to me, and I'd not have taken offence.

'What do you fear?' I ask him. He meets my eyes.

'Everything,' he says quietly. That surprises me. I don't imagine men like my father, uncle, or even Herebrod ever fear anything. They're mighty warriors. They've shed more blood in their lives than it would take men to fill the whole of my father's stronghold at Tamworth.

'Your father has few enemies, but the one he has don't respect him or even try to understand him. Oswiu thinks your father's a heathen.'

'And?' I ask, intrigued by his words.

'And that's all he thinks he needs. Find yourself some strong allies, not just me or your younger brothers. Someone who'll stand with you and support you against Oswiu, should you ever need to stand against him.'

'His daughter is my wife. What more could I need?' I complain. Now he looks fierce, the firelight casting him into one of the old stories my mother used to tell me when I was a child of dragons and demons, his brow all furrowed and furious.

'She'll be your downfall if you let her become it. She hates you. She loves her father and her fucking God. Be careful. Heed my advice. You're not just your father's son, you're my nephew as well. You share my blood and my ancient right to rule Mercia and Ceredigion. You need to remember that.' His voice is so filled with menace when he finishes that I flinch away from him. I'm not used to seeing my uncle so upset about something and so determined to get his viewpoint across.

I realise that he cares for me deeply. And my brothers and sisters, and also my mother.

He stands to walk away from me, and I restrain him.

'Family or not?' I ask. His face puckers tightly, perhaps pleased that I'm listening to him.

'Both. Make yourself invincible with a host of allies, but not too many. Too many allies can be a curse. Your father managed best with just a handful. Too many opinions can make it hard to find a way forward.'

He stumbles away, leaving my father's campfire and returning to his men. I watch him leave thoughtfully, noting that he wears his war gear even in the encampment, almost as though he doesn't trust anyone.

My father's in a position of strength. He has more than twenty war leaders with him, over a thousand men. I know that Oswiu's force will only be small, perhaps less than two hundred men. But why is my uncle so filled with worry for my future? What does he know that I don't?

The thought gnaws at me, as does the conversation between my father and Herebrod. I'm beginning to worry that my attitude toward Oswiu is incorrect. Should I be warier of him? More scared? And what of my wife? While I think her political influence has been removed, others don't agree with me.

I close my eyes, allowing the warmth of the fire to ease its way along my body, forcing the growing swell of conversation around me from my consciousness.

Something is pressing on my mind that I need to let come to the fore and that I need to understand.

Slowly my mind clears of everything apart from the light of the fire dancing before my closed eyelids. Its heat keeps me comfortable despite the chill season that advances in the northern lands.

Clydog is worried for my father's future. I also think that Herebrod is. I'm reminded of my mother's words before I left, demanding assurance from me that I'd return. She didn't command me to protect my father, as she has in the past, to bring him home to her.

What is it that everyone but I seem to know and understand instinctively?

Is my father ill? Does he expect to die on this journey? I think about him, riding his horse before me all day. The horse looks like Gunghir, but has far less temper to go with it. Yet he's still a contrary beast, and my father spent the day arguing with him, as he always did in the past with Gunghir. But I detect nothing that makes me worry about him. He shows no weakness, no infirmity and no desire to shy away from the coming engagement. Damn, it was his choice to pursue Oswiu. It might have impacted his reputation, but he could just as easily have left the little fucker to die of boredom in the far north, devoid of all allies.

My father remains the giant of my childhood, a man of blackness and ferocity who keeps his sword and seax sharp. His shield is painted with the blood of his enemies. He used to scare me until I came to respect him and see beyond the physical portrayal he insisted upon. From a very early age, he allowed me to speak as I wanted, to think as I wanted, and perhaps most importantly, to question him. He does the same with my younger brothers now.

I detect nothing different in him, nothing at all. It's the people who surround him who've changed. I wonder if he's even aware of the scrutiny he's under.

He hates as he always did. He speaks as I know him always to speak, and he commands as precisely as in the past. There's nothing different about my father. Nothing at all.

Apart from two things, there's a touch of grey in his hair and beard, and he's a grandfather. But other than that, he's the man I've always known. He's consistently fair in his judgment, and men and women flock to his side, keen to be directed by him.

Yet.

Yet it seems I need allies of my own. It's this group of men who surround the fire that I must look to in order to find the first one.

Perhaps I should start with my cousin. Osmond is as much my brother as my younger brothers. He and I were raised together, my mother taking control of my uncle's children without even realising she did so. I've never spoken to him about his feelings regarding his father's murder and his mother's death. I know that he accompanies my father every year when he goes to the battle site and mourns and respects his father as he should.

He shows no resentment for his current position. Not that he should. He has just as much right to the kingdom of Mercia as I do and as my living uncle does. Yet he doesn't live the same life we do. He's an excellent warrior, having been trained by my father and Herebrod to ensure that he'll never die on a Northumbrian sword, but he's never fully committed to the warrior way of life. If he could, he'd be a stunning commander, a warrior with great renown. Yet he shies away from it.

I think he might fear dying as his father did, and for that reason, he's content with his share of the kingdom, his wife and his children. He's very fond of my mother, but even there, he's distant, just as he is with his wife and children. Perhaps he's scared of losing those he loves?

Yet for all that, he's riding north with my father, for once determined to show that he can lead men and support his uncle. My father was surprised by his resolve, as were his small band of warriors. He's shown nothing but a desire to avenge himself on Oswiu. I can only imagine that in the absence of Oswald to kill to avenge his father's death, he's decided to take the next best step, to assist in the killing of Oswiu.

I like Osmond. I always have. I love him and respect him, but whether I can subvert him to my allegiance, I just don't know. I don't even know if I want to, but of all the men here, he might be the best indicator of how likely I am to succeed.

I suppose that what Clydog is telling me is that a new generation of men is soon to hold power within our island. If I'm to rule as my father has done before me, I need my power base amongst those younger men. I can't always rely on my father's reputation. At some point, I'll have to make my own. Osmond will be a good start. As will my brothers when they're older and able to support me with their warriors. I'll make it clear to them when I return that I value them and want to earn their respect and support, not just hold it because I'm their brother.

I open my eyes and fix them on Osmond. He's sitting to the right of my father, perhaps listening to his conversation, even though his eyes are closed, and he seems to be soundly sleeping.

He appears, in the gloom of the dying fire, exactly as I remember my uncle looking, even though it's been so many years since I last saw him. He's similar to my father, although he has a more delicate face, his cheekbones showing clearly in the shadows of the fire. He could have been a weak man. I think my father tried to make him strong, but he tends to shy away from trouble.

The land he rules is in the heartlands of Mercia, close to Tamworth, his father's main stronghold, and because of that, he has little fear of enemies attacking him. He's protected from the north, south, east and west by others who'll have to labour to stop any form of attack that might come from my father's enemies. Yet he doesn't deny his responsibilities. He keeps his borders clear and sends men to train with my father and Herebrod after each harvest until the cold weather truly sets in.

As I say, I've always liked Osmond. Can I use that to make him my ally, think less of him as a person and more an entity that adds prestige to my reputation? I don't know. I don't think I've ever thought like that.

In the distance, I hear my uncle shouting something at his men, his distinctive accent and tongue reminding me of his words and my need to take action before he berates me for thinking instead of acting.

I sigh deeply and stand. I'd rather sleep but first I'll speak with my cousin.

The majority of Penda's commanders have filtered away to sleep with their men, to enforce their authority over any who might have drunk too much or decided that they hate their ally more than their enemy. Osmond remains, as does my father and Herebrod, and so does Æthelwald. Perhaps I could include him in the conversation? But I decide against it, and instead, Osmond beckons me to sit beside him, and I do so.

'Cousin,' he mutters. I greet him in the same way.

'We've come a long way today,' he says, conversing with me but not making any effort as he does so.

'Have you been this far north before?' I ask him, and he shakes his head.

'I prefer Mercia. I always have. I hate the fucking Bernicians,' he says quickly. His words are always clipped, as though he's finished speaking, but the words haven't finished being said.

'Why did you come?' I ask because I'm genuinely intrigued.

'My honour demands it,' he spits angrily. 'Last time, your father let the little prick go far too leniently. I've come to ensure that he dies this time.'

It seems I was right to blame revenge as his motivation.

'You know it was my fault,' I begin, but he interrupts me.

'Your father's never done anything he was told to do. My father used to complain about it, saying he was a contrary bastard. He wouldn't have fulfilled the treaty's terms if he hadn't wanted to. No, your father's grown weak in his old age. He lives only on his reputation and nothing else. I'll make sure that Oswiu pays for my father's death.'

I've never heard so much anger in my cousin's voice, as though years and years of pent-up frustration and aggression have suddenly vented themselves all in one go. I shy away from continuing my conversation with him but know I'll never make allies that way.

'Oswiu has no allies. My father won't ally with him again, not after what happened with Onna in East Anglia.'

I don't look at Osmond as I speak, but rather at my father. I'm sure he doesn't appreciate the price of Osmond's unhappiness.

'Your father always has excuses for why Oswiu lives and why he allies with Oswald's sodding son. I'd prefer it if I could wipe out the entire family line, even your damn wife.'

I wish I'd chosen a different first option now. I thought Osmond would be pliable because of our family connection. I was wrong.

'He should have chased Oswiu from Mercia and hacked his shoulders from his head when he had the chance. If I'd been older, I'd have been there and been able to do so.'

Ah, I begin to understand now. I don't think Osmond is angry with my father, he's angry with himself and Eowa for being killed. I can't imagine his life in my father's household has been easy, knowing that his father was killed by his enemy.

Certainly, I'd not want to walk around with the same ember glow in my soul.

'Do you wish you were king?' I ask. I've often considered this. What would it have been like if both my father and his brother had died at Maserfeld, if Oswald had triumphed instead?

'Fuck no. I just don't want any more alliances with the Bernician kings. They speak shit and do so using the voice of their God. I hate them all. Each and every one of them, but I don't resent your father. He's a great man, an excellent king. I'd never have had the abilities that he has. I've never even wanted it as desperately as he did, or my father did.'

'What about in the future?' I don't want to say the words 'if my father died,' but I don't need to. Osmond isn't stupid. He's already made the connection.

'Whoever is the king of Mercia will need a reputation to rival your father's. He'll need to be strong and powerful, and able to compel men to follow him into battle. He'll need to dispense justice well and be generous with his treasure and silver.'

Osmond isn't describing me when he speaks. I know I'm none of those things. But he's not finished yet, and there's a spark of understanding on his face.

'But he can't be your father. Your father is unique. Men such as him aren't born more than once a generation. My father stood no chance. I know that. My sister knows that. That's why there's never been any bitterness. Your father is driven, he's ... I can't even describe it. He's Penda. That's what and who he is all at the same time. Our next king can never be Penda, but he can be someone else, someone just as committed to his thoughts and wishes and to the advancement of Mercian ambitions. Men love your father because he doesn't pray on their minds. He doesn't question their motivations. Provided I think the same way he does about most significant issues, that's all that matters to him.'

I'm stunned into silence. I don't know what to say. What have I achieved? When have I made men determined to follow me into battle? I think my uncle is correct to have spoken to me like he did. I've basked in the glow of my father's reputation for long enough.

'You did something no one has ever done, well, no one who was Penda's ally anyway. You've spoken your mind before him. You've spoken out against his plans. You might not have as many kills as he does or wear the blood of your enemies with quite the same zeal that he does, but men respect you. You might be surprised.'

'I respect you,' he says quietly, 'and you'd be my king if anything ever happened to your father. And I wouldn't plot to take it from you. Never. I don't want to be a king, I want my family and life, but I want to kill fucking Oswiu.'

The menace in my quietly spoken cousin, and how his voice gains in resolve as he speaks fills me with confidence. He's made me see character traits about myself that I've not appreciated before, although I do think that my father probably has. I'm not my father, nor did he ever expect me to be. Neither has he ever held me up to his image. Any pressure I've felt has been self-inflicted. I need to step more firmly, be prouder of what I've accomplished.'

'You do need to get rid of your whore of a wife.'

I wince at the snap and snarl of Osmond's anger. I sense why he might have been distant of late. I've made a bad decision, but one that I've dealt with.

'When her father is dead, she's going to a nunnery.'

'Good. Get yourself a pretty wife or a strong one, but not a Bernician one. And now, I'll bid you good night. I know we rest tomorrow, but I want to sleep tonight. I've a man to kill in the next few weeks, and I plan on ensuring my blade that slices his head from his shoulders.'

I don't shudder at his words as he stands and walks away, but I also don't appreciate his desire for blood. But then, my father still lives and always will, and I've never had to watch my enemy work its way into the affections of my adopted family.

I should have thought far longer, and without the needs of my cock at the forefront of them, before I agreed to any marriage with Alhflæd. I'm almost pleased that the relationship has proven to be so disastrous. It allows me to make amends for the mistakes I've made.

My father continues to speak with Herebrod, the pair of them equally pissed, but there are tears of laughter pooling down their faces, and it seems I look at young men, not two old stags. I hope that Osmond and I will share a relationship similar to this one.

Now I understand him better, I know how to ensure he stays my ally, and now he understands my intentions towards Alhflæd, he'll be able to be more open in his support for me. And all of it without undermining my father because it's to him that we owe our ultimate allegiance.

My eyes grow heavy as I lie before the fire, smirking at the antics of my father and his friend.

I'll have to thank my uncle for speaking to me as he did. But that's a task for another day.

In the glowing embers of the fire, as my eyes half close, I see the burning images of buildings and men, the howls of the dead and the dying, and in them, I see a portent of things to come. My father might be old and grey and hoary, but he's still Penda. And that's all I need to know.

One day I'll be King Paeda, but that's a long time in the future.

19

OSWIU, KING OF BERNICIA
AD655

My kingdom is in an uproar. Not a moment can go by without someone else rushing to Bamburgh to tell me that Penda is once more marching north.

Panic and fear stalk every face that looks to me, and what do I have to offer? Nothing but my faith. Nothing more. My bishop has failed me. He assured me that he'd find allies for me, from the northern lands, from the Church in Ireland, but Finan has lied to me, and my relationship with him is strained.

I've always held firmly to my faith, but in my time of need, it's failed to provide any comfort. What power does it have against a man with over a thousand warriors whom all want my blood?

I erred when I sent my warriors to support Onna in the kingdom of the East Angles. I should have kept my warriors here and waited for Penda to die of old age before I took any further action.

I spent much of last winter on my knees praying to my God, and having letters written and messengers dispatched to the other kingdoms who might support me. Not one word of support have I received from any of them.

My nobility begs me to leave or surrender, anything to avert the coming attack from Penda. In my stubbornness, I refuse to accede to their demands. Bishop Finan told me that my God would provide me with the means to triumph. I'm still holding out half a hope that he will. But I also need to be practical. As such, I'm ordering my warriors to ride out in the morning. In the meantime, my family and monks are to find shelter within Bamburgh and to keep the gates closed no matter who comes calling until I return myself.

The men think we journey to meet Penda, but I'm not that stupid. And I'm not convinced that my God has anything to offer. I'm riding for the northern lands. I'll demand allegiance from the kingdom of Dal Riata and my nephew. I've people ready to take action to subvert them to my will.

I need allies. If the Church doesn't provide them for me, then I'm going to use every other weapon I can to ensure I don't face Penda's huge force with my tiny one. I hope I haven't left it too late to firm up my resolve. Initially, I'd decided to wait for him to come to Bamburgh, and thwart his plans by staying inside the fortress my father built for his first wife to protect her from the men to the north and the south. But I now realise that Penda won't let its steep sides and lack of access be any form of impediment. Not like last time.

He hates me and means to destroy me for making him look like a trusting fool. The mighty king Penda, warrior and follower of Woden, won't take my insult again. No, he means to destroy me, and I, too, mean to destroy him. Somehow.

I've sent a select few men ahead. They have instructions to follow, and although only half of them believe my plan has any possibility of working, they're going to try. We have no choice. I've made it clear to them. And if by some happenstance we succeed, they'll be rewarded with riches and treasure beyond their imaginings.

My wife fluctuates between tearfulness and her desire to help me. She seeks comfort from Bishop Finan and his monks and the relics of my dead brother. When she touches the broken skull of my brother, she grows firm with resolve, yelling demands to her women and slaves, demanding assurances from my warriors. And from me. Railing at God for allowing Penda to advance as he has.

If she could call forth a flood to dispel Penda and his warriors, she'd have done so twenty times over.

If she were one of my warriors, I know I'd succeed against Penda. But she's simply my wife, the mother of my younger children, and must be protected against all the odds. Bamburgh will stand firm against anything, apart from fire, and even then, the wet summer will have dampened the ground and the wooden palisade enough that it'll make burning it almost impossible.

I've spent time worrying about my other strongholds, Ad Gefrin especially, but I'm filled with realism. I can't save everything. I need to prioritise to ensure my family survives and that my God is allowed to provide a means of escape.

But until then, I'll wait for my men to bring their hostages from the Pictish kingdom, and Dal Riata. Then I'll demand treasure and men from my unwilling allies. With the men or the treasure, I'll either kill Penda or buy him off.

There's no other way to ensure that I triumph.

When Herebrod killed my brother, and when Penda hacked him to pieces, they allowed no part of my brother's battle gear to be returned to me other than his white-bladed sword, taken from his dead body by one of my men. My brother may have died clutching his white-bladed sword, but I plan on slicing Herebrod's neck from his shoulder with the same weapon. The man should have been killed years ago.

And then, when Penda is grieving for his warrior and staunchest supporter, I'll offer him the same treatment.

I've many plans in place to bring Penda to his knees. I can only hope that one of them proves successful.

20

TALORCAN, KING OF THE PICTS
AD655

I dismiss the man and send him from my presence. I almost can't believe that my uncle has acted as he has, but desperate men will do reckless things. But this is suicidal.

My family has been under heavy guard since Penda sent me word of Oswiu's rogue actions against him last year in the kingdom of the East Angles. I know my uncle too well, even though I've only met him a handful of times. He thinks to force me to his will and bend me to do his bidding because I refuse to enter into negotiations with him. He doesn't understand how transparent he is. Or how easy it is to say no to him.

He's alone. He has little or no support from anyone. So, he's lashed out and decided that the only way to make men do what he wants is to force them to bend their knee before him and bow to his allegiance.

What a fucking fool!

Why would I support my uncle when I already have the support of Penda of Mercia? He tried to assist my father in reclaiming his birthright, and if it hadn't been for that damn British king, Cadwallon, my father would have been successful. But he was too trusting, almost opposite to his younger half-brother. And I've learnt valuable lessons from studying the troubled history of my father's family. The most important lesson is that family stands for nothing amongst the descendants of Æthelfrith of Bernicia, my grandfather.

I doubt he realised what the long-term effect of his usurpation of Deira's kingdom would be. Or what effect his marriage to my grandmother would have. I never met her, but I refuse to believe he understood it would bring so much strife to his sons and grandsons.

Men should learn to think with their minds rather than their swords and certainly with their minds instead of their cock.

My uncle Oswiu has never fully learned the lesson, and now he's made his most fatal error.

He's tried to kidnap not only my own family but also Herebrod's at the same time. He's failed, and now his men are strung up outside my broch, their lives taken, while their king continues to hope they'll return to him.

Instead, he'll feel the full force of my wrath against him. He has no right to demand my allegiance. I rule a far greater kingdom than he does, and I do it well. I'll continue to do so whether he rules in Bernicia or not.

I keep to my lands, and my uncle should do the same. I've been kind to him, but if he should survive the coming battle, I'll press him on my borders and reinforce the kingdom of the Gododdin. He has no claim to my kingdom, none at all.

This messenger from Oswiu has ridden in to ask me to support him, clearly thinking that my family will be in the hands of those who came to kidnap them. He received a nasty surprise when he saw my wife beside me, my son at my feet, and more, Herebrod's brood of children and grandchildren as well.

Now instead of going back with my agreement for Oswiu, he'll return strung up on the back of his horse, leading my warriors to wherever it is that Oswiu has run away.

For there's no secret to that either. Oswiu stands alone, and to protect his family, he's absconded. He's left them locked up inside Bamburgh. I've never been to Bamburgh. I've never seen the home where my father was raised because he wanted the kingdom of

Bernicia to be at peace when he claimed it as his to rule and before he called me to him. I've always thanked him for that. It meant I didn't die on the end of Cadwallon's sword, as my father did.

I was planning on riding south anyway, keen to show my support to Penda, a man I greatly admire and remember vaguely from my childhood over twenty years ago. Now I have a greater undertaking. I hunger to kill my uncle.

My men, already assembled for our journey to the south, are as irate as I am at the audacity of Oswiu. If they should encounter him before I do, they'll hack his head from his shoulders and leave his body standing, headless. The image makes me smirk with enjoyment.

I'm not a bloodthirsty man, or maybe I am. I like my enemies to suffer, always suffer, for their outrages against me. It's the way of my people, for I think of myself as a Pictish man. I loved my father and admired him. As I near the age he was when he died, I also pity him. He was too trusting, and first Edwin, and then Cadwallon took all that he managed to accomplish from him. I've been unable and unwilling to reclaim it.

The Saxons to the south are an unruly breed. They think the same of the Pictish people, but I know better. Of all the kings to the south, it's only Penda that I feel any connection to. Any loyalty. That's because he understands what it takes to rule. He knows that reputation is more valuable than religion. He knows how to fight for what he wants and yet accomplish it fairly all at the same time.

I admire him, and as a younger man, I was thrilled to listen to Herebrod each winter with his stories of men who see Penda as inferior to them because he worships the ancient Gods of his homeland. I hope to listen to Herebrod again when Oswiu is dead, and he can return to the Pictish kingdom. More kings have died or lost their kingdoms because of Penda than any other Saxon king. I look forward to meeting with him again. It's been many, many years. I desire to see how he wears his reputation and if the stories of him are as true as Herebrod once assured me they were.

The summer is nearing its end when I ride out, Oswiu's messenger before us all, as he leads his horse to where he knows

Oswiu is taking cover. My father told me of the battle of Hæðfeld. Of how he found all the Saxon and British kings hiding within a great forest when they attacked Edwin. I doubt Oswiu has found himself in such a well-considered place to defend. I imagine he'll be high on one of the hills that dot the disputed borderlands, using one of the ancient strongholds built by my Pictish ancestors.

It'll have a water supply but little in the way of food or shelter from the turbulent weather, which one moment can be warm and welcoming, and the next chill and foreboding. He'll think himself in a position of power, but Penda and I can starve him out. He'll not have thought of the long-term consequences because he'll be convinced that his plan to drag me to his alliance will have worked. He'll be sitting there, waiting for me to arrive and unravel Penda's alliances and save him.

I've not allowed anyone south since the aborted effort to steal my family, so he won't realise how monumentally he's miscalculated.

As I say, he's not the sort of man who ever considers failing. That's his worst failure. He needs to spend more time considering alternative action plans than just settling on one.

His lack of forethought will bring about his failure and, hopefully, his death.

He'll have no chance but to attempt to attack Penda's force in an effort to live another day. In doing so, he'll lose all his men and his life. Either that, or he'll need to bribe his way out of his predicament, and I know that Bernicia is not a kingdom with great riches.

It's a harsh place of slopes and valleys, rough seas and interlacing rivers. My father used to tell me that the wind never stopped blowing, and on those rare occasions when it did, it was worthy of note. I know it can be warm and that the animals and crops grow well there, but I also know that harsh storms blow in from the sea and that deep fogs can shroud the land for days. That the rain can fall without ceasing.

It's much like my kingdom, only more exposed to the elements.

Large parts of Bernicia are hilly, their tops sprouting snow long into the winter, just as my mountains do. Those same hills of Bernicia can offer sanctuary and succour for men and women who need to find somewhere to hide from their enemy. It's easy to get lost amongst those hills, and for the unwary, they might never find their way out again.

I also know that the ancient men who built the great wall within Bernicia, after they'd built the one higher up, closer to the kingdom of Dal Riata, could not tame the wild savages who lived there. Some of them were my ancestors on my mother's side, and some were not.

The British once held the land, and they survive in the form of the kingdom of the Gododdin, which my uncle hopes to rule with force. He's already attacked it more than once, and its people are wary of my uncle. He should have lived side by side with them, but that's not the way of either of my uncles. They don't seem to understand what toleration is, and that makes them weak men.

They live by their faith and swords. They'll die by them too.

I'm not convinced that Penda will. I see him living to old age, surrounded by hordes of grandchildren, telling them of the men he's known throughout his long life and regaling them with tales of battles that no other man remembers. I hope I achieve the same sort of peace he does.

I also hope he kills my uncle or allows me to do so. I want to satisfy my father's honour, and as Oswiu's brother is dead, the man who purposefully failed to help him, I'll have to exact what revenge I can on the other man.

Not that they're the only two uncles I have. Not by a long shot, but the other two have done me a favour and died before their time. If I were unkind, I'd suggest it was from drinking too much or from being crap warriors. But I have a sneaking suspicion that their deaths may also be the work of Oswiu. He seems to enjoy killing anyone who gets in his way.

I wonder what penance he's done for the death of his brothers? I imagine that Bishop Finan has found some way that he can atone without sullying his soul.

Fuck, I hate my uncle.

As I travel through my kingdom, I make a point of assessing and checking the majestic marker stones that differentiate the different tribes of my people. Unlike the Saxons, my kingdom consists of three tribes who made a pact to live together, as best as they could, to ensure their survival against both the ancient men with their shining swords and armour and also against the pretensions of Dal Riata. That kingdom has far less history on our island than any realises. Once small tribes dotted this island, now larger ones try to claim more and more for themselves, overriding the wishes of others and in doing so, making themselves lifelong enemies.

The Pictish people chose to live differently, and that pleases me.

We have the stones that tell us who owns what land. Each season the men and women of the tribes stake their claim to their lands once more, informing their neighbours that they yet thrive.

My people come to meet me at these markers, pleased to see me and ask me for boons and favours, to rectify an injustice, or just to see their king. The land is pleasant in the late summer, the harsh winds from the coast failing to penetrate the lush green valleys of the protected basins where our crops grow tall and strong or are being harvested.

We're lucky people. We can grow as much as we need during the short growing season. Then, when the weather turns, we can retreat to our brochs and stay warm and snug throughout the winter snows and storms that cover our majestic mountains until deep into the warm season.

The number of men in my war band also swells at each marker. There are men from these small settlements who're keen to prove their worth to me and also their prowess with their spears and arrows. I encourage the men to accompany me. When we battle against Oswiu, they'll make a name for themselves.

By the time I reach the area where I think Oswiu will have chosen to hide out, I have over three hundred following me. My war band has doubled in size from those men I can call upon in times of war. Amongst their number ride two of Herebrod's sons come to see their father and also to do their duty for their Pictish mother.

They need to make a reputation to rival Herebrod's so that other women, fussier women and their fathers, will overlook their half-blood status in our tribe.

I wish them luck. I've trained with them, seen them fight, and taught them the way of the Pictish warriors. I can see no reason they wouldn't make excellent husbands and fathers. If I encounter Herebrod, I'll tell him as much. He'll find it high praise from the son of his long-dead friend. I'll be pleased to see the smirk of joy on his old face.

Not many men would have chosen to live as he has. But as he informed people, his oath to Penda was binding, and he could little break it when his wife made it clear she wished to remain within the Pictish lands with her sons and powerful family. Other men might have left her or buckled under the pressure, but Herebrod found a way to make it work.

I have outriders seeking out Penda and Oswiu amongst the hills and plains, but I want to find Penda first, ensure he knows I come to stand with and support him.

Yet, of all the kings my riders could find, I'm surprised when I receive a report that tells me Conall of Dal Riata has been sighted on his borders and looking decidedly uncomfortable.

I wonder what it all means and instruct my man to speak with him. The news he brings is unwelcome and unsurprising.

Oswiu has commanded Conall to support him, calling on their family bond. It was Conall's father who offered Oswiu and his brothers' sanctuary after Æthelfrith was slain by the might of Raedwald of the East Angles and Edwin of Northumbria. Yet even my messenger says that Conall's torn. He doesn't wish to ally with a weak king, who has only monks and priests to treat on his behalf, and who steals away the holy men he protects on Iona.

I consider turning Conall to my allegiance, but Dal Riata and the Pictish kingdom have been enemies for far longer than the Saxons and the Pictish. I can't countenance forging a pact with him, even if it would further isolate Oswiu and make him a more desperate man. Not when I know that Penda already has a host of men aligned against Oswiu.

I dismiss Conall. He's no threat to me. I've left men on my borders so he won't take advantage of my absence and distraction to attack my kingdom. It's Penda I seek or Oswiu, but preferably Penda.

Another day passes, and my men, not used to being so far from home, grow a little restless, but before they can talk of returning home, an outrider returns with the news that I want. Both Penda and Oswiu have been sighted, and they're very, very close. And more, Conall hasn't moved from his position. Hopefully, he's seen sense and decided to stay out of an altercation that's nothing to do with him.

Any family tie that Oswiu has tried to call upon needs to be dismissed. Oswiu has done nothing to endear himself to the king of Dal Riata.

Penda and I have been sending messengers to each other throughout the summer, and the plan is simple and easy to implement. My men will stay in position to the north of Oswiu's chosen place of sanctuary. Penda will remain to the south. Oswiu will have no way of escaping.

As I thought, Oswiu is high above the surrounding countryside on a strange outcropping that reaches out from the deep earth at my feet. If we want to attack him, we'll have to do so uphill. But before any of that can happen, I have a discussion to have with Oswiu. I take the man he sent to me and have him ride up the steep hill, myself behind him, surrounded by twenty of my most fierce-looking warriors. They might not be the best warriors, but they look the part. It's the threat I wish to use against Oswiu, not actual brute force.

From our encampment to the north, Oswiu's position of strength looks formidable. There are sharp ridges cascading down from the peak they've chosen to shelter on, but from the south, there's a meandering trail that leads to the top. It's hot and sweaty work, but it's worth it when I reach the summit. Oswiu's warriors, perhaps expecting me to come and pledge my support to their king, scramble to look menacing as opposed to welcoming when they realise I don't come with peaceful intent, but laden with my weapons and wearing battle gear.

I growl at the men, noting their sun-reddened faces. The Bernician men might just be suffering from the windless conditions in the north and their exposed location so high up. I hope they've enough water. And then I dismiss the thought. It's not my concern.

'King Oswiu,' I bellow. I want to speak to my uncle face to face, ensure he understands my rage and unhappiness and my clear-cut decision that I won't be swayed by anything he says to me or that he tries to do to my family.

The men look at their tide-up comrade, clearly on the cusp of death before me, and they rush to have their king brought before me. I've not been kind to Oswiu's man, nor have I been unbearably cruel. He's been fed and watered each day. The way he looks now is because I've had him beaten a little to make it look as though I've been treating him like crap.

My uncle takes his sweet time in arriving. As I wait, I consider what he's doing. Perhaps he's eating, or fucking, or taking a shit. Then I reconsider. I imagine he's praying. Why wouldn't he be? He believes his God owes him everything.

He finally appears, flanked on both sides by warriors in their battle gear.

His men have put up some rudimentary defenses. A twisted pile of twigs and hedge rows lies before their hastily dug ditch, lined with wooden stakes. It's a poor excuse for what Bamburgh would have offered him. I can't help thinking that he's worse than a fool. He's a cocky one who believes the legend that his bishop has woven around him.

'Nephew,' he says, his eyes flickering between my captive and me. He shows no great sign of worry or upset, but I imagine he's had time to weave a mask over his face so that his failure in this regard is unknown to me.

'I've brought your man back for you. I'm afraid that the others didn't survive.'

That does make him flinch, and so I don't tell him what we did to his men and their bodies.

'Ah,' is all he says. I wish I could reach out and grab him by the neck to throttle him there and then. But he doesn't deserve such a quick death. Not for what he tried to do to my family.

'I've come to join Penda,' I tell him. He nods as though he knows this already, although he can't have been sure of my intentions, not until he realised his man was my captive and his other men dead.

Yet his warriors do react to my words, and they look at each other warily. They know what this means.

They have no one to stand shield to shield against Penda. Not unless Conall comes. I already know that Conall probably isn't coming. They hold out little hope as well.

'Then you can die with him,' he mutters. I gaze at him and can't stop my mouth from opening in shock.

'You still mean to fight him?' I ask, incredulous.

His eyes don't even flicker as they meet mine.

'My God will always triumph over pagans,' he retorts and turns his back on me without even saying farewell.

I don't want him to go because I want to tell him he's a fucking idiot, but I hold my tongue. I turn my horse aside, pushing his man toward the rest of his warriors. He turns frantically to look at me, his eyes pleading for me to let him stay with us, but I've heard enough.

My uncle and his men will die here.

They're welcome to their death and my captive with them.

21

ÆTHELWALD OF DEIRA
SUMMER AD655

I don't think I've ever seen a force that consisted of so many men. Penda has outdone anything my father might once have accomplished. He's brought together men from almost every kingdom on this island. There are the men from Ceredigion, Powys, the Mercians' themselves with their commanders and the men who rule small areas of the kingdom in Penda's name, his son amongst them. The warriors from the kingdom of the East Angles are also here, and in front of us all, the men from the Pictish kingdom, their king sitting with us as we feast and talk of tactics for the coming days.

Penda's force has amassed throughout his journey to the north, through my kingdom and then ever onwards, hunting for Oswiu, who's chosen to hide in the northernmost tip of the kingdom he rules.

It's a poor decision for him because he has nowhere to go. He should have stayed within his fortress at Bamburgh. From there, he'd have been able to keep his family alive and fed, as well.

But his decision to leave his family behind and bring his warriors almost to the kingdom's edge has left him exposed and without any real chance of survival. Unless his faith manages to present him with one, and as a man of the same faith, I know that's not the way our God works.

Even if he couldn't have stayed within Bamburgh in the long run once we surrounded him, he would have been able to take a ship and flee the kingdom. Yet, instead, he decided to try bribery, and it failed. Not only has Talorcan warned everyone of Oswiu's tactics, but he's also ensured that any possibility of retreating further north has been effectively stopped. Talorcan has blocking any hope of escape to the northern lands he controls.

The only way Oswiu can flee from his hilltop sanctuary is to sprout wings and fly from it. As that's unlikely, I can only see his death here. That thrills me. If my uncle dies, I can claim his kingdom for myself, just as I should have always held it if I'd only been a little older when my father died and less trusting.

As Oswiu sits on his hilltop, he must wonder what he's allowed to happen. The camps of Penda's allies almost completely encircle him, Penda wanting to ensure that Oswiu cannot flee. For today, Penda's called together all his allies, and we sit in a loose circle, eyeing each other, trying to determine what Penda has decided we should do.

'Allies,' he says, standing and turning to face everyone within the circle. He meets my eyes and ensures he does the same with everyone else, all twenty or so of his commanders and fellow kings. I consider if he enjoys positioning himself before such a coalition or if he's angry that he's been left with little choice but to call them us together. I'd be pleased to have so many prepared to support me in such an open way, but it also speaks volumes about Penda's anger against Oswiu. Is it also a warning to us all, as well as a show of strength? Is Penda saying, 'look what would happen if you attempted to defy me?'

'Firstly, my thanks for bringing your men so far north.' He makes a fine point. None of us thought that we'd have to travel further than Talorcan of the Picts would have to travel south, and yet in fact, he's had the shorter journey to be here; even shorter than mine, and as I share borders with Oswiu I didn't think that would be possible. Talorcan and Oswiu don't even share borders, the tattered kingdom of the Gododdin still in Oswiu's way as he considers expanding northwards, his attempts at quashing the kingdom failing when his brother died. Since then, I believe he's had little time to pursue his ambitions.

'Or south,' Penda also adds, glancing at Talorcan. My cousin grins at the acknowledgement. I meet his eyes and smirk at him. We've only just met, and I find it strange to be looking into the eyes of a dead man, but he's the spitting image of his father, or at least as I remember him. I was young when his father died. Even so, I wonder if he sees the same in me, my father reflected in my eyes.

Penda wears his black battle gear, polished to a high sheen so that the colours of the day seem to be absorbed by its murky face, complete with his midnight sword. He looks menacing even as he speaks, and he moves with such purpose that no one can deny his conviction to be rid of Oswiu, or his right to be known as the greatest warrior on our island.

Behind him, his oldest son sits and watches him as though memorising his stance and movements. Does he attempt to absorb as much of his father as he can, as though that alone will make him as well respected as his father?

I remember my father in his battle gear. He was a warrior all in white, playing on the legend he'd gained as a young man when he fought in the petty wars across the sea for the king of Dal Riata, the man who'd saved him when his uncle took his kingdom from him. He had a blade that shone brighter than the sun and a helm that was polished to a high gleam and rimmed with silver, just to add to the illusion of it being cast from white metal.

He looked fearsome and regal when he donned his battle gear. As a child, I'd always been in awe of him. I consider what he would have been had he lived. I ponder if his lightness would have stayed with him or if he, too, would have succumbed to the tricks my uncle plays. After all, rumour has it that my father could have aided Talorcan's father, and stopped him from being murdered by Cadwallon, but he chose to do nothing but let the rampant British king have his way.

I think my father would have ended up twisted and broken, a mockery of everything he said he was trying to achieve. I don't believe he'd have been a more honourable man than my uncle. Yet, I'd still rather he was here for me to hate than his scheming bastard brother.

Perhaps Herebrod did me a favour when he killed my father. Perhaps it's easier to live with the legend of a dead man than the reality of one who's alive.

Paeda is lucky. His father's legend grows with everything he does. No man looks at him and hopes that he'll fail, no man that is apart from Oswiu. While we might all dream of being as powerful as Penda is one day, we'd not try and topple him from his position to do so, not in such a way.

We wouldn't succeed. We're not as blind as Oswiu. We see the truth of who Penda is, and we all support it. Better to be the ally of such a powerful man than his enemy. Far better, and as if we needed that reinforcing, another twenty or so men are looking one to the other and thinking the same. We work to remember what we look like, calculating our military might and determining our value to Penda, measured against the others, with each breathe we take.

It's a strange experience to be amongst men who classify themselves as my equals. After all, I'm a king. I rule my kingdom through the support of my warriors and ealdormen. But I rule it. Each decision is ultimately mine to make. But then, these men must do the same.

'Talorcan informs me that he's spoken with Oswiu, and returned a small gift to him that Oswiu sent to the northern kingdom.' Talorcan nods as Penda speaks. We've all heard of the attempt on his family. We agree that the choice of tactics was one of a despairing man. Some of the men jeer as well. We know what's meant by the word 'gift'.

'Oswiu is a very desperate man. It won't take all of our warriors to defeat him, but we must be united in our desires to do so. We can't turn away at the last moment. We must not allow any jealousy between us to allow bad decisions in battle, born not by what will be successful but by what might be most acceptable to just one person.'

I listen to the words and consider what's prompted them. Has someone tried to make peace with Oswiu? If they have, they're idiots.

My uncle has nothing and can offer nothing in return. All he's ever done is take.

'I think we should mount an attack against Oswiu. An open attack, cutting off his chances of fleeing. I'd like your opinions on that, but first, I'll explain what I mean.'

He turns and looks up the slope where Oswiu has made his stand against us. Normally, and as the fortress at Bamburgh shows, having a stronghold on a hill is a sure sign of victory, but not in this case. Oswiu has left his fortress stronghold and come here against all the odds and all the expectations. He's a frantic man.

'There's a sharp cliff face behind the fortress. I can't imagine that anyone will attempt to escape down it or try and get in that way either, but Talorcan's men will stand guard there.'

That seems simple enough. Talorcan's men are already in position, their encampment not far from the base of the hill.

'Next, every man here will choose twenty of their finest warriors to represent them in the shield wall.'

This does have my allies looking at each other in surprise. Just twenty men from each ally? But then I reconsider. That'll still mean we have a force at least twice as large, if not three times as large as Oswiu's, according to Talorcan. It'll also ensure that each man here can satisfy their honour and will be able to add Oswiu's death to their reputation. I think it's a good plan, and the men aren't shouting or arguing but instead think of whom they'll send.

It'll be a mark of honour for the warriors as well. Once more, I appreciate that Penda understands the minds of men better than many others. He knows what drives men who live by their sword and shield.

'The idea will be to drive him from his sanctuary, to kill his warriors and make him understand once and for all that he can't stand aloft from our alliance. If he meets his death at the same time, then so be it.' His voice booms as he continues speaking. I can see the image of the future he's painting for us all.

By stressing 'our,' he also makes it seem as though this is something we've already agreed upon, even though we haven't. It ensures we feel committed to the enterprise.

It also, and this is important, means that none of us risk being denuded of warriors while our allies, and closest neighbours, remain at full force should the attack be less simple than we're expecting. This should stop any spontaneous attacks when we return to our homelands by men who might have had an opportunistic advantage if we'd allowed all of our men to attack at once, some faring better than others.

Penda watches us all. I imagine he's determining whom he still has to convince, but I don't think he needs to persuade anyone. We all want the same thing. We all desire Oswiu's death

But he's not yet finished.

'The men should be Christians, if possible.' This causes a ripple of unease. I feel a slow smile crossing my face. Impulsively, I stand and begin to clap. Others look at me in surprise, but then they realise who I am. They consider Penda's words and why he's spoken them.

'It won't be a war of religion then?' I nudge loudly and slowly those who've not yet understood the restriction nod in understanding.

'Oswiu thinks his priests will make him invincible,' I continue while Penda watches me with a nod of approval, allowing me to speak for him. 'If we stand against him, with our faith worn proudly around us, even his God won't be able to do anything for him. He doesn't make bargains. He's not the same as the old Gods.'

'When will we attack?' Æthelhere of East Anglia shouts. Penda glances at him. He's another of the kings who owes his kingdom to Penda. He would have nothing without Penda's aid.

'Tomorrow, but in the evening, not in the morning. It'll be a battle of but a few moments, nothing more. I don't want him to have any warning that we're coming. We won't even be offering the opportunity to surrender.'

Æthelhere considers those words and finds that he agrees with them Everyone agrees with them as no one raises a concern.

'What of Conall?' Talorcan queries into the bubbling hum of conversation.

'He's not coming? Is he?' Penda questions. Talorcan grunts a noncommittal answer.

'He wasn't, but he might change his mind.'

'Should we send a force to the north to stop him from joining Oswiu?'

'It might be the cautious thing to do,' Talorcan admits grudgingly.

'Then we'll do so. I'll send my men, led by Herebrod, because he knows the land well.'

Talorcan's face lightens at that. He doesn't want to risk his men, but Herebrod is also pleased and I understand why. Herebrod is as pagan as his Penda. This way, he'll have the opportunity to serve Penda as always and not have to watch the battle from the sidelines.

But Penda hasn't finished yet.

'Oswiu has put himself in an unenviable position. But we're not invincible. Mistakes could cost us dearly. We need to be unified, forget any discord we hold amongst each other.'

'Who'll be king in Oswiu's place?' I wanted to ask that question but veer away from it. I don't want everyone to see my desperation. I'm pleased that one of Penda's commanders has asked the question. Immin is a firm supporter of Penda's wife, and if he speaks, it'll be with her voice. That gives me pause for thought, but I'm too busy listening to Penda's response to consider all the implications of the exchange between the pair.

'That'll be decided once Oswiu is dead and not before. There are many here and elsewhere with good claims to the kingdom. It's not my place to determine who next becomes king. I can only advise and support the man I think should be the next ruler. He'll have to be a fine warrior and a man acceptable to the rest of the Bernicians. But also to the king of Deira and Dal Riata, not to mention the kingdom of Gododdin. If a weak man rules there, then the Gododdin may seek their revenge.'

This is the answer of a man who knows he's in a delicate situation. He wants Bernicia to be loyal to him but he doesn't want to be seen as an interfering over-king, even if that's what he'll be.

Also, and perhaps more importantly, he has many men here who see themselves as king of Bernicia, myself included. He can't disillusion us before we've made war on Oswiu. It wouldn't be impossible for one of us to change our alliance and slink back to our kingdom in the hope that Penda somehow fails in his attack. It wouldn't be advisable, but in the heat of battle, men act in strange ways, even more so when they're in hostile territory and suddenly realise they're not fighting for what they thought they were.

Penda asked that we did not fire every settlement along the way, and yet much of Bernicia is in ashes now, a reminder of our pathway through the harsh landscape and forbidding landscape. It's the way for warriors to take what they want and consider the consequences later, if at all. The people of Bernicia are fearful, wondering where their king has gone and why his warriors aren't there to protect them. I envisage the fortress at Bamburgh burgeoning with additional men and women, fleeing attacks from Penda's allies, and I once more question Oswiu's right to rule.

Neither am I blind to the fact that those who did the burning are those who don't want Bernicia as their own. I think Clydog of Ceredigion was particularly gleeful in his firing. He's a British king, and given the opportunity, he'd probably burn all of the Saxon kingdoms, aside from Mercia. He'd more than likely leave his sister's kingdom for her sons rather than risk them coming after him demanding retribution, but his men might see events with different eyes.

'Choose your men wisely,' Penda offers as a final thought. Then he turns to bow heads and talk to Herebrod. I'm left, still standing, feeling a rapid beating of my heart. Despite what he said, we've not discussed our intentions but rather look set to follow his wishes.

The prospect of success here has been wavering on the periphery of my thoughts. It's been too fleeting ever fully to grab hold of and enjoy, but now, seeing all these men, and realising how precarious Oswiu's position is, I truly feel that this could be it. Penda will crush Oswiu.

I've chosen my ally well. Even if Herebrod, Penda's closest friend, did kill my father, it was his own damn fault. He should have stayed within Northumbria and focused only on extending northwards, not southwards, or on just holding what he could legitimately claim. He should have thought of his children and his legacy, and not about stealing another man's kingdom.

As all the men in our circle stand, the clunking of so much war gear echoes through the air. I consider how much wealth and how many years of training these men have in combination. How many swords are sharpened to deadly points, and how many shields have been freshly daubed with bright paint? How many blacksmiths have spent half their lifetimes fashioning the weapons, ensuring the weight and the haft are correctly aligned? And even further back, how many women have laboured to bring these warriors into this world, to succour them from their first breath to the day they took their first steps and swung their first practice sword.

This is a monumental moment, the visible representation of one man's lifetime spent warring and cajoling, of bringing men to his alliance, of speaking with them, not often threatening them, of knocking aside those who stood against him, of killing some of those men. This is the physical representation of one man and his belief in the old Gods and his ancestor, Woden, pagan king and warrior, and of his God-given strength to be the most powerful man on our island.

I'm a Christian man, but even I can see the potent symbolism that Penda represents, and I'm drawn to it just as everyone else here is.

With Penda as our leader, we can't fail here.

22

PENDA, KING OF MERCIA
AD655

I gaze at Oswiu's temporary fortress, and I suppress a shudder of unease.

I can't believe that I've travelled so far only to be faced with the image of the place that's haunted my dreams since my father's death.

I can't quite comprehend that I've journeyed so far to kill a man who stands as a solitary voice against my ambitions and power, only to discover he will be the cause of my downfall.

I shake my head in anger once more. Freki is fractious beneath me, and I'm unsurprised. If he's Gunghir's descendant, he must feel the prophecy that stalks us both as we gaze at the view before us. I spoke to Gunghir of my worries when I was a much younger warrior, and it's just possible that his offspring shares his knowledge. He and I understood each other well and shared much I've never confided to others. We understood the fire within our bodies that made us want to be the best at everything in honour of our chosen God and his ideals.

When I spoke to my allies last night, when I sent Herebrod and his men to intercept Conall of Dal Riata, I had no idea that when I woke the next day I'd be faced with the stark image my father had filled my head with on his death-bed. my head heavy with too much ale, I'd ridden around Oswiu's hideaway to see Talorcan's camp for myself and sighted the thing I never wished to see.

But here, and just as my father whispered in his gravelly voice, the cliff face is stark, sheathed in white chalk, and lit at its peak only by the blueness of the sky, hazy with cloud cover. The cliff face is ragged and ringed with birds nesting in its shelter. Halfway down its side nestles a great tree, its branches reaching outwards into nothingness, not skywards, and in its branch lies a great crow's nest. It's this, more than anything else, that has convinced me this is the place of my father's prophecy. It's unlike anything I've ever seen before. I know that in his lifetime, my father would never have seen this place. He spent his life in the kingdom of Mercia, fighting for land and titles. I doubt he ever saw mountains as huge as this one, for Mercia is a place of hills and meandering valleys, not rough peaks and exposed outcroppings.

For some time, I try to turn away from it, to look at anything other than the shape that's burrowed deep inside my mind. But I've never shown fear, and neither will I here. Whatever fate has stalked me hasn't managed to catch me yet. I resolve, now that I must face the alleged manifestation of my downfall, to ignore it and go about my original intentions.

I can't leave now just because of a worry that if I crest that cliff face, I might meet my death. How would I explain it to my allies? To my son? To Herebrod, who travels to the north for me?

Instead, I stare at the view. I consider the actions I've chosen. Oswiu is marooned on that hillside. It will take less than a handful of men to overcome him. I've asked my allies to send only twenty of their warriors. They must all be Christians. I'm turning the tide of any last-ditch efforts Oswiu might be trying to make with the local Christians, in Dal Riata and perhaps Iona, by sending Herebrod to intercept them.

I've no intention of waiting around for Herebrod to return, not now. I'm pleased I called the attack for this evening. Oswiu and his men's corpses will soon be rotting on the ground. I don't envy the men their task of rushing up the steep hillside, but I also know that I would want to be there if I weren't a pagan and Oswiu hadn't made this altercation about his Christianity and my belief in the old Gods.

By tomorrow morning, I could be on the way home to Mercia. I would know that Oswiu's dead. I would have outrun my father's words, which have little bothered me within Mercia and East Anglia, but which have manifested themselves here. It'd be an agreeable way to end this vast expedition to the north, although it'll hardly add more to my reputation. But then, Oswiu is so weak and alone, his death now, brought about through my vast coalition, will never be perceived as anything but the last stand of a cornered man. The last stand of a Christian man who believed in his God instead of himself.

Oswiu should have given up long ago, before he lost everything he had, apart from the ties that bind him to this mortal world.

He should have fled his kingdom, taking his wife and children. I'm sure his old allies in the kingdom of the Dal Riata across the sea would have welcomed him. If not them, perhaps the kingdoms over the short sea to the east, the homeland his ancestors once came from. His final desperate effort is a pitiful attempt to survive, and his reliance on his bishop and faith has made him a laughing stock.

No man in their right mind would ever follow a king like him, and few do. Yet he must still hold out some hope. Otherwise, he'd not have left his wife and sons behind at Bamburgh and travelled to the north with nothing but his weapons and his men. If he's hoping for some last-ditch intervention from his God, I think he's waiting in vain. The only surety is that his death is a few breaths away and his heartbeats are limited.

Surely he must know as much?

Yet, something is keeping him alert and determined as he gazes out over the vast number of men who've come to attack him. That thought worries me. I've never been a man sure of his success until it was a surety, but here, in the wastelands of Oswiu's kingdom, does he have something to thwart me with finally? Is there something that he knows and I don't?

The thought chases me all through the long, hot afternoon as the men, twenty of them from each of my allies, make themselves ready for war. Their priests speak to them and praise them for their efforts to make the kingdoms peaceful. I listen with a wry smirk.

I should have brought more than my horse and my inner faith with me. I should have also brought Woden, and allowed him to stride with me through all the men, but it would have been inappropriate. I've tried hard not to make this about my God for all that Oswiu believes it's the only way for him to succeed. If I donned all of my battle gear would these Christians have shied away from me and have seen me as Woden as so many of my followers do?

I little know, and as the sun begins to cast pink and orange tendrils through the finely laced white clouds, I decide it's no longer important.

I've clarified that this is about Oswiu and his desire to stir up war between the different kingdoms and not accept the status quo. When Oswiu dies, it'll be because, unlike all of my other allies, he wouldn't acknowledge me as his overlord. After all, he wants to be his brother. He doesn't object to the idea of one overlord over all the Saxon kingdoms. He challenges it being anyone but himself, and he dresses it in religious overtones.

His reasoning is irrelevant. I watch all my allies and their men. When they're ready, and I'm sure that Oswiu knows what's coming, I beckon them onwards, a grin on my face as I remove my helm, but still wear my black byrnie and weapons belt. I sit on Freki, who preens as though he finally knows his worth. If I wasn't trying to look so fierce, I might just smirk at my horse, but instead, I glower as he does. The men take heart from my rage and anger as they surge up the steep slope.

I hope Oswiu has made peace with his God.

23

PAEDA OF THE HWICCE
AD655

Unlike my father, I have a very high-profile baptism to my name so that I can take part in the coming attack.

I've not told my father as such, although I suspect he already knows my plans so that when I walk past him, leading my men, he shows no sign of surprise, none at all, and that pleases me. I wouldn't want to be reproached for taking my part in the attack. I've endured a Christian wife all this time, and it has been an endurance, so I should now benefit, even if only in some small way.

I take with me twenty of my warriors. They all profess to some belief in the Christian God, not spurred on by my wife's endeavours but more by my mother's. They're the sons of men who came with her when she married my father. They've been my playmates, and now they'll stand with me in the shield wall.

When my father told us all only to take twenty men, it seemed like such a small number compared to the vast horde arranged around us. But it's still over four hundred men. As we all begin the steep climb, already in a tight formation so that our shields go before us, I take the time to look behind me over the rocky terrain and the straggly grasses. I take heart from the rows and rows of men who watch on with hungry eyes, cheering all the same.

They wish they stood with me, and that they don't is more a matter of Oswiu's terrible choice of refuge than anything else. With just four hundred men, the trackway is crowded. Already we're three deep in places so that we can attack uniformly.

There's a rugged camaraderie between all the men. Even though we don't share the same language, we all share the same intent. Killing Oswiu will give us a great reputation. Whether we carry swords, seaxes, war axes or spears, we all know the language of war, and we'd not be here if we weren't skilled in its intricacies.

One of the men, I know he must be one of my uncle's men, begins to chant as we labour higher and higher. The sun, although not as high in the sky as at midday, is still warm on our back, and weighed down as we are with our weapons, the heat makes the going particularly difficult. The sound of voices raised cheers us and makes us move quicker and quicker, ready for the final battle to begin.

We've chased Oswiu throughout his kingdom, never expecting him to come so far to the northern lands. We were sure, all of us, that he'd be hunkered down in his fortress at Bamburgh. For that very reason, my father had ships following our movements, brought by Æthelhere of the East Angles, so we could attack via sea and by land. In the end, the ships weren't needed. Now they wait far to the south. They've not been sent home yet, but with little to do but stay out of the way of any Bernician who might be keen to try their hand at seeking a little vengeance for their current king's strife.

I never expected to be making war on a strange outcropping of rock, more likely to be a home for birds and gulls than for Bernicia's king, but if this is where I must make my name for myself, just as my father did in his youth, then so be it.

I feel the battle rage begin to build inside me. This is the special gift that Woden gives my father's family, or so he tells me. He says that other men have the same rage, the same desire to kill their enemy, but that Woden sustains it within our family to make it last all battle long. Woden gives us the strength of a giant and the cunning of a fox.

I let it begin to burn inside me, starting as an ember and then building higher and higher until I, too, feel as though I'm a giant, taking huge steps toward the peak. Then, when I feel my strongest, when my grip is tight on both my shield and sword, and when I know that it'll be like smiting small children, rather than the best of Bernicia's nobility, I see a sight I wish I didn't. No matter what my father hoped, this will be no great battle. This won't be Oswiu's death, for he has one last desperate attempt to make, and it's both a shocking and one that will stop many of the men who stand with me.

For standing in front of us all, a holy cross at his back and his cloak as white and flowing as the clouds that surround him, is none other than Bishop Finan, the holy bishop of Holy Island, or Lindisfarne. A man that many here will know of and revere.

Despite my father's best intentions, he's not appreciated the level of Oswiu's desperation or deviousness. Oswiu's learned from his brother's victory against Cadwallon when he prayed to his God and won a great victory against him at the battle known as Heavenfield by relying on his God. Or has he?

At Bishop Finan's feet are chests and chests of deepest oak, open to the fading sunlight. In the dimming glow of the evening, I can make out the vast riches contained within each chest.

Oswiu knows he can't win this battle, so he's decided on two attempts to escape here with his life, his bishop and his treasure.

I know many men won't engage in the battle now. Some will fear for their Christian souls, but really, most of them will want their share of the treasure that Oswiu has on display.

Fuck. There'll be no battle tonight. I call the men to a halt and think of my father.

He'll not be pleased, and his black byrnie, sword and shield, will stand as a stark contrast to Finan's white glow.

This might all have been for nothing.

Oswiu might just live through this attempt to hound him from his kingdom, and take his life.

Fuck.

I turn to Osmond, standing at my right, his eyes focused on the spectacle of the white bishop. I see emotion in his pursed lips, all that I can see of his face behind his helm, and he turns to me.

'I'll get King Penda,' he mutters, and at that moment, I wonder why he doesn't say his uncle or my father, and then I understand. This isn't a matter for family, but rather for the war leader who brought us all here, who organised the vast force waiting at the bottom of the steep hill and who wants to make an example of Oswiu. And more, who wants to make this not about religion.

Yet it seems that king Oswiu has a different opinion. Even now, he hopes his faith might save him, so although my father tried to mitigate his efforts to make this about religion, Oswiu isn't prepared to do the same. He plans on using his faith and his wealth, two very potent emblems for the men who stand against him.

'Go,' I say, and in that one word, there's a whole wealth of anger and frustration as I stare at Bishop Finan.

He's not changed since he baptised me in the freezing river. He's neither aged nor gained or lost weight, and he stands with the strength of his faith behind him, if not the force of his king, for Oswiu has nothing to offer him apart from his unfailing belief.

That's clearly not enough for Finan, for he looks terrified. I've never seen a man so scared in all my life. He's a warrior of his God, not his king's warrior. Oswiu, with nothing to lose, has placed his bishop between him and four hundred men who want his death. In doing so, Oswiu appears even more cowardly, and even less honourable. I need to know little of his faith to appreciate that he's not acting in the same way that his older brothers would.

I feel pity for Finan and also, bizarrely for Oswiu. Not only has he brought his men to the edge of his kingdom, abandoned his young wife and family, allowed his kingdom to be over-run by his enemy and his people terrified for their lives, he's also managed to earn the enmity of the Christians before him.

They might not respect Finan as they do the bishops in the south, but they know who he is and what he represents. For all that the monks and priests pray and scream for their faith to be vanquished with swords and shields if necessary, these warriors aren't to be how it's accomplished. Just as King Æthelfrith, Oswiu's father, did all those years ago when he sacrificed the monks in his attack on Gwynedd, so too does Oswiu subvert his alleged belief to his ends.

I feel sick with disgust and as Finan meets my eyes I know he feels the same as I do.

Whatever my father does now, he's still won the contest of wills.

If he allows Finan to live and by implication, takes Oswiu's treasure, his reputation will grow, for Penda will have better understood the faith of his fellow Saxons than Oswiu could ever do. Even though he supposedly shares it.

24

OSWIU, KING OF BERNICIA
AD655

I watch with apprehension as my bishop stands alone before four hundred warriors.

I didn't want to put him in this situation, but until reinforcements from Conall arrive or I receive news from my men scouting for Herebrod, I have no alternative.

My men are unhappy with the decisions I've made regarding their bishop, and the treasure they think should be theirs. But I'm the king here, not them, and I make the decisions that will either see us live or die.

We can't hope to beat the thousands of warriors who ring us. Still, if my men can capture Herebrod, or better kill him. And if Conall comes to reinforce me. And if the religious men that Penda has forced to come against me can be convinced that if they kill Finan or ignore his peaceful words, they'll lose their right to heaven, then we might just live through this to return to Bamburgh.

If all those events fall into place, then Penda will be hobbled. He'll be unable to attack me again anytime soon because he'll have failed in his greatest attempt.

He won't have his battle against me as he did against Edwin and my brother at Hæðfeld and Maserfeld. He'll have nothing but a handful of gold and treasure. Provided he can be convinced to disband his war bands and take the treasure I have on offer.

Of course, my kingdom will be denuded of wealth, but we'll have the superior claim. My men and I can fight to reclaim our lost jewels with the might of the Church at our back.

Finan is unhappy and uneasy with my actions. I could curse him repeatedly for his refusal to present me with an alternative or accede to my demands as soon as I made them. Instead, I've been forced to tie him up and deprive him of food and water for the past two days. I told him the only way he'd ever be fed again was if he stood before the enemy to offer them eloquent words to deter them. He must speak of his God and faith with the same fervour that he uses amongst his monks and to my wife.

I've rarely seen such hatred in the eyes of a man, but Finan and I will, quite probably, never be allies again after this. Not that I concern myself too much with that. I don't think this will work. I believe Penda will simply strike him down and continue his advance to my position. In that case, I'll have done Finan a great favour. He'll have died as a martyr to his faith. He death will have been quick, whilst the rest of us must suffer.

I watch him carefully while I wait for my enemy's next move. It was no easy matter to get him to leave the dubious safety of our hilltop refuge. It was easier to carry the wooden chests, as heavy as they were to their position. Yet, I couldn't tie Finan to a wooden cross and make him a martyr. He needed to walk to his position.

I don't know what finally swayed him to leave my encampment, but I'm pleased he's done so. Now I can do little but wait.

Not that I have to wait for long. Penda and his monstrous war horse quickly come crashing through his line of men, the shield wall parting to either side of him. Just as at the battle of Maserfeld, and when he stood before my fortress at Bamburgh, he comes sheathed in black. His helm, shield, sword, and even his war axe, carry the shine of night, as does his horse. The beast is monstrous, gnashing its teeth and kicking out with its front legs.

Bishop Finan quakes before him, but Penda doesn't so much as meet his eyes. Instead, his gaze has picked me out from amongst my men. His eyes threaten to burn a hole through my head. He comes with the intensity of a warrior who knows his worth. He carries himself in the way of a god-infused fighter. There's no hesitation about him.

I can't imagine that he could have foreseen these events, and yet he acts as though he has.

'Bishop Finan,' he calls, his horse breathing into Finan's face, not even dismounting.

'King Penda,' Finan manages to retort. He neither steps away from the horse nor attempts to look back toward me. If anything, he stands a little straighter. Penda slides back the two panels of his black helm, etched all over with a detail I can't quite determine. I see a smile on his face.

'My son tells me that you might require protection,' he utters, looking at his men and not at me anymore. 'I'll happily provide it if you find yourself without the ... support you need to continue your work.' I stiffen at the words and watch with dismay as Finan relaxes from his tense position at the conciliatory words. A ripple of amusement runs through Penda's alliance.

I swallow as my men groan with unease. I might have sacrificed my bishop and treasure and still, Penda will hold the initiative.

'Prince Paeda is here?' Bishop Finan thinks to ask, his voice raised just enough that we can all hear it, and even I can hear the relief in his voice.

'Paeda is no true Christian,' I think to shout, but my solitary voice is ignored as Paeda brings his weapons and himself to where his father and Bishop Finan are talking. I wish Finan would hurry up with proposing the truce, ensuring we can leave here without injury. But he seems far more intent on greeting Paeda and inquiring how my son and daughter fare.

Can I have misjudged so poorly once more? Have I made my death even more certain?

Paeda, for all that we all know he's no longer truly of the Christian faith, and perhaps never was, allows himself to be blessed by

Bishop Finan. He turns his back on my line of defense. If I were more skilled with a spear, I'd take the opportunity to kill him. I'd forget all about my attempts to use religion to thwart Penda, and I'd bloody well kill his son. Paeda has cast my daughter aside and made her a laughing stock. Penda might have more sons to replace Paeda, but I know that Penda would lose his warrior detachment if I made the attack personal.

But as I can't attack Paeda, I must rely on my small force sent to intercept Herebrod's attempts in the north. I pray that they succeed.

With Paeda at his side, Bishop Finan finally finds his strength and courage.

'My children,' Bishop Finan begins to speak. There's a hush from my warriors and Penda's. I think Penda should kill Finan now, not let him speak. That's what I'd do.

'I come before you to propose a treaty between King Penda, and his allies, and between King Oswiu, sealed with our faith and with this treasure you see before you.'

Finan gestures to the wooden chests at his feet, so enticingly opened and filled with all the gold and silver I have, or rather, they almost are. I've kept a small proportion for myself. I'll need to pay my warriors when I return to Bamburgh. Should I return.

'The time for treaties has passed,' Penda growls, not angrily, but with intent.

'This will be a treaty sealed with more than just marriages and children,' Bishop Finan tries to elaborate to make it more appealing.

'King Oswiu has so far failed to adhere to any of our treaties,' Penda continues, just loud enough for everyone to hear, 'and he entices others to make war on Mercia.'

I want Finan to deny the truth of those words, but he doesn't.

'This treaty will be agreed with the Church of Lindisfarne and King Oswiu. We'll ensure that he adheres to his holy vow. King Oswiu will return to his family. As soon as his son, Ecgfrith, is old enough, he'll allow him to rule in his place and become a monk, serving me on Holy Island, as he should.'

'No,' I howl, rage in my voice. Bishop Finan is determined to punish me for my acts against him, for questioning his God and for blaming him for my failure.

My men look at me in consternation. They know I've not spoken these words, and yet Penda grins at me now, his joy at seeing my last-ditch attempt at securing my kingship and future failing. It makes his own thwarted attempt seem insignificant.

If I had a spear, I'd be content to kill Finan now. How fucking dare he attempt to make a treaty that suits him and which makes me nothing but a spent force in the Saxon kingdoms. I don't miss that it will allow his faith to continue without being wholly dependent on me.

'I thought you'd speak for your king, but it seems you don't.'

At that, Finan mutters something far more quietly to Penda, out of my hearing. Whatever it is makes Penda's entire body start a little. I can't see his face, though, to know if he laughs or is surprised by Finan's comment. My men, dejected at seeing their bishop so close to the enemy, are becoming fractious. They call to me, demanding that I rescue their beleaguered bishop. I shake my head empathically. We'll only survive if Finan does what I demanded.

'Tell me of your treaty then,' Penda demands, his voice loud and carrying to all the warriors once more.

'In exchange for our retreat from here, the Church on Lindisfarne will give you and your men all this treasure before you. It'll make your men rich without the need to kill others and without imperilling their souls. In turn, the church will ensure that Oswiu respects his borders and never again meddles in the affairs of other kingdoms.'

'You think this is enough when my men are merely a few paces from engaging in war with Oswiu? From killing him? And you?' Penda adds. Finan, for all he trained as a warrior and a priest, allows a squawk of horror to escape from his mouth. Penda laughs at the fear on the bishop's face and looks to his men as though it's already a done deal.

Only Paeda takes the opportunity to whisper to his father. Whatever he says makes Penda hesitate to give the final command. It's then that I notice that the warriors have fallen to silence. Finan has moved away from his position close to the treasure. He walks amongst Penda's warriors, offering blessings to those who ask for it and simply praying with others.

I suppress a grimace of annoyance. This isn't at all what I'd expected Finan to do. I thought he'd understood what was expected of him. I was wrong.

Before my eyes, Penda and his son continue to speak. Then, first one, and then two, and then more and more of his warriors, his commanders and allies join the small discussion taking place until almost more men stand around Penda than they do around Finan.

I can't tell what's happening. My men grow quiet at my side. They think that this might just resolve into a favourable resolution for us.

I might never rebuild my relationship with Bishop Finan, but I might be allowed to, after all. I consider seeking out Penda amongst the rabble of men by running from my temporary refuge to strike him down with my brother's sword. I know that it'll also mean my death. While Bishop Finan moves to negate my authority over my followers, I've every intention of leaving here alive and working out a way to get my revenge on Penda. I must ensure he dies for humiliating my kingship.

Abruptly, Penda steps from the mass of men who surround him, his cheekpieces back in place so that it's impossible to determine his thoughts from his lips that show below the nasal piece.

'We'll take Bishop Finan with us and return at first light with our answer.' His voice is powerful and dominating. I sense nothing from his words that could give me cause for hope, but that Bishop Finan is being listened to is enough for me.

Come the morning, I hope I'll have a treaty, and then I can slink my way home, hopeful that at least Herebrod has met his death on my warrior's swords.

25

HEREBROD

AD655

As I ride through the day, mindful that Oswiu might have outriders anywhere and that he might also have men sent to help Conall find him, I feel relieved to be away from Oswiu's entrapment.

I can't understand how he's allowed himself to become marooned as he has done, far from home and on an outcropping that's inherently less easy to defend than Bamburgh. His father built the fortress at Bamburgh. I can't fathom why he's left its safety, not when he knows that every Saxon kingdom is against him, and almost all the British ones as well.

His desperate efforts to have Conall come to his aid speak of futility, as does his attempt to force Talorcan to become his ally by stealing away his family. Men in such precarious situations will do strange things, and I fear he might have more plans that I've not foreseen.

I know he hates me and blames me for his brother's death. I find it strange. Oswald's son doesn't hate me as much as Oswiu, but then, Oswald's son hates Oswiu for usurping his kingdom. Perhaps it's not so inexplicable after all.

I've warriors who ride with me. Some are spread out in front and while others follow on from behind. All seems to be as it should be, but still, I feel uneasy. That worries me. I've ridden this track before, I know these mountains and lakes, and I should feel at ease, almost pleased to be home, but I'm not.

My men sense my unease. As dusk begins to fall, bringing with it a chill breeze, and my back-rider fails to materialise, I take matters into my hands. I summon my men to me and make the best defensive structure we can, with a small cave to our back where the horses can be kept safe. To the front of us, we hack the prickly brambles from the ground and lay them out. They'll only serve as an inconvenience should my imaginary enemy appear in their battle gear. Still, if we set light to the brambles, we'll have an opportunity to see an enemy who only thinks to attack at night.

While my men and I spend the night taking turns to ensure no one attacks us as we sleep, nothing happens. In the morning, I feel foolish, especially when my back-rider appears, filled with an apology for his lateness, walking beside a limping horse.

I swallow back my unease and order the men to ready themselves for the day's journey. Only, and I'm not sure if I should be angry with the man or not, my back-rider and his limping horse have brought a full force of men to our hideaway. My twenty men must face at least thirty. I'm surprised, although I shouldn't be, that Oswiu is still determined to bring about my death and that he'd waste so many men when he has so few.

Quickly, the men realise our peril and form a line of interlocking shields behind the brambles. The men are too professional to abuse the back-rider for his part in the attack. Yet it's clear he feels his failure keenly.

I clasp my hand to his back. He jumps at my touch.

'Kill the bastards for me,' I mutter, and he nods, ensuring the grip on his war axe is tighter. He checks his byrnie, and his weapons are easy to access in the heat of a battle. I can't blame him for what's about to happen. Somehow I've been expecting it ever since I left Penda's side.

Still, I'm surprised by the anger and rage on the faces of the men who quickly encircle us. If we'd not had the cave at our back, we might have been fully surrounded. As it is, we have much in our favour. Although Oswiu's warriors are hardened men keen on revenge, I imagine they once fought for Oswald. My men are more detached. They don't see this as a moment to exact revenge but rather a test of their skills.

I offer my men the same encouragement.

'For Penda,' I shout, and that's all they need to hear. Their rumble of battle joy begins deep in their chest, with weapons pounding on their shields. I have time to grin.

I can't imagine that Oswiu's warriors will beat mine, but, as Penda would say, it never pays to be too sure.

Trying to salvage some sort of initiative, I shout for the attack to begin. As I do, I have the satisfaction of seeing the surprise on the face of Oswiu's warriors. No doubt they expected me to try and treat with them first, but I've no time for that.

Immediately, I'm moving forward to meet one of my attackers. My shield is firm in my hand, and my seax in my other hand. This will be close fighting, and my sword and war axe might be too big to use in such a confined space, so they're left on my weapons belt. If I need them, I can reach for them quickly.

We meet in a clash of metal and leather. I feel the strength in my arms that I've so often relied on in the past. My years might sit more heavily around me than in the past, but my experience ensures my movements are well-measured and routine.

Immediately I can feel the weight of my enemy against my shield. A weapon tries to sneak its way around my shield. I know this movement far too well. I step back and allow the enemy to unbalance himself. Then, I stab my seax into the exposed area beneath his raised arm. Immediately blood drenches my gloved hand. The warrior growls in anger and pain, dropping the arm that holds his war axe. He only has his shield to deter me, so I raise my shield and stab the man's neck. Better to kill him quickly.

He collapses to the ground. Another warrior comes to take his place. The man's eyes are black and hooded. He stands slightly taller than me. His shield is a huge piece of curved linden wood, much larger than the average warrior, and for a moment, I consider a change in tactics.

My foeman is a large man. His shield shows me his strength and height, but like all men, he'll be vulnerable in the same ways, provided I can get beyond his shield.

Around me, I can tell that my warriors are victorious. The cries of wounded and injured men mingle with those who're jubilant. I'm almost pleased that the late return of my back-rider has hastened this altercation. Once the men are dead or have retreated, I'll resume my journey for Penda and ensure that Conall doesn't manage to reinforce Oswiu.

I think all this as my arms and upper body work to find a weakness in the large warrior attacking me. The warrior drops his shield before he attacks with a smaller war axe than normal. I can see the sharp sheen on its edge. He prefers a sharp blade and manoeuvrability to brute strength and the ability to break bones.

The next time he swings at my head, I dance toward him, drop my shield, and stab at the exposed area between his neck and shoulder. My seax encounters some resistance but slices through the edges of the byrnie, and blood blooms from the gaping wound. Before I can twist the seax and make my strike more effective, the man raises his shield to bat my arm aside while attempting to ensure his war axe hits my body.

I swing my shield to knock his war axe aside. As I do so, my seax continues to scour down the man's body, leaving a trail of blood in its path. More and more of the man's blood gushes from the cut. He looks at me with true hatred, realising his death is only a heartbeat away. But he's determined to fight to his death. I stand back to admire my work, allowing my shield to drop slightly, and as I do, I feel the weight of his war axe across my stomach. It's my turn to look surprised. What is this?

Only it's not the man's axe that I feel striking through my byrnie, but that of another, his mouth rimmed with blood. He chuckles around his battle pain, mixed with his battle joy. The man who should have stood beside me is writhing in pain on the floor. There are bodies everywhere, mostly of Oswiu's men, but also a handful of mine.

Oswiu, it appears, was determined that I should die here. The few of his men who still survive are focused on me, their weapons bloodied as they step over comrades and their enemies.

My men seem unaware of the danger I'm in, but I don't despair, not yet. I'm wounded, but only slightly. I feel a steady trickle of hot blood over my skin, but still stand tall, hold my shield and swing my seax.

The man I was attacking has fallen to his knees, his neck pulsing blood and his eyes turning blank. He's swung his war axe for the last time. I spit at him, pleased he's dying quickly. I turn my attention to the three men close to me. They leer toward me. I appreciate this could end badly for me. I take a moment to close my eyes and think of my god, Woden, and to ensure that his gaze is on me before I die or kill my attackers.

Despite my injury, I dance into the first two men, knocking one to the ground with the weight of my body. I attack the other with my seax, threatening to swipe across his exposed chin. The man flinches, and as he does so, one of my warriors attacks him from behind, a firm and solid connection between his war axe and the enemy's helm. He stands stunned as my warrior slides his war axe to the side and attacks the man's neck. He stumbles and falls, and now I have only one enemy to attack.

Yet I've forgotten about the man on the floor. Before I take even one more step, I feel the metal slice through my leg. I suppress a shudder of pain. I swing my seax down and stab the man through the arm. As I do so, I feel my stomach rip open, hot blood cascading over my sliced byrnie. This wound has the potential to kill me.

Angry because I've not come here to die, I stab the man through his eye as his helm tumbles from his head. I feel the sharp blade grind on bone, and I watch the man die with satisfaction.

Then there's just the one warrior remaining, once more, but I can feel my strength leaving me. I've half a notion that Woden watches me with approval on his face.

If I should die here, at least I know, I'll see Eowa in the next life and can finally apologise for my error that saw him die.

But first, I must kill the remaining warrior so that my residual men can fulfil Penda's wishes. I leave my seax in the dead warrior's eye and reach for my war axe. With its weight, I can slice the man's head from his shoulder.

The thought gives me strength. As the man menaces toward me, I balance my legs and swing the war axe behind me to have as much force as possible in the final blow. The man, only seeing the blood pouring from my body and not the menace of my war axe, steps exactly where I want him to. The weapon's impact is so great that it drops me to my knees as the warrior gasps in surprise at the weight of my axe on his helm. Whether it stuns him or kills him, I don't know because I sink to my knees, my last hope that my wound can be staunched and that I'll see Penda once more.

26

PENDA, KING OF MERCIA
NOVEMBER AD655

It's late in the year to be returning home from a battle. The damp, chill mist swirls around my returning warriors and their horses.

We had the victory here. Yet it wasn't what I expected.

I'd hoped to strike Oswiu's head from his shoulder and leave him hacked to pieces as with his brother in the past. But I'm returning with yet another treaty, and one I'm not happy about.

Oswiu, in his attempt to evade me, travelled further and further north until he was almost within the Pictish lands, and by then, many of my allies felt that they'd travelled too far and gained too little.

They were as unhappy as I now am, or so I must assume, and so I was left with little choice but to conclude the campaign as quickly as I could. I followed their wishes instead of mine, especially when Bishop Finan and his treasure appeared. And now, on the long journey home, with my sworn men shearing away from my main campaign far more quickly than when I convinced them to join the attack on Oswiu, I'm unhappy. They're keen to be home with their share of the treasure with which Oswiu paid for his life.

I should be happy, but I'm uneasy. Oswiu spoke to the minds of my allies far more convincingly than I did. He gave them gifts of gold, treasure and silver. Riches that they wanted and which they gained without having to do more than threaten to bloody their swords and shields. Or rather, Bishop Finan did. It was he who spoke to the minds of the men.

I thought they were keen to kill their enemy, but they only wanted treasure. Bishop Finan gave them all the excuses the Christians amongst my allies needed to change their mind about killing Oswiu. As the alliance's leader, I, by necessity, gained the most treasure. It's that which weighs me down on my journey south, that and the feeling that this isn't quite as over as I think. I have half a mind to journey to Bamburgh again to assure myself that Oswiu's family are there and that they've been reunited with Oswiu for what time he has left to be king. I dread that he tails my movements, yet I thirst for vengeance against him.

My son thinks my fears are only half-formed, but I understand the way the minds of men work, especially men who want to be powerful. I know because I'm a powerful man and a devious one at that. I have the proof of Herebrod's terrible wounds to show me just how desperate Oswiu is to visit revenge upon me.

It took years of planning and building my reputation, losing my brother, to gain what I wanted. Oswiu has had that many years to do the same. All he lacks is any allies, any at all. He's been abandoned by everyone, and that makes him more of a threat than a man who thinks carefully. It makes him reckless. As such, I have a despairing man who's been plotting his success for over a decade and has been constantly thwarted.

He might have seemed desperate enough when we had him hemmed between our own attacking force and that of Talorcan of the Picts. But now that my allies are bleeding away from me, more quickly than icicles with the thaw, I imagine him reconsidering. Perhaps he thinks of all the treasure he gave me to leave and worries that he'll never rebuild his reputation. No doubt, he hates Bishop Finan, who's promised to ensure he rules wisely until his son, Ecgfrith, my hostage and ward, is old enough to rule without the aid of his father. Then he must step aside and give his kingdom to his son and become a monk. I can't imagine he's thrilled with that part of the treaty; for all that, it was his use of Bishop Finan that stopped his inevitable death.

I shouldn't have let the rest of the men decide our course of action. I should have demanded war, and, if they refused, ordered my warriors and those of my son and son-in-law to engage against Oswiu. I fear there'll never be peace as long as Oswiu lives.

I should turn around, head back the way I came, and trap Oswiu again. He thinks he's safe. Only the weather has turned torrid. The men and I have already endured three days of heavy rainfall. To head back now would be asking too much of them, of us all.

It's long past the time for fighting this year. Now we should be slaughtering animals, not men, and spending our days in lazy slumber, endless eating and the occasional walk or ride into the bright but frigid countryside. We lingered too long in the north, joking about our newfound wealth and treasure and watching Oswiu slink his way home.

My son is buoyant at my side. He believes we've won a great victory against his father-in-law. That makes him happy, far happier than his wife's made him. I wish I could share his enthusiasm, but when I'm dry and warm again, I'll regret the missed opportunity. I'll wish I'd turned the men around, even in the rain and the grey clouds.

Instead, I've men riding to the front and others to the rear of our journey south. I hope that if Oswiu attempts a desperate attack on my retreating allies, I'll have the time to find a good site to defend easily. It might rain throughout the battle, but if Oswiu comes, as I think he must, I want to be ready. It would be better if he were killed only by the combined might of Mercia. That way, I'll claim responsibility for his death. I'll gain from the death of a third member of the ruling family who tries to claim Bernicia for themselves. That Oswiu's also tried to kill Herebrod adds to my anger at my agreement to the treaty. It fuels my desire to seek revenge and attack Oswiu once more.

It little matters that Herebrod still lives. Oswiu's been trying to kill Herebrod for many winters. I've kept Herebrod close to me. The only time I've let him fight away from me, Oswiu took full advantage, even though he should have been marooned on his hilltop refuge.

I smirk through the rain, the mist and the gloom. Even though I'm cold, wet and shivering inside my cloak, I still hope for another battle of great renown to rid myself of Oswiu finally. I'd rather gain with my sword than with my words or even through fear of the damage I could inflict upon my enemies.

With every river valley I ride my horse through, every hill I crest, I look through the grey day to search for a site that would be defensible and allow us easy access to water and food.

Oswiu's force was only small when he treated for his peace, yet it was filled with men who knew this land and how to fight in it. If he came upon us at a moment of weakness, it would be a far harder-fought battle than my son thinks. Nothing in this life is ever as easy as it at first appears. Our victory will have angered Oswiu, as will Bishop Finan's antics. Until I step foot on Mercian land again, the threat from Oswiu won't diminish. As small as it is, it could still prove deadly.

I want to send my son home and ensure he safely returns, but he refuses to escape my fears and worries. Instead, I send part of the treasure trove we've won home on a fast horse, with an extra horse. My wife will be waiting for my homecoming and anticipating more and more treasure with each man who makes it safely back. But I feel its weight as a physical thing around my neck. I never felt like this when I killed men who were my enemies. But seemingly, letting one live, albeit because my allies demanded it, is a heavy burden.

My son says I worry too much. That angers me because I don't worry. I take action. I'm a warrior, first and foremost. If I'm worried about Oswiu's ultimate intentions, I think my son should listen to my caution as well.

'Father,' Paeda calls me from his position at the rear of our straggling line of drenched warriors. I hear no fear in his voice, only intrigue. I pull my horse out of line and wait for him to catch me. His eyes are quizzical, his expression perplexed, and I look to where he's pointing.

Along the line of hills we weave between, there are strange

outcroppings on the top, and on this particular one, not far from where I know Oswiu's stronghold of Ad Gefrin is, he's looking upwards and upwards.

'Was it built by the Romans or by the ancient British?' He has a keen interest in the landscape and in the men and women who lived on this land before our people claimed it.

'Woden knows,' I mumble. My interest is only in getting home or fighting Oswiu, not in enjoying the journey. He laughs and kicks his horse to rejoin the train of horses.

'Never mind,' he says, riding onwards, but I feel my gaze turning to the north. I can feel shadows in the wind.

'Paeda,' I call. He turns back to me with a question in his eyes. His hair is long and lank, laden with rain.

'Take your men. Burn Yeavering, Ad Gefrin – it's over there.' I point to where I know Yeavering is. There should be a faint smudge of smoke on the horizon to show me where it is, but if there is, it's mingled with the rain and the clouds, obscuring any sign of the settlement.

'Father?' he asks but knows better than to question my decision. Soon he and his contingent of just over seventy-five men are ready to ride toward Yeavering. I'll feel better when Oswiu's home is burned to the ground. It'll be a mark of my strength if my men scorch it. We should have done so on the journey north, but there was too much of a rush to meet Oswiu.

I ride on. I remain haunted by the image my father once described to me of the place of my death. I'm keen to be away from it, and yet I feel the pull to stay behind because it's not killed me yet. I want to beat this prophecy, as I couldn't the previous one about my brother and me. I trust those Gods my father worshipped, that gave him his insight, and I don't want them to be thwarted.

The quandary makes me grumpy and petulant. Even Herebrod, as ill and wounded as he is, shuns my company. My allies shear away from me more quickly than a sheep's coat under the knife. They have their treasure, and they want to be at home, in the warm, to enjoy it. I don't even have the desire to keep them close to me. If Oswiu does attempt to attack me now, he'll find that I have only a force of pagans to support me, and that means that if he wins, he'll have his Christian victory.

Fuck the man. I wish I'd killed him four years before. I wish I'd never left Mercia.

I wish I'd sent an assassin to steal his life with a knife.

Rather his death than mine.

When the smoke from the nearby settlement of Yeavering colours the drab horizon in a wet and murky haze, I feel I've done my best to taunt Oswiu. If he wants to continue his defiance against me, I've advertised my position. If he doesn't come soon, in the next day or two, I'll know I've defied my Gods and my father and that I'll live another year yet.

If not, well, at least my Gods will have been proven correct in everything they've ever allowed to happen in my life.

There's some comfort in that.

My Gods are true to their words. Oswiu's God lies and offers half hopes in reward for a few half-mumbled prayers.

I know for whom I'd rather die.

27

PAEDA OF THE HWICCE
NOVEMBER AD655

My father's strange mood worries me but not enough not to do as he commands.

I find Ad Gefrin silent and sullen under the grey skies that have marked our journey south. The turning of the seasons can be felt in the taste of dampness on my tongue and in the chill that permeates my clothing despite the thick layers of fur and leather.

Yet my father is victorious, and his acclaim has been reinforced once more. Not only is he a man of his sword and shield, he's also a man of inaction. He knows when it's not worth his while to attack an enemy that has nothing to offer in return but treasure.

It would have damaged his reputation more if he'd taken Oswiu's life when he had such a small band of warriors to counter my father. If Oswiu's truly given the alliance against him all his wealth and gold, then I don't see how he can continue to be a lord. He has nothing to reward his followers with, and he has the acrimonious reputation of having to give away all he had not once but twice.

Oswiu is a spent force. When I return to Mercia, I'll follow through with my intention to have Alhflæd, my wife, sent to a nunnery. I have a son now, born to me from my liaison in my uncle's kingdom, or so he tells me. While I might not want her as my wife for all time, I'd rather she warmed my bed than it was cold and sterile with Alhflæd lying in it.

No, my father has accomplished a great deal, and this harrying of Ad Gefrin seems punitive, a petty act of revenge. That worries me, for my father has never been petty.

It takes time for the fire to light the wet timbers on the great hall, on the strange stage constructed so that Oswiu's bishops could preach to the men and women of Northumbria. My men are exuberant at finally being able to do more than just sharpen their blades. The people of Ad Gefrin have long fled, no doubt seeing my father's long trail of warriors as a threat. It's only the rats and field mice that stream from the burning logs into the grey and misting day.

We passed this place on the way north. I know that in the east, Oswiu's fortress of Bamburgh lies huddling on the rocks and cliff faces. I imagine my father has demanded the fire's set to warn those who remain in Bamburgh. The outline of the fire, which on any normal day would be visible from their position, will cause fear in the hearts of those who remain within Bamburgh, whether Oswiu is returned yet or not.

I lick my wet lips, looking around with little interest. There's nothing of value at Ad Gefrin. It's as though they understood it'd be a victim of this campaign. I wonder if Oswiu did the same with his other great halls, dotted around the landscape and from which he used to dispense justice and receive his tithes.

Once assured that the settlement is burning as merrily as it can in the damp conditions, I order my men to rejoin the main body of returning warriors. It's then that Osmond rides to join me. His face is chapped with cold, and I feel a moment of pity for him. He didn't bring a thick winter cloak with him, not realising how cold the conditions would be in the far northern lands where Oswiu ran away to hide. He's been cold for much of the last few weeks.

'Paeda,' he shouts, riding his sweating horse toward me. He sounds worried but not terrified. I'm unsure why there's such urgency until he opens his mouth to speak.

'Æthelwald has taken his men and ridden for home.'

'I thought my father had agreed he could?' I ask, surprised this is what worries Osmond.

Osmond grimaces. 'He had, yes, but Æthelwald's gone without his treasure. That's not right. Your father isn't saying he's concerned, but he's ordered every man to wear his war gear. He fears treachery.'

Instinctively, I tighten the grip on my sword, ensuring my byrnie's tightly fitted against my body. My father has been waiting for this.

'Was it the burning of Ad Gefrin that sent Æthelwald running?' I ask, wondering why my father has brought this disaster upon himself. Osmond shakes his head, rain dripping from his long hair.

'No, a man came to see him. I thought he was just a monk, but I don't think he was. It was a disguise. As you left, Æthelwald ordered his men to saddle up and ride on.'

'Did you apprehend the messenger?' I ask, but he shakes his head.

'This is all second-hand. I didn't witness it myself.'

'Fuck,' I mutter angrily. 'What bloody game is Oswiu playing now?'

'I don't like it,' Osmond replies just as angrily. 'Half of Penda's allies have ridden on ahead. We're no longer the force that faced Oswiu in *Urbs Iudeu*. It might be that his two hundred men against our own, smaller force, on land we don't know well, could defeat us.'

Osmond isn't being dramatic. He's right. The alliance, which started with over twenty war bands and allies, has dwindled to half that number, especially with Æthelwald's disappearance. None of those that remain know this kingdom well. The only man who might have been able to help my father is lying half-dead on his horse and spends most of his time delirious. Herebrod is lucky to be alive.

'Fuck,' I say again, wishing I'd not followed my father's orders and set the fire. 'Hurry up, men,' I shout. 'We need to get back to the main body of the force.'

Osmond turns his horse, and we race back the way he's just come, but my thoughts are a riot of confusion and stunning clarity.

I don't know if any of this was planned, but having Penda running for Mercia will be a psychological advantage for Oswiu. He might be watching even now, tired of licking his wounds and determined to make something of his ineffectual leadership and an empty treasury.

My uncle remains with Penda, as does Æthelhere of the East Angles, Coenwahl and Ealhfrith, but Cadafael and the king of Powys have headed for home. The king of Strathclyde and Talorcan have both, by stint of where their kingdoms are, sheared away from the mass of men who rode to hound Oswiu from his kingdom.

They were the men keen to barter for heaps of gold and treasure, jewels and delicate jewellery with which they could festoon their wives and children, and who, despite our advantage, decided it was best to accord a peace with Oswiu instead of a battle. They blamed the presence of Bishop Finan, but I know they're simply greedy men.

Fuck. I feel that we've been forced into making errors where we'd only taken perfectly timed steps.

As I race to the rear of our line of retreating men through the steep hills and meandering valleys, where the cloud clings to the outline of valleys and fields, my father awaits me. His eyes aren't bleak, but neither do they hold the fire I expect. He seems tired. Herebrod's more than likely mortal wound is plaguing him. He blames himself for Herebrod's injury, but that's not a concern for now.

'Son,' he calls, beckoning me to him.

'You've heard?' he asks, looking at Osmond without rancour. Osmond has ridden to get me without asking my father's permission, but on this occasion, it seems that the oversight is to be ignored.

'We should find a peak, make our stand there.'

'We should, yes,' he says, but his voice holds no warmth for the idea.

'Winter is coming, the snows will fall soon, and it would be better if we tried to return to Mercia or at least Deira, where we can apprehend Æthelwald and discover why he's run off, than wait for Oswiu to find us. We don't have the food or supplies, not this late in the year.'

Why do you think Æthelwald's gone?' I ask, but it's not the most important question. It's what we choose to do now. My father's assessment of our situation isn't dire. It's more annoyance than anything.

'Have the men pick up the pace,' he orders Osmond. My cousin streams to the front of the snaking line of men, now encumbered with their swords, shields and coats of mail, as well as their fur cloaks for warmth. Every single man who remains has fought in more than one battle in the past. I'd trust all of them with my life. They'd easily put off any attack, but the weather is, as my father said, on the turn, and just as many battles have been fought and won because the victor knew the area better than the loser than have been fought through sheer strategy and military might.

'Paeda,' my father's voice is stern as he reaches out and grasps the reins on my horse. He wishes to restrain me.

'Paeda,' he says again. This time I take a deep breath and listen to him. This is something that he's suspected. It doesn't come as a surprise to him, although it does to me.

'You must promise on Woden and your young son that no matter what happens in the next few days, you'll make it back to Mercia and protect it.' His voice is steady, his eyes even more so. He's telling me to leave him should the opportunity present itself. 'I've not spent all my life working to make Mercia strong to have it torn down immediately,' I shake my head, trying to deny his words, but he reaches out with his other hand and holds my head in place. He leans toward me.

'Listen to me, son,' he says the words quietly, and it's that which stops my denial and makes me truly understand how hard this must be for him.

'Paeda, you're my oldest son, my greatest achievement. I want you to promise your lord and your father that you'll follow my instructions, no matter what they are. I love you,' he ends, and for some reason, I find I can't speak. My throat is tight, and my mind is filled with a hundred images of all the times I know my father has acted in my best interest or the best interest of Mercia. Men think he wanted to rule because he was an arrogant sod, but he had a vision of something greater than had ever existed in the Mercian kingdom.

He wanted to build Mercia, make her strong, secure her borders and make her rich in allies. That he enjoyed doing it doesn't detract from his accomplishments.

'Father,' I manage to squeak. He pats my cheek. There's no condescension there, only the love of a father to a son.

'Your mother knows my fears, and so does Herebrod. I pray to Woden that my father's dying words will be proved false, but if they are, it means our god is false too, and I'd rather not accept that.'

I want to know more. I want to know what his father said, but he's turned away. He's looking back toward the strange view on the horizon, where the smoke of Ad Gefrin mingles with the drizzling clouds.

'This kingdom is a shit hole,' he mutters. I laugh at him, amazed that he can be so irrelevant in the face of his worries and fears.

'I wouldn't want the damn fucking place,' he reiterates and kicks Freki to action. 'Come, let us ride for Mercia and hope we find it before Oswiu finds us.'

28

OSWIU, KING OF BERNICIA
NOVEMBER AD655

The weather's grim as I race as quickly as I can through my sodden kingdom. It's done nothing but rain since I ventured forth from my ultimate humiliation in the far northern reaches. None of my plans came to fruition there, and I was forced to accept Bishop Finan's terms to the treaty that I'd wanted to dictate.

The experience tastes bitter in my mouth. It drives me now, through the sleeting rain and the waist-high rivers, to overtake Penda before he leaves my kingdom.

I can't allow our altercation to end in this way. If I sneak back to Bamburgh, my head low, then that's all I'll ever be remembered for. I'll be no great Christian martyr as my brother is remembered. No, all that will be written about me is that I lost all my treasure, all my wealth to a pagan king who fought with Christian warriors and that I lost my kingdom in all but name as well to the holy man I thought would help me keep it.

All that will be recalled will be my inability to realise when I'm beaten and to accept the obvious and move on.

I hate fucking Penda. I always knew I did, but now the knowledge that he lives burns within my soul. I've no choice but to attack him once more. To seek him out and kill him, if I can. Anything to undo the harm that's been caused to my kingship and my reputation.

If I don't make good on the catastrophe that's befallen me, then men won't follow me, and why would they? I've nothing to give them but the seemingly empty words of my God and the possibility that they must face Penda in battle again. He has Christians amongst his warriors now, so no war will ever be one of the righteous Christians against the pagan. And certainly not when I'll be going against the words that my bishop spoke when he made the treaty.

I must be grateful to the allies who convinced Penda to settle for gold and treasure instead of my head.

Penda exacted a heavy price from me, but only because his allies demanded it, and my bishop offered it. I was surprised that he listened to them and demurred to their requests to ensure every man stayed alive. I was also relieved. Or rather, I was relieved.

Now I'm angry, angrier than ever, because the anger masks my utter humiliation. I'm the son of Æthelfrith of Bernicia and Deira, the brother of Oswald of Northumbria, the great Christian king. But I've been whipped by Penda of Mercia, a pagan with more power in his little finger to command men than I have in my entire body. I've been humiliated by my faith.

I should have settled for his alliance four years ago, but I didn't, and now he has my gold and treasure, my daughter, my son and my other son. He has everything, and I have nothing. Currently, he has complete control over the man who will become king after me if Bishop Finan has his wish.

I'm a desperate man with nothing to lose and a wave of anger that could shake the hills I rush through.

I must intercept Penda, especially now many of his allies have scurried home to avoid the coming winter storms. Penda stands weak and alone, with only twice as many men as I can command, not four or five times as many as he had when he encountered me, and that wasn't even including Talorcan's warriors to the north.

This is my kingdom. I know it intimately, and I know what this persistent heavy downpour means. It means the ground will be sodden, the rivers flooded and impassable. More importantly, it means that Penda, devoid of his guide after the kidnapping of Æthelwald's son by some of my most loyal men, a task I know has been carried out, will become lost and then trapped. I'll have my opportunity to undo all the harm Penda's inflicted upon me.

When I catch him and his retreating army beside a river or on top of a hill, I know all I need to do is win a resounding victory. All the damage that he's done to my reputation and my future will be undone with one success. But first, I have to catch him.

He was at Ad Gefrin only two days ago. The fire he set there, despite the heavy clouds and lingering fog, was easy to see even from the north of my kingdom. I've since sent men far and wide to track his movements and if possible, to shepherd him toward a difficult river crossing.

For the last year, I've done little but panic about Penda's impending attack. Now that I've lived through it, I feel more confident than ever, provided I can intercept him on his journey home.

My men, so sullen throughout the last year, so scared that they'd lose their lives fighting for a man out of favour with their God, are imbibed with new vigour. They, too, can see how we can win this after all.

It's a risk, but we're all prepared to take it. Anything is better than living with the infamy of what we've just endured.

Penda must die. It's that simple. I'll be the one to do it. Then when I've killed Penda, I'll begin disposing of his children and his nephew and niece and any other child who shares the pagan's blood. I'll win back the support of my God by ensuring that paganism is eradicated from my kingdom, from Mercia and then from the rest of the island. If I have to kill Bishop Finan as well, then I'll do that as well.

29

ÆTHELWALD OF DEIRA
NOVEMBER AD655

My uncle is a fucking bastard. I've always known it to be the case, but now I know it's true.

In light of his total failure to stop Penda and his unstoppable advance, he's taken it upon himself to further involve me in his campaign by having my young family kidnapped. They're being held as a surety that I'll withdraw my support from Penda, and because I don't know where my family is, I've had no choice but to agree to his terms. Or rather demands.

I felt sick with worry and fear riding away from Penda's retreating force, rushing through the grey, cloud-laden hills and valleys until I reached the smoother ground that leads towards York.

It was one of my warriors who came to me and tracked me down in the far northern hills of Bernicia. He carried a gaping wound to his shoulder, and he was delirious with the pain. He managed to cough out his message before slumping from his horse and dying before my eyes.

How he made it to me with his life-destroying wound, I'll never know, but I thank him all the same. I'll reward his family as soon as I've retrieved mine.

I have no idea where Oswiu may have taken my wife and two

young sons. I know he won't have sent them to Bamburgh. No, he's tried very hard to steer everyone away from Bamburgh because it's where his family and monks have sought safety. No, he'll have had them taken somewhere within my kingdom, called on some old bastard's misguided sense of family loyalty to keep the whereabouts of them from me.

I could cry with the un-justice of it all.

My uncle stole my kingdom, and now that I have part of it returned to me and a strong ally, he steals my family instead.

Oswiu needs to die, and soon, but I won't be there to witness it if he does make a last-ditch attempt to attack Penda because I need to find my wife and sons.

My horse flees over the gentle terrain, released from the restraint that we needed to show through the twisting valleys and hills. Still, it feels as though I'm making no headway, and every time I breathe, I feel like I've already lost my family. Whomever Oswiu managed to convince to breach the safety and security of my home at Goodmanham, I know they'll not be kind men. No, they'll be animals, used to getting what they want with their fists. No matter what Oswiu thinks he's accomplished, all he's really done is put them in extreme danger. If they anger the man, if they incite his wrath, they could be dead in a heartbeat.

When I can get my hands on Oswiu, I'll kill him myself for his underhand tactics. How can he pretend to his Christian God when he acts in such a way? For all that I don't believe in Woden anymore, with his lust for blood and power over men, I find that the attributes that Penda ascribes to his god, and which he lives by, are more to my liking than Oswiu's, who pretends to his faith.

Penda is a man of his word, a man of honour. He'd never kidnap a family and hold it to ransom for their father's behaviour.

Oswiu is a snivelling piece of turd. Once my family are found, and are safely hidden once more, I'll ride back to Penda and make my apologies and protect his back as he retreats through Deira. I'll make my peace with Penda, not with Oswiu.

30

PENDA, KING OF MERCIA
NOVEMBER 15TH AD655

Despite the rain and the flooded rivers, my men and I have made excellent progress through Bernicia and into Deira.

I've sent messengers to Æthelwald, and the man he sent back to me, shaken and terrified, earned my highest regard for coming before me and telling the truth of the matter. I wish Æthelwald had spoken to me before he left, but I also understand why he didn't. Nothing is more important than family. Nothing.

I understand Æthelwald's desire to be gone from my presence, but his betrayal will need to be dealt with eventually. Just not today.

I have men riding to the rear of my retreating warriors. Every warrior is alert to possible danger, their war gear hanging around their bodies like a spider's web around the corners of my great hall. They wait to catch their prey, and they fear to do so all at the same time. They don't want to be caught in a difficult situation. Still, as it's done nothing but rain for nearly a week now, and I can already hear the gushing sounds of yet another shoulder-high, swollen river, I feel that the time is near for our altercation with Oswiu.

I know he took away my guide, Æthelwald, so I'd become lost and disorientated, but it's not worked. I know some of these lands, and poor Herebrod, barely alive unless I shake him roughly, has enough sense to know where we are and to direct me ever onward. He's taken these paths almost every winter and early summer, travelling to be with his family or to return to my war band, and he's ensured we've stayed true to our path.

Yet, the news from my outriders this morning was bleak. They've seen Oswiu on the horizon. He comes faster and faster, too fast for my men to carry Herebrod and our treasure. I'm considering leaving it, only I don't want to cause panic amongst the men. They serve Penda of Mercia, overking over almost all the Saxon kingdoms. I don't want them to know we're fleeing for our lives. We're the victors, yet because my other allies demanded the treasure and not the death of Oswiu, we ride as though we lost. Even though my son understands the mistake now. I don't want it to be the last one he ever has the chance to make.

We're all cold, wet and miserable, dreaming of good food and warm beds. Oswiu dreams only of exacting his revenge against my men and me. I know that he'll take his chances today. I can feel it in the dampness of the rain, the persistence of the steady grey clouds, merging with the undulating shape of the land around me. Everywhere I look there's grey. No colour, no sound other than wet hooves on sodden ground.

My son rides at the front of the men, as does my nephew. I ride to the rear. His horse, despite his protests at the pain, is carrying Herebrod, and as soon as the three of them are over the swollen banks of the river before us, Æthelhere and I will arrange our men and make ready to battle Oswiu.

Æthelhere is keen to show his loyalty to me, his overking, and the reason he now holds the kingdom of the East Angles. I've told him the battle will be bloody and deadly. He eyed me with surprise. Never before have I cautioned anyone not to stand at my side, but this time I know that the battle might not fall in my favour.

Ever since I saw the object of my father's vision in the far north of Oswiu's kingdom, I've been keen to return home, to know that I'll live to fight another day. Now that I'm sodden and chill, with an enemy at my rear who won't leave off chasing and harrying us, who'll try any means possible to ensure my allies shear away from me, I've realised the object of the vision might have been wrong.

My father thought I'd die there, at the place he described. I didn't, but its eventual appearance in the changing fortunes of my life might well presage my death. For that reason, and despite the calmness of the last few days, I suddenly wish to rush. I want my men to live, regardless of my future.

I want to know that Paeda and Osmond, and Ealhfrith, my daughter's husband, make it back to their homes in one piece. The boys are all too young to die. They're not hardened warriors as I am. They were all raised as the pampered sons of renowned kings, trained by the best men in each warband. The battles they've fought in since haven't been the heaving, sucking mess into which this attack is about to disintegrate. They've fought before. They all have reputations that their generation admires but they don't know what dirty, filthy, hate-inspired battle is.

Oswiu detests me. I hate him too. He means for me to die. I mean for my sons and nephew to live.

The two objectives aren't mutually exclusive, and they mean that my focus is different to Oswiu's.

My wife will keep Mercia safe without me until Paeda returns. She has great warriors who'll fight for her, amongst them my brother, also dispatched ahead of my retreat. Coenwahl must live. My father told me as much when sharing his prophecy.

I almost await the outcome of the battle with impatience. I want to know that ultimately, it's Woden who has the most power, who has the biggest part to play in the stitching of my life. I don't want the Christian God to have had any impact on it. None at all.

Ahead of me, the line of men has slowed perceptively. The rain rushes down in great torrents that make it impossible to see, despite the earliness of the day. The sun is little more than a watery orb in the sky, it's light failing to disperse the fog and low-lying clouds. We slept under the dubious shelter of a small pine forest, so we dried out with the use of our fires, lit because there was no need for secrecy. Oswiu knows where we are. I've ensured that. But now that we're riding through the rain again, we're all wet and cold for all I demanded a warm breakfast be served to everyone, the remains of last night's meal. Men can't wade through rivers when they've no energy to do so, and neither can kings fight other kings.

I've been keeping myself as warm as I can throughout the long ride, making myself walk beside Freki, so that steam rises not just from his body but also from mine. Æthelhere follows my example, and so too do many of the men who know what I expect of them today.

I spoke with Paeda first thing, and wished him luck for the day. I believe he knows what I suspect will result from today's activities. I've never spoken to him of my father's words. I've also refused to burden him with any similar truths, whether glimpsed or half-glimpsed, that I might have seen of his future.

My father was a hard man, a warrior through and through, a great follower of Woden, who strongly believed in the value of blood sacrifices and cared little for whether his sons were scared of him. I'm not the same man my father was, just as Paeda isn't a mirror image of myself. Each man, each generation, must be something different if they are to survive the ever-changing fortunes of our kingdom.

My father wrote my future for me, I refuse to do the same for Paeda, other than to ensure he's safely over the gurgling river when Oswiu attacks.

While Herebrod is ill and close to death, his men have followed my orders with the same level of secrecy that Herebrod has always demanded. Early this morning, one of his men whispered in my ear that he's managed to get close enough to Oswiu's encampment to hear him telling his warriors of the plans for today.

They mean to rush us, to come at us as we try to cross the river in an orderly manner to ensure that no man drowns in its twisting torrents.

The heavy rain and the torrent it's released have brought down the wooden bridge that once spanned it. Now nothing more than the stone struts remain, and Æthelhere and I, with the support of Herebrod's men, have decided to set our shield wall behind our warriors.

We'll send the men to safety across the river while we arrest Oswiu's attack.

It's an attack born of weakness and a lack of ability.

I would always attack with a river at my enemy's back, but I'd make my presence known, and announce my intention to use my shield and sword. No such word has come from Oswiu. He thinks we don't know of his presence and means to kill us or force us to panic in a cowardly attack.

Oswiu has no honour.

I'm glad I know of the attack and welcome the chance I've had to come to terms with what must now happen. I can only hope that Oswiu drowns as well. It would be a fitting end for him. He believes submerging his head in water has cleansed him of his sin. I imagine a full-blown experience will excuse him from almost anything in the eyes of his false God.

Herebrod and I have spoken, at length, about the future. We both laughed a little at ourselves. How foolish it seemed to him to speak of a future he doesn't think he's to have, and I am, but we'll both know the truth by tonight.

I don't fear dying. No warrior should. We ride to battle or walk or run, and we know the possibility of dying is a high one. That I've lived through so many great skirmishes and battles speaks of my skill, my luck and my affinity for Woden, who rides with me today.

He's shown himself in small ways. He's turned my fractious beast into the very image of Gunghir, even down to the nipping of my ear. He's ensured my blade has stayed sharp throughout the bleak weather and that the same has happened for my warriors. This dampness should have caused our shields to buckle and our weapons to dull, but none of those things occurred. He's also ensured that we slept warm last night, had wood to burn and food to eat and that my friend has lived to travel this far south.

I feel him walking with me as a shadow on my shoulder. Woden gives no more hint of today. That was left to my father, and he did it well.

Woden is a god who rewards his followers well, and who directs their lives, but only a little. It's to others that the task of weaving my life fell. I hope that today proves the veracity of their words.

I feel the presence of others. Men who died long ago fighting for my cause. My brother and father are here. They embolden me and give me the youth they died with to empower my older body. I've lived longer than the pair of them, and yet they don't begrudge me that.

I mount Freki, and force him to the front of the straggling line of men. The noise of the river has long obscured any sound that the men make as they use a hemp rope to offer guidance across the turbid river. We passed this way on our journey north and it was little more than a tinkling stream, its sides covered in the weeds that so enjoy the dampness of the riverbank.

Now it's a seething mass of grey and brown, far expanded outside of its riverbanks, the first stirrings of its contents reaching my horse's hooves and making him raise them in a strange little dance. I tug on his reins, and he turns and bites my knee. I laugh.

Whether the beast is Gunghir or not doesn't matter. Gunghir rides with me today. Woden's spear made flesh, and I want him to live as well.

The men who've already made it across the river are beginning to stream out on the flatter land, looking for somewhere and some way to dry out from their dunking. They've worked well. A series of ropes run across the river, allowing the men to hold onto them and guide their horses if they ride and allowing those who simply walk a way of knowing that each painful step brings them a little closer to the other side.

The treasure that Oswiu forced on me, which hasn't been sent on ahead, has been placed into small sacks. Each man carries some small part of it with him. The large chests of treasures gleaming in the grey day are the only source of colour or light. I spit in their direction.

I'd rather have had Oswiu's death than gold, but I feared dying so far from home, convinced that Oswiu had found the place my father had told me about all those years ago. I should have been firmer in my resolve and ignored that image imprinted on my mind, but I confess fear took control of my reason. I allowed myself to be swayed when I shouldn't have been.

That's gone now, replaced by my determination, hatred and anger, and as I signal to my son, almost across the river, my nephew with him, I sigh deeply, the belief that they're safe making everything else seem irrelevant.

There's no way that Oswiu would risk his men in the deluge. None at all, especially when I see that on the other side of the river, Æthelwald has returned to me. He's brought his men, and I hope his family as well, to ensure we make it in one piece. I'd speak with him, offer him my thanks, but at that moment, a roar of anger at the rear of my men alerts me that Oswiu has been sighted.

The bastard.

The rain falls even harder, the sound harsh on the swollen river. It's almost impossible to tell where one drop of rain ends and another begins. It's as though the god of weather has simply released all the water in his domain in one go.

From his place across the river, I see the shock on my son's face, the anger, and then the flash of understanding. He can hate me later, for now, I need to turn and race to where Æthelwald's men, and Herebrod's, are beginning to form up. Our shield wall won't be long, but it will be deep, protecting the full half of my force that still waits to cross the river.

I turn and meet Paeda's eyes one last time. In them, I see his youth and fear and tears mingle with the already pooling rain. I raise my hand to him, a farewell gesture, and he copies the action without even realising it. I hope he knows how much I love him.

Yet before I can go any further, I hear a strangled cry and turn to see Herebrod about to enter the water. His horse meekly follows the animal in front, but Herebrod has realised my peril and tries to turn his horse against the current. Angrily, I rush down to the riverside, mindful of those who yet wait to cross and also the slippery conditions. Herebrod screams at me from his twisted position on his horse, but I can't hear him against the raging river, the flooding rain and the roar of my fear.

Herebrod has lived this long, he'll longer yet, provided I can get him across the river.

Without even speaking to Herebrod, and fearful that he'll drown himself and the horse he rides, I ride my snarling monster toward his horse and the poor animal, terrified by the river and the rain and by the beast I ride, takes its first steps into the chest high water. I watch with satisfaction, almost unable to meet Herebrod's eyes. He knows now why I spoke to him as I did this morning.

'You bastard,' I hear him shout, but his voice breaks on the word. I wish I could call him back to my side. He's my oldest friend, my most loyal warrior, yet he's no good to me in this attack. He needs to get across the river and stand with my son.

'You bastard yourself,' I roar back, my anger making my words fairly thunder from my mouth. 'Get to the other side, you fucking cock,' I continue, and the tears I felt for my son threaten to overwhelm me and perhaps would if not for the surge of men and beasts that threatens to force me into the river as well.

Angrily, I tug on my horse's rein, forcing him back up the embankment. I don't look back. I can't bring myself to organise the chaotic stampede across the river, and I can only offer an exhortation to Woden that Herebrod makes it in one piece.

I have work to do. I think of killing Oswiu with hunger.

No two men, such as he and I, should have been allowed to live at the same time. It truly is a convergence of strange worlds and new religions that has brought this moment to pass.

Oswiu is nothing. He has nothing. And yet he wants it all.

31

PAEDA OF THE HWICCE
NOVEMBER 15TH AD655

The Battle of Winwæð

My eyes open in horror as I see events across the swollen river.

Damn my fucking father. Somehow he knew this was coming. He knew to expect it and knew to get me away from him.

He knew what I'd do if Oswiu tried to attack him again but he's ensured that I can be nothing but be a useless bystander.

He meets my eyes across the surging water, its surface topped with detritus from the flooded fields, and more, with the members of our force who are trying to escape from the enemy to the rear. The three ropes that we've managed to string across the river's widened width, one between the standing stone struts and two others between well-placed trees, are filled with men and horses, Herebrod amongst them. To get back to my father, I need to either crash through them all or forge my own path above or below it, and the river is more than a torrent. It's a swirling mass of seething river and flotsam, some pieces as wide as a tree trunk, others as sharp as a knife. Neither of the options seems possible. Not now.

He knows what he's done. He knows what he means for me to do, but I can't. I simply can't leave him to whatever fate he thinks has come upon him. He needs to kill Oswiu. He needs me at his side to do so.

Half of our force has made it to this side of the river, and men stand, shivering, numb with cold and fear. The remainder is split between those crashing through the waters and those who've rushed to the shield wall that Æthelhere is calling to order.

I curse once more. Æthelhere knew of my father's plans, and I feel resentment that my father trusted him and not me. I note the exchange between my father and Herebrod. He too, is raging against my father, but Penda is determined. I can see it in his stance. He knows something that I don't and that Herebrod doesn't. My father means to fight himself and finish his argument with Oswiu once and for all.

Fear constricts my breath. The weather is atrocious, the ground slick, and the men who still need to reach safety are in as much danger as those who stand in the shield wall. The river has so far taken at least three horses and several of the men. I hope they'll be found further downstream, but I don't hold out much hope. The river is a terrible surge of freezing, dirty water, and any piece of floating debris might have struck the men and horses. They might drown and never even realise because the sense has been knocked from them.

Regardless, I rush to the riverside, hurrying the men to get out of the way, helping those who stumble over the slick riverbank to stay on their feet, the water up and over my boots. I can't take my eyes off Herebrod. My father has rushed the horse he rides through the water, but Herebrod's attention is exclusively on my father. He won't care if he lives or dies. His heart is to be with my father, and just like myself, he'll be angry and fearful all at the same time.

But I must rescue him. My father has made it clear. He expects Herebrod to live, and if all I can do now is ensure that happens, then I must do so.

The rain stings my eyes, almost blinding me, and men cry with fear and relief as they make their way through the thundering river. The sky's grey and menacing, the river thundering down the swollen banks, and there's no let-up in sight. To add to the urgency of those retreating, the sound of battle is starting to swell. I try not to look up, try to focus only on Herebrod, ignore the thundering rain and the stray echoes of anger that reverberate from the two shield walls.

I can hear my cousin urging our men to stand far from the river, to stand away from the under-assault riverbanks. He shouts his orders to those remaining on my father's side of the river to hurry and reinforce my father. But his voice can't combat the rain or the river. I feel a surge of panic from the men trying to cross the river. They know that men with swords are at their backs, but because the river is lower than the area the shield-walls have met, they can't see above the riverbank to know how many men there are. The panic causes them to make mistakes and to think only of themselves and not those in front of them or behind them.

I need them to remain calm, but no one is listening to reason. I'm amazed that men, who are normally so staid and ready to attack their enemy, suddenly fear to turn back and face Oswiu and his warriors.

But my focus remains on Herebrod. He's been tied to his horse, ropes snaking around his legs to keep him atop the beast. But the animal is as terrified as all the others in the river. Herebrod is still seeking my father with his eyes even though he's gone to fight, and he can't see what happens either. I shout to the man in front, asking him to help the ailing horse, but his eyes are as wide with panic and fear as the horses. I can tell he doesn't hear me. Angrily I look around, trying to find some way of helping Herebrod, but there's nothing for it. I'll have to go to him and risk crossing the river once more, or Herebrod will be lost.

Desperate to make myself less susceptible to drowning, I shrug my weapons from my side and my byrnie from around my shoulders. It all takes precious time, and men and horses buffet me from side to side. I know I stand no chance if I just launch into the river. My horse barely made it through with me on his back. On my own I'll be vulnerable, but I have to get to Herebrod.

His horse is barely afloat. Its eyes are crazed with terror. Bracing myself for the freezing water about to reach above my shoulders, I crash into the water, trying to avoid impacting anyone else as my breath catches and I feel my heart pounding far too fast.

Fuck, I hope I don't die here.

Men watch me with disbelief, their resolve clear, my own more difficult to determine, as I wade through the thick water, my head only just above the water line. A smaller man would have drowned already. I know where Herebrod's horse was. I feel my way along the damp and fraying rope, trying not to grip it too tightly, my breath harsh in my ears. I don't want to kill another man by knocking him into the river's current, but I must get to Herebrod.

With relief, I grab the reins of the distressed horse and tug him angrily to follow me. Pleased to have someone directing him, the beast follows without further argument. I reach out to hold Herebrod in place, grabbing his leg to keep him upright. Much of his body is underwater, his face locked in shock and fear. He meets my eyes without seeing anything. I know how he feels. But even I'm worried that he doesn't recognise the peril he's in or me.

His wounds to the chest were wicked and deep. My father thought he'd die, and that he didn't was taken by all as a good sign, but there's still time yet. I need to get him warm, get him out of the river.

Each step is agonising as I feel unseen items in the water crashing into my legs. Tomorrow I'll be covered in bruises if I make it to tomorrow.

The flood of men across the river seems to have lessened as I encourage the animal to clamber up the steep embankment. Before I can even think to turn and see how my father fares, a man rushes to take control of Herebrod's horse. The man is somehow dry, having not been forced to swim through the river. I realise it's Æthelwald. He looks at me in understanding as he reaches for the horse's reins.

'There's a hall, not far from here. I have people with warm food and dry clothes. Let me take Herebrod. Look at him, he's blue with cold.'

I'm torn, I don't want to leave the river, but I can also see that Herebrod is shivering uncontrollably, his breathing too fast. He'll die if I leave him here.

'My thanks,' I mutter, handing him the reins.

'I'll ensure he's well looked after,' he says somberly. 'Now help the rest of your men. I'll send everyone I can find to help the other survivors. Order the men to follow me.'

Stunned and frozen warriors look across the river, their discomfort forgotten as they watch events befalling their king. I know how they feel, but Æthelwald is right. These men need to get warm.

'Go with Æthelwald,' I call. Others take up the cry on the wrong bank of the river, Osmond amongst them, Eafa as well. The men are so used to following orders from them that I hope they'll simply do as they're told.

I glance at Herebrod, but his face is stony. Whatever he sees, it's not what's happening here.

'Go,' I say harshly. Æthelwald kicks his drier and fresher horse to action. Men follow him, some sullen and others tripping over their feet with exhaustion. Most have dismounted from their horses now that they're safe. The animals look sullen and cold as well but follow Æthelwald without complaint. The smell of damp wood smoke fills my nostrils. It mingles with the low-lying cloud to make it even more difficult to see events that befall my father.

Every so often, I hear a cry of battle rage, the gurgling sound of a dying man brought to me in the intermittent swirls of sleeting rain that hit me full in the face. It'll blind the men who fight for my father and help those who work in Oswiu's shield wall. I wish I could go to my father and assist him in this battle, but even as I think it a great cracking sound fills my ears. I watch in disbelief as a small flotilla of ships surges down the river. They were more than likely pulled clear from the river by their owners, but they've been caught by the flooded river and now thunder toward where I still have men in the river, trying to get to safety, and there's no time for them to get to safety.

The noise is so loud that none fails to hear it, even amongst the crying and sobbing, the growls of fear and pain. Those who can rush back to the riverbanks to either side, but those who can't watch with fear on their faces.

They're warriors. They should die with their swords in their hands, not be bludgeoned to death by floating debris.

I watch in horror as the first ship cleaves its way through the men still in the centre of the river. Those on the rope closest to the stone struts have managed to tie themselves to the stone or find shelter out of the way of the coming river surge.

For the rest, I imagine they see their deaths coming toward them.

I meet the eyes of one of my men caught in the middle of the river, a fine man, someone who taught me to first hold a sword and a shield correctly. He looks at me with resignation on his face, a wry smirk on his lips. This wasn't how he saw his death, but he meets it face-on, as I know the rest of my father's men will. The crashing ships, some of their planks coming loose, and dragging their heavy chains behind them, roll over the remnants of my father's war band.

I watch. I can barely turn my head away from the loud shrieks and cries of fear from the creaking groan of the ship, stuck on the stone strut and then lifted over its top by the sudden unplugging of the river further upstream. The water level somehow doubles, risking the lives of even those men who are firmly held in place.

Long moments of panic and shouting men, heaving timbers, and even heavier rainfall, suddenly pass, and an eerie calm falls over the remnants of our force still in the river. Those on the river banks capable of moving, rush to help their comrades, but the silence has mingled with a sudden break in the cloud cover. I turn to gaze once more at my father's shield wall, and at that moment, I know true fear.

Oswiu might not have a huge force of men, and my father and Æthelhere might well be holding them off, but not for much longer, not at all, as I see more men rushing to join the wet battle from Oswiu's side.

I can only wonder who they are, but somehow, Oswiu has found some reinforcements. With only the river at my father's back, there's little he can do to hold off the heave of the new attack.

32

OSWIU, KING OF BERNICIA
NOVEMBER 15TH AD655

The Battle of Winwæð

I turn in surprise. I'd not expected any reinforcements, and I don't know where they've come from, but I'm grateful all the same.

I'd expected to catch Penda and his men here, in this place of weakness, just before they reached the safety of flatter, drier land, but I'd not expected the resistance to be quite as deadly as it has been.

I've been watching him carefully for the last week, trying to determine how many men and commanders he still had control over. Still, I'd not appreciated how desperate frantic men can be. I was worried I'd still lose the battle, despite my better placement and the knowledge that the men stand little chance of managing to retreat across the flooded river. But now I don't see how I can.

With so many of Penda's allies rushing away to return to their homes before winter begins in earnest and with so many already across the river, I have more men than he does. I plan to make excellent use of them.

By the end of the day, Penda will be dead, and his son will be subject to me. Mercia will lie under my control.

Yet, for now, I need to focus on the battle.

It began quickly, the men forming up under cover of the overhanging clouds and then rushing to the position I'd deemed as the best one for the battle to take place in. I didn't want my men in any danger from the river. I want that to be Penda's fear, not mine.

I'd decided to direct the attack from the rear. Still, when Penda's shield wall met mine, I realised that somehow the man knew of my attack. He'd already arranged for many of his warriors to have crossed the deluged river. His arrogance that even now he can beat me had turned my blood to fire. I'd leapt from my horse and rushed to meet my men.

Penda has humiliated me too many times already. Not again, never again.

So now I heave and sweat with the rest of the warriors, even though a chill wind blows from behind, bringing with it stinging clouds of freezing rain.

I can smell Penda's men where we toil, shield against shield. I hear the grunts and groans as they try to combat the renewed vigour of my men, buoyed by the addition of some other, as yet, unknown, group of warriors.

I consider if my wife has sent them. Or perhaps Bishop Finan could finally tempt some of his Irish warriors to fight on my behalf.

My hand's slick with rain and blood, for I've already killed one man, but now comes the time for the real work. I must work as close to Penda as possible and Æthelhere as well. To avenge my brother's death, I must be personally responsible for Penda's death, and then, well then, I'll visit on his body the same wounds he inflicted on my brother. I'll display his head and his severed body for all to see.

No more will people think of me as the weak brother, the one who failed to capitalise on my brother's death.

I'll make much of Penda's death. I have it all planned. Even though he, of all men, knows that the body I retrieved from Maserfeld was not my brother's, I'll make much of the fact that I've visited the same wounds on the murderer of my brother.

I could only wish that Herebrod was fighting with Penda, but I suspect he's already dead. He was wounded in an ambush far to the north, the only success I've so far had this year.

I have my brother's white-bladed sword strapped to my warrior's belt, ready to use against Penda. But until then, I use my axe and seax to wriggle between my shield and that of my enemy and use it to festoon the day with the bright red of dying men.

I'll have my skalds sing of this day when I finally became as powerful as I always should have been. I'll ensure they contrast the red of the dying with the grey of the clouds and the sucking brown of the deep mud.

My boots are slick with blood and mud, water and filth. I'm forced to step carefully to ensure I don't slide on the surface and unintentionally allow men to kill me. I would have preferred it if the rain had stopped, but it's done nothing but rain for a week, solidly, every day and every night. I don't think my prayers, uttered from our hiding place before I began the attack, will be heeded by my God. He's too busy listening to the terrified prayers of warriors who fight for their life.

If I don't win here, I'll never rule Bernicia again or have even the slightest claim to Deira. I'm a desperate man, and reckless men will do all they can to win. I don't think that Penda realises that.

A juddering reverberates through the shield wall. I look around in confusion. I've fought in many shield walls, but nothing like this has happened. I turn in surprise to see that my reinforcements are forcing their way to the front of my shield wall and hammering their shields in place across those of the men who already stand there.

It will make it difficult to manoeuvre. I turn angrily to glare at the men to my left and right. They meet my eyes but don't explain their intentions, and as grateful as I am for the support, I wish I knew who directed them and why they were doing this.

The men brace themselves on the slick ground. Suddenly we're moving, powering against Penda's shield wall, and I think I know what the men plan to do. I react angrily, abandoning my shield where it is and going to look for whoever's men these are.

I don't wish the men to drown in the river. I want to cut them down and feel their hot blood gush over my hands and face. But my unknown ally has other plans.

I fight through the four lines of men, not caring whom I unbalance as I do so, and at the rear of the shield wall, I finally come across a man on a white horse. I gaze at him through the sheeting rain, blinking in confusion and not a little fear.

The man looks like my brother, exactly like him, as though he's risen from the dead and come to fight for his vengeance because I've failed to procure it throughout the last thirteen years.

The warrior sits on his white horse, wearing a white cloak and with a white helm on top of his head. The helm stops me from seeing who it is and why they've thought to fight with me. As I turn to look at the havoc being caused on Penda's shield wall, I almost forget that I care.

These reinforcements, no matter where they've come from, are turning the tide of the battle in my favour. I close my eyes and offer a brief prayer to my God. I've been wrong all this time. My God does wish me to win, and to ensure that all of Mercia becomes as Christian as Northumbria.

Yet it seems that my prayers are short-lived and ineffectual, for in the blink of an eye, I see men reinforcing Penda's line. I consider where the fuck they've come from. Surely they've not crossed back across the turbid river to fight at his side? No man in his right mind would think it a good idea to cross the river in spate once, let alone twice.

I look at the men, feeling a little frantic. I can't not win this battle, not now. I've staked my entire reputation on it. Yet it seems it's still not enough.

I hear Penda roaring at his men through the heavy falling rain, but it takes me time to work out that he's berating them, calling them fucking idiots, and demanding that they make their way to safety.

I don't understand why he'd do such a thing. Surely he wants to be reinforced?

The cloud cover is so low, the steam rising from the men so great, that I can barely see the river. I hear it, and I can hear the men on the other side if I listen carefully enough, but I can't see it.

'It's blocked,' a voice says behind me. I turn to see that the warrior on his horse has leaned down to tell me the news. I look back at the river and then up at him.

I recognise his eyes, but I still don't know who my saviour is.

'It's blocked,' he says again, his voice trying to tell me something my muddled brain doesn't understand.

'They can't fucking get across,' it finally growls. 'So, they're coming to fight for their king, their commander.'

It's then that I finally begin to understand, and I also appreciate that my position of power has become a thing of weakness. I have few men, and I wanted to use the river at Penda's back so that his men had no choice but to escape into its waters. But if the river is blocked, they have nowhere to go, and despairing men will fight and fight and fight. They have nothing to lose. Nothing at all.

I growl angrily. My choice of the battle site has just become a curse.

'Call the men to retreat,' the voice offers, the accent still not revealing who speaks. I tear my eyes from my shield wall and meet the dazzling blue eyes of the man. And then I swallow. It's Conall, from Dal Riata, a man with whom I'd long thought a lost ally. Certainly, he didn't come to me when I first hid from Penda in the far north of my kingdom.

I grew up with Conall. He's one of Eochaid Buide's sons, who gave my brother and me sanctuary when Edwin became king. Unlike his brother, he's prepared to ally with me.

'What? We can't retreat. This is our only chance.'

'Then it's a poor one,' he offers from his vantage point about the fray. 'You'll lose all your men if you continue, and you don't have that many to start with.'

Sudden anger stirs in my soul.

'What the fuck do you know?' I snarl, but my anger's greeted with derision.

'I didn't bring my men here to die. I brought them here to fight for your kingdom and make you loyal to me. You can be my sub-king in Bernicia. I'll let you hold the kingdom for me.'

I turn to glare at him in rage. I can't believe Conall thinks he will get away with this. Why would I suddenly acknowledge him as my overlord? I have one fucking overlord, and the idea here is to do away with him.

'Retreat. You'll die otherwise.' His tone is reasoned, silky almost, as though he speaks of which piece of meat I might eat next at a feast and not my future.

'I can't retreat. Penda needs to die.'

'Penda will kill your men. Look,' he points and I see that all my fears are coming true. Despite everything, despite all the precautions I've taken to ensure that Penda and his men will meet their death here, it seems that I've been denied.

I scream with rage and anger, my voice rising above the clash of the battle, the roar of the river, and above Conall's derisive laughter.

Fuck it all.

33

PENDA, KING OF MERCIA
THE BATTLE OF WINWÆð

November 15th AD655

I don't know who the warrior is on his bright white horse, nor do I know why men I've sent to safety are suddenly flooding into my shield wall, reinforcing it and undoing any good that the warrior in white has managed to accomplish.

Even through the cloud of sheeting rain and my sopping wet hair, I see in this white warrior a reminder of Oswald riding to his battle against me. I see the same arrogance, the same belief in his religion, and it fuels my anger.

I shout to my men to get back to the river, to make it to safety. But I also want them to remain with me and help me kill this unknown warrior and the help he's giving to Oswiu, who I also want to kill.

It seems that my faith is to be tested just as much as Oswiu's in this battle.

Men have died fighting for me, and men have died fighting against me, but the battle is still in its infancy. I hope to use my shield and sword to much greater effect than they've yet been put.

When I spoke to Æthelhere of what would happen here, I made it sound hopeless, a last stand and a way for our men at the front of our slowly retreating force to make it home alive. He agreed with my terms, even though I cautioned him against it. In all honesty, I gave little thought to how I would stand, and how I would position my men. But now, this last stand is anything but that.

I have more men than I thought I would, and the same goes for Oswiu, and despite my best efforts it seems that my men simply won't fight without me. That means I need to deploy some tactics. Apply more thought to the battle and do everything in my power to win it.

I don't think my father lied to me when speaking his prophecy of my death, but much of what he said hasn't yet come to pass. It's just possible that I might yet be the victor here.

I'll consider what that means about my feelings toward my father later when the battle is won. For now, I call on Woden, have him made flesh before me, and take courage from the knowledge that no matter what my father said, he still wishes me to win here. Woden wishes me to triumph against Oswiu. And why wouldn't he? He's a God as much as any other, and he needs followers and adherents to keep him alive in the minds of those who don't yet know him.

Æthelhere is fighting in the thick of the shield wall. I can't call him to me because it would cause a flurry of worry. Instead, I beckon for my warriors who've recently joined the battle to come to me. They're soaking wet and blue with cold, but their eyes hold menace. I appreciate they want to play a huge part in our victory.

'We need to get behind them, attack from the rear and the front.'

It's an obvious tactic for me but one that was impossible before the number of men fighting for me swelled to such great numbers. Those who I've trained know exactly what I'm asking from them, and it's not an easy request.

Everything and everyone is sodden. The men aren't encumbered with all their normal fighting equipment. Some have borrowed shields and swords. I can only assume that some catastrophe has happened at the river, but now's not the time to worry about it.

The men are keen. They know what I want.

I seek out the eyes of any I know well, of someone I can call upon to command the men once they get behind enemy lines and settle on Wulfnoð. He fought with me at Barrow Hill and Maserfeld, and he shares my hunger.

He meets my eyes, understanding quickly what I want him to do. He steps toward me as the men ready themselves for the attack.

'My lord,' and I fear to know what he's going to say, but listen all the same, reaching out to grasp his arm and squeeze it tightly, even if it's the last time I get to do so.

But he surprises me. 'We'll kill the bastards,' he snarls, and I jerk back in surprise as he winks at me and prepares his men for their coming attack.

No one is prepared to die today, no matter the odds.

I try and count my men to determine how much larger our force is to Oswiu's. Still, in the swirling rain and the low cloud cover, everything has become a hazy grey, with the occasional slash of bloody red, the grey of the inside of a body, and the flashing of a piece of metal.

The rain has drained the colour from everything and everyone, leaving us all as a uniform mass and making it almost impossible to tell an enemy from an ally. Instinctively, the men know who wants to kill them and who aids them.

I decide my numbers far outweigh those of Oswiu's, and although it gives us an advantage, I need to do more to use that advantage. We have no men with bows, and the spears we do have are too slick with water to be effective. The men's gloves are waterlogged, making it impossible to grip them well. Some men have found strips of leather and used them to tie their axes to their wrists, if not to their hands, but the same can't be done with the swords and seaxes.

My weapons glimmer in the dull light of the day, but I know it won't be long until the short winter's day is done. I need to hurry up the attack and get to Oswiu sooner rather than later.

I narrow my eyes, still sure that I can do something better than just force my men against the enemy, but Wulfnoð is looking at me. I realise I must organize the men in the shield wall so that Wulfnoð can attack. I decide to see what happens when my warriors mingle with Oswiu's before taking further action.

Hastily, I pass a shouted message along the line of my shield wall and satisfied that the men have all shared it because they won't hear me if I rely on my shouted voice, I turn to Wulfnoð and give him the command to proceed.

He licks his lips, hammers his helm in place, and, just as I've done, passes the word to the men on either side of him. A ripple effect of growling men, trying to gain some traction in the slick mud, unfolds before me. I watch as the rear of the shield wall lowers itself. They'll help the men rise high about the two quarrelling lines.

This was my brother's favourite movement in battle. A tactic I always thought would never work, but he proved me wrong. I've made extensive use of it ever since. The panic that ensues throughout an enemy line when their enemy infiltrates it is a sure way of bringing the battle to a hasty end.

I watch the men, keen to see the movements they make. I hold my breath as I watch the men move as one. They rush to the rearmost man in the shield wall and lift a leg to stand on top of the first shield. They gain as much lift as the man beneath the shield can give them to enable them to step onto the next shield and then the next. The game is one of slippery balance as they try and keep themselves, their shield and their weapons in the correct place so that when they run out of shields to mount, they can turn and meet the rear of Oswiu's shield wall without even pausing for breath.

The majority of the men make it, but I watch in horror as one of my warriors slips on the linden shields and crashes into the breach between the shield walls. His cry of terror is matched by my mine.

It's no place for a man to die.

But he's the only one of the thirty or so men who falters. The rest are successful as angry noises erupt from Oswiu's shield wall.

Keen to take advantage of the disorganisation filtering through my enemy, I urge the men to greater efforts, rushing to reinforce my men and add my weight to the shield wall.

The ground is drenched with blood, rain and piss, but I laugh with delight. I can feel Oswiu's force starting to falter, their emphasis going from one trying to force a mistake from my side, to just trying to maintain their position.

A thundering crash of something at the river makes me jump in surprise, but I don't swivel my head to gaze at it. Whatever has happened there, other men will have to contain it.

The warrior to the right of me turns to meet my eyes as we begin to take giant steps forward, crushing warriors underfoot as the line moves together. Eni grimaces at me, or grins. It's hard to tell beneath the mess of his teeth and broken nose where blood pools into his mouth.

He's been the victim of a shield to the face, and I wince in sympathy.

'It doesn't fucking hurt,' he shouts exuberantly. 'My face is too damn numb.'

The blood slurs and broken teeth he now has slur his words, but I laugh all the same. This is the talk of men too buoyed on their battle courage to consider anything else.

'Let's fucking kill them,' I roar and he nods his agreement.

'And make sure you get bloody Oswiu,' he adds.

34

PAEDA OF THE HWICCE
15TH NOVEMBER AD655

The Battle of Winwæð

I watch with morbid fascination as those men unable to cross the river because of the hulking great pieces of wood and broken ships that bar their way, turn to assist my father. The timbers are too precariously stacked to risk crossing on them and those caught against the stone struts know it. It can only be hoped that another surge of water crashes down the river to clear the impediments, but until then it's a waiting game. Those on the far side of the river have decided that if they must wait to reach sanctuary, they'll do it fighting by my father, their war leader.

I wish I were with them but having rescued Herebrod from his unstable position, I'm once more shivering and soaked through. If I stand here for much longer, I'll fall victim to the shaking disease and slowly lose my reason.

I need to get warm, but I don't want to leave my father. Even just trying to catch a glimpse of him through the sodden downpour, is better than turning my back on him.

Yet, just as Herebrod before me, my father has made his wishes toward me clear. He wants me to survive this battle, even if he doesn't. With a sinking heart, I realise I need to seek Æthelwald's hall. I need a change of clothes, something warm inside me, and then I should be able to return to the bank of the river.

Yet I don't know how far the hall is that he speaks of, and I don't want to leave. Not now.

Men struggle past me. Some have been catching their breath on the river bank, too exhausted to move despite their discomfort. I encourage them and order them to follow the line of men who make their way slowly to where Æthelwald has directed them. I hope it isn't some trickery on his part, but I'm too exhausted to truly question his motivation. Instead, I see men with lit brands, and shields over their head, trying to light the way.

It'll be dark soon. I can already see the tendrils of the early winter's day being sucked from the sky in a mix of dull blood red and even darker purples, despite the terrible gloom that has pervaded all day. I know this battle will not be fought for much longer. I have a decision to make, and quickly before my shivering becomes too pronounced.

I've managed to find a horse. I sit on his back, and his heat warms my body, not mine, as my teeth chatter. I clamp them shut to stop biting my tongue and drawing blood.

From my vantage point, I can see the men in the river, still holding on despite the water's surge and the pieces of timber that block the curve of the river lower down. The water is rising around them, and I know they're stuck in a position from which they can't escape. Not until the blockage of the tangled, broken ships and the branches and pieces of hedge are torn away by the power of the water and taken further downstream.

I want to help them, but I feel helpless. What can I do? I'm a warrior with failing strength. I've already shown that I can't wade back into the river and move the wood myself. I barely made it through the first time, and rescuing Herebrod was pure luck.

Yet as I watch anxiously my eyes are drawn to a point of brightness on the other side of the river. I'd guessed that Oswiu had received some reinforcements, but I'd not realised from whom. I still don't know who the man is, but the horse he rides, even across such a distance, is a thing of beauty. Whomever the man is, he's a king of somewhere, and just like the legend of Oswald before him, he comes as a man of his faith, imbued with the light of it.

If I had an arrow, and I knew the wind would be kind to me, I'd aim at the man, strike him from his horse and ensure he died in the dirty filth of the battlefield.

But I don't have an arrow or a spear for that matter. Due to the lay of the land, sloping gently toward the river, although now the river cuts a new wickedly cruel scar through the land, the men who fight for my father can't see the warrior. Not from his position above them all.

I'd take the time to watch him, to determine who he is, but I can see that my father and one of his men are deep in conversation. I watch in relief, and with held breath as the men who've gone to reinforce my father decide they will attempt to crest the shield wall and fight Oswiu's men from the rear.

It's a move I've practiced many times. My father insists on using it because he says Eowa was always keen to prove it's worth, which he did in the end. It's almost as though Eowa joins my father whenever he carries out the attack.

I watch, my eyes shielded against the heavy rain, falling like stones across my chill cheeks, leaving gouges in their wake, and causing my face to bleed even though I'm not in the battle. If this movement should succeed, or so I tell myself, I'll run for Æthelwald's hall, change my clothes and then come back, with other men who're drier and warmer, and see what we can do to help the men trapped in the river.

An ominous creak of timber drags my attention from the shield wall. When I look back again, the men have already begun their movement, striding high above the shield wall and dropping down into Oswiu's force. One man falters, but no more, and the response is immediate. My father's shield wall takes immediate advantage and begins to rush the shield wall of Oswiu's, encumbered now by his enemy from the rear as well as the front.

I think the battle might be a short one. My father, and I have no idea how he's managed it, seems to have gained the upper hand and I offer a blood sacrifice to Woden should he enable my father to truly win here.

Despite my earlier resolve to leave, I find that I can't turn away. I want to watch this victory and see my father persevere despite so many odds stacked against him. As though a warming wind has blown through the southern side of the river, I feel that all of the men, even those numb with cold, are turning and watching their fellow warriors. Some have a hunger in their eyes for their missed opportunity. Others watch as though they can't believe what they're seeing. But we're all watching the unthinkable. We're all watching my father and Æthelhere succeed.

A rugged cry of appreciation rips from my mouth, and is soon followed by more and more from the men. We can do little but offer our vocal support, but that we can do, even above the howling wind and surging river. Even those in the river, as though stirred by the knowledge that their king is going to live to fight for another day, are starting to make an effort to free themselves.

I call for ropes and help, and Æthelwald's warriors notice my cries and rush to help those they can. They have fresh rope and drier horses and somehow the men in the river, those for whom the water has nearly covered their mouths and noses, manage to grasp the ropes and step by step, make their way to the riverbank, to safety.

My eyes are torn. I want to watch Æthelwald's men labour to save my own, but I also need to watch this victory.

A surge of brightest red works through the shield wall, almost too bright in its intensity, causing me to shield my eyes. When I manage to focus again, I realise that many, many men lie dead and even better, I can see the warrior on his horse slowly backing away.

It's clear he came here for an easy victory and that's not to happen.

I wish I knew who he was, but the man's helm stays firmly on as he signals for his men to retreat, resulting in a great bellow of rage from a figure that erupts from the shield wall, sword in hand, shield in the other, seeking my father.

This must be Oswiu. Oswiu the failure.

I see my father consider turning to attack him, but he's busy commanding his men, ensuring the enemy doesn't escape. Men are screaming in pain but Penda is relentless. He knows how to win a battle and he must kill Oswiu, but not yet.

Instead, another man greets Oswiu and I smirk with approval. Even from here I can tell it's Æthelhere. He hates Oswiu and he has a grudge to settle with him. If not for Oswiu's support, his brother might not have tried to make war on Penda, and met his death doing so.

Æthelhere means to kill Oswiu. I'm surprised my father is content to allow it, but then, he knows that Æthelhere needs the boost a good kill will give him. His followers are still uneasy under him because of his alliance with Penda. If he slays Oswiu, they'll rest more easily and be more exuberant in their support for him.

Before the two men can even swing their swords at each other, I hear the ominous noise of creaking wood and look in horror at the river. It's so full now, backed up behind the broken ship, behind the stone struts, that I imagine the whole lot will give soon, causing another great rush of water down the riverbank.

Many of the men have been rescued but some still flounder, and despite knowing that to return to the northern side of the river might result in them being caught by one of Oswiu's warriors, they know they can't make it to this side.

Almost in slow motion I watch the combined moves of the three men and the battle playing out between Æthelhere and Oswiu. With horror I realise two things. The men in the river won't make it. The creaking timbers will give long before they can return to safety, and the other? Æthelhere is no match for Oswiu and his rage at being abandoned by his only just found ally.

With trepidation, I watch as the two events converge, the wooden timbers rising high over the stone struts, releasing a flood of water rich with stray items of buckets and branches, even the corpse of a sheep, as Oswiu lashes out at Æthelhere. With no sign of training with a sword, only anger and luck, a bright slash of red obscures my vision as Æthelhere succumbs to the first cut, one to his neck. The men in the river have their heads cracked open by heavy logs, before being swept down river, their bodies floating without resistance.

I cry out in horror and shock, but it seems my father is already aware of what's happening to Æthelhere. Only, with the removal of the ships, the river level has temporarily fallen to just above knee-high. This gives my father and his men, who yet live the opportunity to escape and to flee the battle that's raging in the growing gloom of night.

I shout to my father. He must ensure he gets across the river before the flood waters return. I know he hears me because at that moment, the rain abruptly stops, the wind dying to a whisper, and my voice carries across the river, even Oswiu stopping his action to glance my way.

I can't see his eyes, but his body starts when he sees Penda so close to him. His head swivels just as my father meets my eyes. Oswiu is looking for reinforcements and my father is trying to determine if he can engage Oswiu before the floodwaters return.

Æthelhere yet lives. Although his bright blood is the only point of light in the day, he staggers toward Oswiu, axe in his hand. His helm covers his face. His body is barely obeying his commands, but he swings all the same, his axe impacting Oswiu's back and knocking him sideways. It's not a brutal blow, but it's enough to worry Oswiu. He stops looking for reinforcements, realising his enemy yet lives and instead jumps out of Æthelhere's way, being careful not to step too close to Penda.

He too is trying to determine how much time Penda has before he must retreat.

I can only imagine that there's another blockage further upstream and that it's preventing the water from flowing freely. I have no idea of how long it will last and I understand my father's hunger and his desire to be rid of Oswiu once and for all.

I think of ordering the men to join him, to rush across the river and send Oswiu and his men scurrying there and then, but my father's men are aware that they can escape now as well. This makes them fight with less desperation and more skill.

Already many of Oswiu's men have fallen and in places those of my father's warriors who infiltrated the rear of the shield wall are meeting their comrades and just managing not to attack each other.

Oswiu has realised his peril and is scampering to where the greatest concentration of his warriors still fights. My father goes to follow him.

'King Penda,' I shout, desperate to get his attention and again, I know he hears me.

I watch him, my mouth open in shock, willing him to take advantage of the respite he's been given against the encroaching black of night, the long moments stretching out so that I think he'll do as he wants and not as he must.

But then I hear the cry I've been waiting for, and I shout for the men to bring their flaming brands closer to the river as darkness descends for the night.

'Retreat,' Penda cries, his voice rising high and carrying the full distance of the shield wall.

Although the men had carried on warring, they must have been alert for the command, for immediately they turn and run for the low river. I'm pleased I'm their ally and not their enemy. They look fearful in the strange half-light, their faces, where they're visible, covered in a grimace of war, festooned with the gore of dead men.

In their wake they leave men who are dead and dying, some simply falling as soon as their enemy moves away. I know that my father and his men have killed many more of Oswiu's men than vice versa.

As soon as Oswiu is back with his men, I experience a moment of fear. Now I do order those men who yet stand and who have weapons with them to stand against the riverbank. I don't want Oswiu to try and rush across the river as my father's men are doing.

We need Oswiu to stay on his side of the bank, otherwise this battle might well rage for days longer. But I think we have only moments before the rain and the floodwaters return. I think this is Woden and his fellow Gods giving my father the opportunity to live to fight another day.

It might not be what he wants, but it's the only sensible course of action to take.

As my warriors form up, offering helping hands to those who're exhausted from their fighting as they struggle up the side of the riverbank, I lose sight of my father, my eyes flickering constantly upstream. I think I'll be able to see when the river returns in full spate and I want to use that warning to hasten the men who're managing to flee with their lives.

I look upriver, across the river and then upriver again. My eyes rest on my father and Oswiu. As though they're not surrounded by their fellow warriors and the corpses of those who've already died, they glare at each other. The gaze is heated and with more intent than they've yet managed to bring to bear on their animosity toward each other. I have a terrible feeling that my father will attack, will stay no matter the inevitability of the water's return, and I can't let him. He doesn't need to die here, but he needs to accept that his enemy will also live.

At that moment, Æthelhere intervenes. I'd forgotten he yet lived. He moves between Penda and Oswiu, his axe in his limp hand. He begins to scythe the air before him, the movements uncoordinated, but Oswiu doesn't want to risk being hit by him again. Oswiu begins to back away into his warriors.

'Father,' I shout again, stepping down into the river. This time, finally, Penda turns decisively and rushes toward the river. He still wears his helm, its blackness seeming to absorb the drabness of the day, adding a sheen to it against all expectations.

I've not seen him, other than through the sheeting rain, for some time. Now I notice the deep slashes of other men's blood that continue to drip down his black byrnie and the gashes of maroon that daub his shield. He looks every inch an avenging warrior, and once more, I'm pleased I'm an ally. As he runs, he's trying to slide his sword back into its holster above his shoulder. I gesture frantically for him to hurry up.

I glance fearfully upstream again. The water remains low, and my warriors add their voices to call for Penda as well.

Now, the river is no impediment. It'll take my father no more than ten steps to cross it. I reach out my hand to help him, but at that moment, I hear a cry of rage from Oswiu. I watch as Æthelhere has his head severed from his body. It tumbles wetly to the drenched ground. Oswiu's remaining warriors cheer and taunt Penda as Oswiu stands triumphant.

I know Penda won't let this go without returning to the fray. I rush to meet my father, to force him back to my side of the river. He must know, as all warriors born to make war do, when a battle is worth fighting and when it isn't. I forget my fear of the river and the worry that we'll be cut off, with only each other to defend the other. As water sloshes into my boots, reminding me that I have feet, although they've been too numb, I tug urgently on my father's arm, where he's turned to glance at his ally. He looks at all of his men, slain here on the banks of a rising river by a coward who'd not only already made peace but who'd also thought to attack men in such a difficult place.

Oswiu knew how full the river would be. He knew exactly what he was doing.

'Father,' I exhale breathlessly, and he turns to meet my eyes. The depths of rage and blackness exhibited there make me realise that my task is useless.

My father will re-cross the river. He'll aim to strike Oswiu's head from his shoulders, as Oswiu's done to Æthelhere.

'Go,' I whisper instead of imploring him to follow me. I follow him into the middle of the river and then across it to the side where Æthelhere's body still twitches despite its missing head. The blood and gore pools and mixes with the stale water from the river and the muck and filth of scared and dying men.

Oswiu hasn't moved but watches my father with surprise.

'Get his shoulders,' my father shouts to me. I start. I don't want to touch the body, but my father is right. We need to move his body before Oswiu desecrates it. Penda reaches down and grabs hold of his head, a grizzly trophy. I watch in horrified fascination as he tries to tie it to his weapons belt, only his hands are too slick. The head drops to the floor with a dull, wet thud. I wince. My father wants to take all of Æthelhere back, but it's impossible with just the two of us.

It's then I realise we're not alone. Osmond stands at my side, and he lifts Æthelhere's feet, freeing my father to take his head.

The body is heavy and burdensome, but Osmond is as strong as I am. Between us, we hoist the dead man, my father standing watch and retreating back into the water as we go.

I've not even glanced upstream this time. My eyes are focused on Oswiu, where he stands motionless, and on Æthelhere's dead body.

I've never looked quite so intently inside a headless body. I feel my stomach turn to bile as I see the inner workings of what made the man who he was. The contrast of bone on blood is so stark in the almost black day that I have to look away. It's then that I realise we've delayed too long.

From upstream, I can hear the water beginning to rush toward us. Overhead, the torrential rain has started again in a downfall that lands more water on my head in just that one moment than there has been there all day.

'Hurry,' I shriek, although I don't think of dropping Æthelhere. My father doesn't seem to hear my words. Our warriors are all shouting. They can see the danger, and ropes are being thrown at us so that we can grab them if we must and stay safe when the surge makes its way to us.

The brands reflect the water back at me blackly. All I see is the darkness of death and the knowledge that I'll never see sunlight again. I stagger to the riverbank and suddenly many hands are reaching for the body as I turn back to grab my father.

I take with me one of the ropes, threading it about my hand. I just reach my father as the tidal wave of debris and water washes over us. He turns, his movements strangely slow as he reaches for my hand.

The force of the water is monstrous as it gushes over my head, filling my boots, as objects crash into me and take my feet from beneath me. All that holds me is the rope I'm just about tied to and my father's hand.

His eyes are wide, though not with terror, as he launches Æthelhere's head above his own and sends it toward the riverbank to join his body.

With both hands free, he reaches for me, but at that moment, I know that he understands he won't survive this. There's acceptance and understanding in his deep black eyes as he pulls himself close to me and plants a last lingering kiss on my rugged cheek.

His words are taken from me as tears glisten in my eyes. All I can say is, 'hold on, hold on,' but my mouth is filled with water. Wood, and carcasses rushes past me, and then the majestic remains of what must once have been a great sea-going vessel, with its high sides and heavy ballast. This, I think, must be what blocked the river upstream. Its unblocking is what casts my father away from me through the grey gloom of the dirty water, festooned with so many other items I almost can't believe my eyes. But it's my father who holds my gaze as his grip loosens on my arm, as the rope tugs on my other arm, as my entire existence comes down to this one moment in time.

My father is leaving me, and he knows it.

The rope bites into my arm, the pull from my father and those on the bank who try to save me almost tearing me in half, but I can't help it. I won't let go of my father, no matter what. Yet he tears one hand from my arm, fiddles with his sword behind his back and holds it reverentially. He won't allow himself to be cast downstream without his weapon of choice.

He's not going to die on a battlefield, but neither is he going to allow his lifetime achievements to go unrecognised.

My mouth fills with water, my breath catches, and before my eyes, my father releases his hold on me. He's torn from my side by the sudden force of the river, as I'm propelled back toward the riverbank by men who've managed to save me but not their king.

I take a huge breath to roar my battle rage, to honour my father, but instead, my mouth fills with water. I cough and hack to gain some air as I take a final look at my father, and then he's gone. I'm gasping for breath on the side of the river bank as men watch me with wide eyes.

My father is gone.

I can't believe it.

35

OSWIU, KING OF BERNICIA
NOVEMBER 15TH AD655

The Battle of Winwæd

I don't even take the time to assure myself that Penda has truly crossed the river, before I call for my men, who yet live to follow me as we rush for our horses, stabled away from the battlefield.

This skirmish has been a disaster for me. I'll not recover from the ignominy of failing to thwart Penda when the odds were so heavily stacked against him and his survival and so patently tipped in my favour.

Neither, I imagine, will my relationship with Conall ever recover.

I'm still seething with anger over his arrogant attitude toward me and his belief that he'll be able to take a predominant position of power within my ailing kingdom.

I can't believe how fleeting his assistance was. He decided I would lose almost as soon as he arrived, and his men did the same. They might have helped for mere moments, but as soon as Penda sent his man over the shield wall to attack us from the rear, his support bled away quicker than a winter's sunset.

I stumble over the dead, and nearly so. My God has forsaken me, and I need to get home and reassert my claim over my kingdom before news of this reaches those who would replace me. Men such as Æthelwald, whom I thought hobbled when even that hasn't gone the right way for me.

I don't even stop to close the eyes of those who stare at me without seeing or think about taking the precious jewels and metals they might still possess.

I have no treasure to call my own, not after I gave it all to Penda and his allies. But I want to live. I can't risk the Mercians attacking me again, not when I'm so weak.

If they continue to travel south tomorrow, I could return and strip the bodies, but right now, I can only think of getting home.

I'm not possessed of the same battle prowess as Penda, and patently, I'm never going to be. I should have left the status quo alone, not tried to force his hand. It's a damning acknowledgement for me to make, one that others have been telling me for much of my life and which I've been ignoring.

After all, I'm not my brother, Oswald Whiteblade. No, I'm just Oswiu, his brother and the man who claimed his kingdom after his death and stole it from the hands of his son. I've been punished every day since.

Once I'm reestablished and safe in my stronghold, I must consider my next steps. But right now, exhaustion wars with my grief. As I rush over the staring eyes of dead men, their hideous wounds exposed for all to see, the dull grey of flesh merging with the dull grey of the low-lying clouds and the chill of the coming night, I know the truth of what I am. I'm a failure.

This was no day to fight a battle and certainly no day to achieve a victory.

My horses were stabled what felt like a brisk march from the battle site this morning. But as I encourage my weary and wounded men back along the path, it feels as though the walk is endless, without even the flicker of a warming light from the men on guard duty; the old and the too young, almost all that's left of my small war band.

I came here with two hundred men, I imagine I leave with less than a quarter of that, and, still, I'm grateful for those who live. And worried. I'll need to present this battle as more than a total failure from beginning to end. The survivors may prevent me from saying what I wish. I might have to take more action than I want to prevent this story from becoming the one that stops me from ever ruling again.

Not that I can do much about Conall. But men won't even believe he made the journey to fight with me, let alone that he did so. I can belittle his claims just as easily as I can disparage his actions here, should it ever become common knowledge.

Slowly, under the deep black of night and the howling wind-soaked rain, we reach the spot where I foolishly wasted my time praying before the battle began. I look at it with a disgruntled twist of my mouth. Was it all a waste of my time? I think it was.

Behind me, the men follow, but they're too tired to talk. I can find no words to comfort them either. We walk in silence, only ever broken by the cry or panting of a man in pain or agony, physical or emotional.

We're broken. We might never recover from this.

We've all lost someone in this ill-advised battle. Having already lost my treasure to Penda, each and every one of these warriors knows that the reward for their work today is nonexistent, nothing more than a promise of better times to come, and even now, I can't see any better times.

In my future, I see more war and my death, much too soon for my liking.

My thoughts are as black as night, as miserable as the saturated ground underneath my wet boots, and yet, finally, out of the gloom, I see three brands flickering bravely in the rain and the wind. The sound of hooves on grass greets my ears. I could almost cry with relief.

Cold faces follow the brands. I have no words for these men

either. Where will we spend the night? It needs to be far from here otherwise, Penda might return for me. He still has a huge force of men, despite those who've left him to this final battle against me, and he could still track me down and kill me.

I saw it in his dead, black eyes. It's what he dreams of, and I want to deny him that possibility. Only I have no idea how I can accomplish that. I have nothing left but my small group of warriors, my family and bishop.

Penda has the allegiance of every leader on this island and more. He walks with Woden at his shoulder, taking what he wants, ruling by reputation alone, although not by fear. Perhaps I should have appreciated that lesson before today. That's what grates the most. He rules well. Not just with his sword and strength but also with his reasoning and his understanding of what drives men and women to act as they do.

His warriors are rewarded well, and his allies the same. And his enemies? Well, his enemies he crushes underfoot, replacing those men with ones who're more loyal to him, and if he lets his displaced enemies live, he spends the rest of his life thwarting any ambition they might have to regain their position. Ceonwahl of the West Saxons, he who married and then repudiated Penda's sister, a brave man indeed, even now has no kingdom or allies . His countrymen rule well without him and Onna, the king of the East Angles who was his supporter, is dead and rotting in his grave, the work of Penda once more. At least I still live. For now.

'We must ride north,' I call to the men who've been minding the horses, not even bothering to explain that we've failed. The men I left behind to guard my horses have realised as much.

'We need more brands, and we need a local guide to take us to a place of warmth and safety.'

I'm not forgetting that my warriors have been fighting in the sleeting rain all day. I'm soaked through, even the inside of my boots squelching when I step, and I've not even been in the river.

The rest of the men will be just as cold. Those of us who thought ahead can find our saddlebags and take out dry cloaks from them and fling them around their shoulders, but other men won't be as lucky, although they might be able to take the cloak of a dead man.

I want to search for my commanders and ensure they live, but now isn't the time.

The men on guard duty had been nursing a small fire. I direct the men to warm themselves as best they can and to eat what's left of the small feast they've had here, under their bare canvas, that's open to the elements, but that has at least sheltered the fire. I should have chosen a better site, somewhere far more protected, with a wood or forest at our back. Somewhere we could have slipped into and never been seen again.

I appreciate that every man here will have a horse to ride home, and that means we can make our escape far more quickly than if we'd had to walk.

Those men who still live call to one another, friends and relatives both, and they also call for their horses. My beast has been kept close to the fire. I reach him with relief, slumping against his heat and warmth. He bends to nip my ear, and I allow his horse breath to mingle with my cold exhalations. Anything to be warm again. I don't mind his stink or the aroma of dampness that covers him. I imagine he's as cold as I am and keen to be away from here.

I imagine I stink as well.

One of the men tries to help me unbutton my saddlebag and remove my cloak, but I wave him tiredly away.

'See to your comfort and ensure there are enough brands. I want to leave soon.'

My voice is laced with exhaustion and defeat, but he obeys my words. I wrench open the saddlebag and clasp the cloak within. It's a luxurious fur-lined cloak of sealskin, perfect for this weather. It's been made from the wealth of animals living within my kingdom, the seals caught on the sandy shores around my fortress in a more hospitable season, the wolf being caught when he tried to steal my sheep from their fields.

In my weary arms, it suddenly feels three times heavier than I know it to be. It takes all my strength to fling it behind me and then secure it around my neck. Heat immediately shoots along my shoulders and around my frozen back. I turn and attempt the next part of my escape.

Mounting my horse.

He's a patient beast, but he's been waiting all day in the rain. I smell of blood and piss, and he shies away from me. I have to call back my man and ask him to hold the damn beast still for me. He does so quickly. I force myself onto my horse's back and survey the rest of my warriors once I do so.

'My thanks,' I mutter to my man, but he's gone to find his horse. I'll need to remember to thank him later.

I look around at my reduced force. There are so few men and so many horses. We'll need to tie the unused animals to the back of those being ridden and hope they're pliant enough to follow us home. Warriors' horses aren't known for enjoying a sedate walk through the countryside, and certainly not a wet and dull one, without the comforting weight of their owner on their back.

The men's faces reflect in the dull glow of the scattered firebrands. There are at least fifteen bright points of light trying to beat back the darkness and the rain. But it's the men's faces that are highlighted that have me fearing the most. There are some who're so drained from the battle, so frozen with cold, that I doubt even all of these few will make it back to Bamburgh.

I shake my head, mocking my arrogance of the day before, the week before. I offered Penda a peace, I should have held to it. Anything would have been better than seeing this.

Just thinking his name has me looking back along the path we've just walked, hoping he doesn't stalk me and that his god, Woden, has had enough of a battle sacrifice for one day. I can see no more than a few horse lengths in front of me. It offers no reassurance that we're truly alone.

The men and I aren't being quiet. There could be anyone out there, skulking in the gloom, and I'd have no chance of defending my men and myself. No chance at all.

I want to hurry the men, but they're numbed with cold, and those who've fought beside me are all struggling to find their cloaks and mount their horses. I can't berate them when I've just done the same.

Dull voices speak, but only as much as must be said to accomplish what's needed, and then a small wooden cup of something hot and smelling of meat is passed to me. I drink it hungrily. Its taste ignites my exhaustion and hunger. I know there's not enough for every man here.

I need to find a place of shelter, or we'll have to ride all night, and the men will drop from exhaustion. I must return to Bamburgh with at least some of my men still living or everyone will know I'm a lord without care or thought for their followers.

My reputation is already in tatters. I can't allow it to suffer any more damage.

A hand on my arm.

'My lord,' I hear a croaking voice and look into the eyes of Anahun, one of the newer additions to my war band. He's barely thirteen winters old and looks about ten. For that reason, I've not allowed him anywhere near the fighting.

'There's a hall not far from here. We should go there,' he offers, and I realise that he's my local guide. That was why I let him join me. He was born and raised in this area.

'Can you lead the way,' I ask, my voice rough with exhaustion and need. 'On a horse,' I add, and he looks at me in surprise. He's not from a family with wealth. He'll have ridden rough ponies before but perhaps not great war horses.

'Yes, my lord,' he swallows down his fear. I try and smile at him, but my face is tight with cold, my cheeks red raw from the stinging rain, and I dread to think what he sees.

'Hlothere, fetch Anahun a horse,' I command above the howling wind. Hlothere does so without even questioning why I would issue such an instruction. It seems he's aware that Anahun knew the local area.

In this moment of need, I'm discovering that my allies are the men who serve me, who ride with me, not the kings in their fortresses with their wealth and their warriors to command. I feel humbled and overwhelmed all at the same time.

I should have known this a long time ago. Perhaps this is the source of Penda's great success. I'll have to think about it.

Eventually, all the men are ready, some slumped in sleep, others taut with pain, and yet more bewildered by this rapid change of fortune.

'Ride out. Follow Anahun' I command, and the animals are keen to be on their way, readily forming a line as they follow each other. I'm leading two horses, and most of the men lead at least one. They have the stamina that I now lack, and provided Anahun doesn't get us lost, I hold out half a hope that we may reach some safety, some sanctuary from where we can assess what we have and how I'm going to get us back to Bamburgh.

As I ride out, taking the position to the rear of the rest of my warriors so that I can protect them from any sudden attack from the river, I look behind me, desperate to know whether we're being followed or not. But all I can hear is the heavy fall of the rain on the dying vegetation and the shriek of the wind.

There's no one out there tonight who lives and breathes. Only the dead remain and they can have this night for themselves.

36

PENDA, KING OF MERCIA
NOVEMBER 15TH AD655

The Battle of Winwæd

I keep my eyes open as the water covers me. I want to take this time to see my son one last time on this earth before we're reunited in Valhalla.

His eyes show his fear and understanding of what's about to happen, but also his anguish. I can only be grateful that he'll be saved and that he'll go on to live his life and become the king I know he can be.

I thought I might have cheated my death, cheated my father, but I'll see him soon and I'll tell him that he was right. No doubt the old bastard will simply laugh at me, slap my back and tell me he knew all about it.

I imagine he'll sit with Aldfrith at his side, the two old men reminiscing of their youth, feasting their enemy, alongside my brother.

The only advantage is that fucking Oswald won't be with them. No, he'll be rotting wherever he is. I hope he won't be in his heaven. I don't see how he can deserve it.

The water moves too quickly, and my son, also submerged with me under the water, disappears from my view all too quickly. I've often wondered what it would be like to drown. I never thought I'd find out.

I've worked my sword free from its place behind my back. I might be about to die, surprisingly not on a battlefield, but I'll hold my black sword and take it with me to Valhalla. Its weight comforts me as I turn back, my son already lost to my view.

I hope the men manage to pull him to safety. I hope he manages to find my body. I dread to think what that bastard would do to me if he were to find me first. I imagine he'd hack me apart, just as I did his brother before him. Yet I didn't kill Oswald, that honour falling to Herebrod. I'm ecstatic that he's not had the honour of killing me.

The river is filled with debris, and it crashes into me, the air I'd been holding whooshing from inside me to bubble before me. I thought I'd given up on my chance at life, but as I watch the bubbles before, I appreciate that I could push my way to the surface, and I could live to fight another day.

Yet the weight of my war gear is difficult to overcome, as I'm turned head over heels again and again, not knowing which way is up and which way down. I begin to feel my strength weakening. Should I fight it, should I give up and allow myself to drown or should I make one final effort?

I look through the black mass of the water, trying to see if any of my God's allies will come to my assistance, but I see nothing. My ears are ringing with the sound of the river in spate and my rapidly beating heart. I feel my feet impact the base of the river. As I look above me, I see a glimpse of light and know a moment of joy. If I can just reach it.

But my lungs are empty, my strength seeping from me with every beat of my heart. I need to breathe desperately, but there's no air here. The weight of my byrnie, war axe, helm and shield means that my weakened push-off from the bottom of the river is ineffectual.

I know this will be it, that the light was just a temptation to make me fight the inevitable.

But I have nothing left to give. I clutch my sword tightly and finally allow my mouth to open and breathe in the water of the river.

I'll see my father and my brother in Valhalla.

37

PAEDA OF THE HWICCE
NOVEMBER 15TH AD655

The rope cuts into my arm, wrenching me against my will toward the side of the river.

My father's gone. I can't quite believe it, but as I feel the urge to breathe and know that only water surrounds me, I know it's true.

I also know that he knew what this day would bring, although I have no idea how.

Pieces of timber and sharp, spikey branches hit my face. I feel a long, long moment of panic before my head finally makes its way above the force of the river in full flood. I've already gasped in one hasty breath and been submerged again. This time I hope I stay clear of the water. The men are shouting, some pointing down the river, others just hauling on the rope that's grown alarmingly tight under the pressure of my weight dancing on the end of it.

Tomorrow, I will feel as though my arm's been wrenched from its socket, although I'll be pleased to be alive.

Unlike my father.

My ears are filled with the storm surge, the keening of men who've just watched their greatest king perish in a flooded river, and the outraged cries of those who've not yet realised the full extent of the tragedy here.

I kick my legs so that I'm doing what I can to aid my rescuers. I'm not a small man, and with the added weight of my shield and byrnie, it's a wonder that the rope hasn't frayed and sent me tumbling to my death.

I see the raised side of the riverbank coming closer and closer to me. I see where Osmond is holding out his arm to reach me. I flail in the water. My free hand feels heavy, useless, but somehow, I manage to grab my cousin, and he uses all of his strength to pull me clear of the water.

I lay on the bank, gasping and coughing up dirty, filthy river water as men surround me with their brands, and in the reflection of that light, I see the fears of all these mighty warriors.

Their king is dead. We all know it.

My cousin is the first to speak, and his words are weighted and heavy, spoken slowly and yet with a calm assertion that they're correct.

'My king,' he acknowledges, bowing to me whilst offering me his arm once more so I can stumble to my feet.

I'm aware then that even though my father is no doubt still tumbling through the water to his death, I must now stand in his place, command in his place, take control of our current predicament and assert my right to the kingship of Mercia.

I know it's what my father would have wanted for me, but as I feel the chill on my face, feel the icy tendrils of grief wrack my body, see the droplets of water that cover my hair, my helm having been lost in the river, I wish I had more time to adjust to what's just happened.

Only, we're at war with Oswiu and many of our men lie dead on the other side of the river. Somewhere over there, Oswiu might be watching our predicament, might be sending out men to search for my father's body.

I can't let that happen.

My cousin's eyes are shrouded with grief and understanding. He knows what it is to lose a father on a battlefield.

I swallow. My uncle is here, perhaps he should be king in the place of my father, but I know he doesn't want that.

He's the brother of a king, of two kings really, and now he'll be the uncle of one. As though conjured by thought, my uncle appears beside my cousin, the men clearing a path for him to walk through.

As Osmond did only moments ago, he turns his grief-hazed eyes my way and bows his head before uttering, 'my king' as well. I hope they don't mean to make their pledges to me here. It's neither the time nor the place.

I grasp the hands of both of these men and stumble upright. My uncle has thought to bring a cloak for me, and he peels the wet one from my back and replaces it with a warm one. The smell of my father washes over me as I notice it is indeed his cloak, black as night and laced with the fur of a black wolf.

I hold back a sob of anguish. Coenwahl is thinking more clearly than I am. He knows how important this rite of passage is.

Yet his hands linger on my shoulders. He uses the opportunity to offer me his support in a physical way as well, squeezing them for long moments as though he can give me his strength.

I know what I must do, and I cough again, ensuring that when I speak the men will hear me clearly.

'I need twenty men to ride downstream, retrieve my father's body before Oswiu can find it.'

Immediately Osmond takes control of the group of men who've benefitted from the warmth and the hot food that Æthelwald has provided.

'I need another twenty men to remain here, guard the crossing and let me know if Oswiu comes back to try again.'

These men immediately turn to Coenwahl, and I know they'll be rigorous in their duties, despite the unceasing rain and the grief of knowing that Penda is dead.

'I need five men to ride for Tamworth, to inform the queen of what has befallen my ... the king,' I stumble slightly, but no one notices. This is perhaps the least pleasant task, but Ealhfrith announces he'll go. He can ride faster than the wind, and he assures me the queen will know of what's happened. But before he and his men can go, I call them back.

'Instruct Queen Cynewise to secure Ecgfrith and my wife.' I don't need to say anything else. My mother will know what that means, and because the message comes from Oswiu's son, now a son of Mercia, she'll even understand his reasoning. He'll want to put as much distance between himself and his father as he can. He won't want any man to accuse him of plotting with his father.

He might have been born as a son of Oswiu, but he loved my father, and certainly, he loves his wife and son. He'll not want to jeopardise that.

A full half of the force that surrounded me has sheered away to carry out my wishes, but I know I have much more to do yet. With a last lingering glance at the river that's claimed my father's life, I turn and walk toward my first allies, my uncle Clydog and Oswald's son, Æthewald, who wait for me respectfully behind my men. My men, I think with wonder.

I need to bind them to me as surely as they were bound to my father, for one thing is very clear after this battle fought in a frenzy on the bank of a river in full flood, in a welter of blood and freezing rain, in the ferocity of a winter's gale, on the flatlands just outside King Oswiu's kingdom of Bernicia, my father is dead, and I'm now King of Mercia.

EPILOGUE
OSWIU OF BERNICIA, 16TH NOVEMBER AD655

We've ridden hard all day, barely taking the time to sleep in the hall that Anahun found for us the night before. We're all exhausted, but none of the men shares my fears, and I feel as though I ride alone toward whatever awaits me at Bamburgh.

I wish I were home already, tucked up against the winter storm. The rain still sheets from the heavens above. I don't think I've ever been this wet in my entire life. No part of me is dry, other than perhaps my legs, where they rest against my horse's back.

On the horizon, the cusp of the ending of another day toys with my tired mind. I want to make it to Bamburgh today. I've forced my men through trickles of water, now risen to raging torrents and across huge expanses of saturated ground where the horses had to step carefully to avoid slipping and breaking their legs. If we don't make it home tonight, it'll all have been for nothing.

All day I've felt as though I'm being chased, but as the men argue about trying to light fire brands to light our way home, I see a welcoming glimpse of the headland in the far distance that means Bamburgh is close. I allow my tense body to relax a little. I wasn't sure we'd make it, convinced that Penda and his men would immediately seek to take out their retribution against me. Now it seems I'll have some time alone to regroup. I urge the men onwards, my thoughts turning to the comforts of home and not the atrocities of war.

At some point, I'll need to send men south again to bury the dead and reclaim what little value my dead warriors had, but for now, it's imperative that I return home, and ensure everything is well within my kingdom.

I've still not fully thought out what I'm going to say about the failure of my attack but I know my men will agree with anything I say. They've already let me know as much. They don't wish to be known as failures, either.

Perhaps I'll have a praise poem written, just like the one about the men of the Gododdin, and the names of my warriors who died and those lucky enough to live, will reverberate through the mead halls of my warriors and enemies alike. All men enjoy a good story of battle and courage, somehow not caring where the men are from, provided there's enough mead on hand, and they've drunk enough of it.

As I think the thought, I turn to look back at my bedraggled collection of followers and feel a moment of pity for them, and then a deep pit of fear wells within my belly. So close to home, and yet we're not alone. Fuck.

There are riders following us. I can see at least ten of them, and there might be more. I make my men aware of our peril, and all of us look around quickly, trying to determine if the men have split a small force and are trying to attack us from the left or the right, from in front of us or behind.

I swallow convulsively. We're so close to home. Surely we can make it all the way? Yet the men are exhausted, the horses fractious from being forced through the terrible rain and being made to ride with another horse tied to their saddle. The animals are plaint enough, but I doubt any of them would welcome a sudden sprint through the wet land, and many might lose their footing and plunge to their death taking their riders with them.

At the moment, I need every man I have and every horse as well. I can't afford to lose anything, and at that moment, I notice a glint of blinding light from the helm of the man who rides at the front of his small force. I have a feeling that this might be Conall. Despite leaving the battle before me, it seems he and his men travel more slowly through my kingdom.

I feel my anger and rage resurface. I wish I had more warriors with me, and those warriors were happy to make war on fucking Conall.

I'd like to slice his neck open and leave his blood pulsing all over the slick floor. But my men could no more fight another battle than they could run for home. So I have little choice but to wait and see if Conall wishes to speak with me, to apologise for his desertion, or whether or not he just comes to brag once more.

He must see me as soon as I see him, and immediately he dispatches one of his warriors to come toward me. He doesn't exactly race across the land, nor is he slow. Soon I can see the colour of the man's eyes through his helm.

I convince my horse to walk back a few steps and settle before the rest of my men, waiting to see what Conall wants now.

'My lord Oswiu,' the man says, his voice deep and sombre but with an added inflexion that I don't understand. He's a huge man mounted on one of the tallest horses I've ever seen. I feel small next to him, and yet I'm not.

'King Conall requests an audience with you.'

The man's voice is respectful, the complete opposite of what I was expecting, especially considering the disdain with which Conall spoke to me the day before.

'Tell King Conall I'd be pleased to speak with him,' I manage to stutter. The man rides back the way he's just come, and along the same path comes Conall, his white armour and cloak dazzling in the dull day. Somehow he still looks dry despite the horrendous conditions. I'd ask him how he's managed it, but the open smile on his face and the fact that he's removed his helm makes me forget all thoughts of asking him.

'King Oswiu,' he calls when he's within earshot. 'I'm pleased I caught you.' I don't know why, but I wait for him to continue. His grin is one of sheer delight, and again, I'm curious about what he knows that I don't, but I can't exactly ask him, so instead, I glare at him, hoping he'll hurry up. If he's come here to gloat, I might just have to release my blood-encrusted sword from its sheath and slice it across his throat.

'Penda is dead,' he says, his voice filled with meaning and far too much enjoyment.

My mouth drops open in shock, and he laughs, the sound muffled by the damp conditions.

'Penda's dead?' I ask in shock. He grins again.

'I knew you hadn't fucking killed him. I just fucking knew it.' And with that, he turns and rides his horse back toward his men, not even looking back at me as he does so.

Fuck, I think. Penda's dead.

My heart pounds in my chest, and I turn toward home with renewed hope.

'Penda's dead,' I call to my men and a small ripple of shock is quickly replaced by cheering. I don't care that I didn't kill him. All that matters now is that he's dead, and his son is weak.

'Penda's fucking dead,' I shout to heaven, the deluge that covers me in response, feeling like my baptism all over again as I spur my horse for home. There's much work to be done.

I'll be King of Northumbria now, and perhaps Mercia as well.

I'm no longer a weak man and an even weaker king.

I'm Oswiu, King of Bernicia, and soon Deira, and even then, Mercia.

CAST OF CHARACTERS

Penda – King of Mercia
    Cynewise – his wife (sister of Clydog of Ceredigion – but this is my assertion)
    Paeda – his oldest son
    Coenwahl – Penda's younger brother
    Wulfhere and Æthelred – Penda's other sons
    Cyneburh – Penda's daughter, married to Eahlfrith (Oswiu's son by his first wife)
    Freki – Penda's current horse
    Gunghir – Penda's old horse (now dead)
    Alweo – Penda's niece, daughter of Eowa
    Osmond – Penda's nephew, son of Eowa (family stayed powerful into the eighth century)

Penda's allies

Herebrod – his commander (fictional)
    Immin – in this story a Welsh man, loyal to Cynewise
    Eafa and Eadberht – brothers and noblemen of Mercia
    Cadafael of Gwynedd

Clydog of Ceredigion

Oswine – King of Deira until 651 (Oswiu's cousin?)

Æthelwald – King of Deira from 651 (Oswald of Northumbria's son)

Æthelhere – King of the East Angles (brother of Onna)

Coenwahl – Penda's brother but I'm not sure I agree with this as he was barely married to Penda's sister).

Talorcan – King of the Picts (Son of Eanfrith of Bernicia who was Oswald and Oswiu's brother and also Penda's ally at Hæðfeld)

Eanfrith – King of Bernicia in 632 after the Battle of Hæðfeld (son of Æthelfrith and Bebba?) (he might only have been a half-brother to Oswiu and Oswald).

Cadwallon of Gwynedd – Penda's first ally at Hæðfeld

Eowa – King of Mercia until his death in 642 at Maserfeld (Penda's older brother)

Glaedwine – Penda's warrior

Domnall Brecc – King of Dal Riata (dead)

Wealdhere – Æthelwald, King of Deira's warrior

Brother Wilfrid – Oswiu/Æthelwald's man

Penda's enemies

Oswiu – King of Bernicia (Eanfrith and Oswald's brother, son of Aethelfrith and Acha)

Ecgfrith – Oswiu's son (youngest son???)

Alhflæd – Oswiu's daughter (married to Paeda, Penda's son)

Aelfwine – Oswiu's son

Ealhfrith – Oswiu's son from his marriage to a princess of Rheged

Bishop Finan – of Lindisfarne

Bishop Aidan – of Lindisfarne (dies August 651)

Ceonwahl – King of the West Saxons (Wessex)

Onna – King of the East Angles (also written as Anna in some sources)

Edwin – King of Northumbria until his death in 632 at Hæðfeld (Acha's brother)

Oswald – King of Northumbria until his death in 642 at Maserfeld (son of Aethelfrith and Acha of Deira)
Willyn, Oswiu's warriors
Ealdorman Alduini, Oswiu's ealdorman
Cedd, priest who escorts Alhflæd to Mercia
Bishop Birinus, Bishop of the West Saxons
Æthelfrith, King of Bernicia (killed by Edwin in order to become king)
Raedwald, King of East Anglia
Conall of Dal Riata
Anahun, Oswiu's man
Hlothere, Oswiu's man

Battles

Hæðfeld – 632 – Cadwallon, Penda and Allies against Edwin of Northumbria – Edwin dies

Heavenfield – 634 – Cadwallon against Oswald of Northumbria – Cadwallon dies

Maserfeld – 641 – Penda and his allies against Oswald of Northumbria – Oswald dies

Winwæð – 655 – Penda and his allies against Oswiu of Northumbria

Places

River *Ad Murum* – site of Paeda's baptism

Urbs Iudeu – site where Oswiu made his last stand against Penda (exact location unknown but Stirling has been suggested, as has Jedburgh)

HISTORICAL NOTES

As I've previously mentioned (apologies), our understanding of events from this obscure period in British history have survived in the written words of men who were able to write down a history of events as they knew them, either through an oral tradition or because it was 'commonly held knowledge'. This, by necessity, means that much of the history of Saxon England is couched in religious terminology. It was the monks and priests who could write, not the lay folk. Not until Ealdorman Æthelweard and his Latin translation of the Anglo-Saxon Chronicle, the *Chronicon*, in the middle to late tenth century, do we have evidence of something not written by the men of the Church and even then, it was a scholarly work and not a piece of social history, although some of his bias is intriguing as it strays from the events mentioned in the 'official' Anglo-Saxon Chronicle (but that's a story for another time).

The emphasis on when Saxon England became 'Christian' has influenced much of our understanding of this period, and I've striven to show that this conversion was overtly political in nature for the men and women who ruled kingdoms or who wanted to. It can have been nothing else. Not that I'm saying that some didn't profess true faith, I'm sure they did, but the gains made from the bargains that these men allegedly made with their conversions are too massive to overlook. In the inherently secular society we now live within, it's difficult to be anything but deeply suspicious of religion's effect on the minds of men and women. Religion has almost become a swear word in itself. (Please note I use the word religion, not faith, they are two very different beasts).

It's almost impossible to separate the history of the reigns of the kings of Mercia and Northumbria from the religious overtones they've been given posthumously, but I believe it's time that some effort was made to see through the fiction of our early 'historians' (yes, the speech marks are intentional), to determine that there was a huge amount of bias, and to allow that thinking to provide us with a more balanced view of why events happened, and just why men were prepared to make such monumental changes to their lives.

However, and on detailed study, much of what happened from Hæðfeld to Winwæd was a matter of family politics, muddled by the many marriages these kings may have made and the horde of children they fathered who had opinions and aspirations of their own. Just as the War of the Roses many centuries later, this was a time when family loyalty meant little or nothing to some people and everything to others.

Penda achieved a great deal throughout his lifetime, regardless of the debate about how long he reigned and when he could officially be known as King of Mercia. The bias of Bede and his list of bretwaldas (wide-rulers) ignores Penda and, in doing so, makes people cast their eyes only on events in Northumbria, seeing Penda in the same light as Bede would have us do, as a pagan who continually thwarted the advances of the Christian doctrine either from the north (Celtic Christianity) or the south (Roman Christianity). In fact, he could reasonably be said to have achieved far more than Edwin, Oswald or Oswiu ever did. It's a great pity that he met his death in the way he did, allowing Bede to skewer his narrative even further, to make Oswiu, the Christian, the victor over Penda, the pagan.

History can be cruel.

Yet recent historians cast Penda in a more complimentary light.

D.P. Kirby calls him 'without question the most powerful Mercian ruler so far to have emerged in the Midlands.' Frank Stenton has gone further, 'the most formidable king in England.' Whilst N J Higham accords him 'a pre-eminent reputation as a god-protected, warrior king.' These aren't hastily given words from men who've studied Saxon England to a much greater degree than I have.

Events after Penda's death could fill another trilogy without too much difficulty and I apologise if anyone was expecting Oswiu to slaughter Penda at Winwæð. After following his rule for the three books, I simply couldn't allow Oswiu that honour, and neither perhaps should our history books. The wording of Bede is vague, as in all these things. He could speak directly when he wanted to, or so it seems, but for some events, he applied a little haze of Northumbrian drizzle to obscure the facts. Still, on the fact that more men died in the flood waters than on the battlefield, he is clear, so I've allowed Penda a watery ending, rather than Oswiu's God-ordained one.

PRIMARY SOURCE MATERIAL
HISTORIA BRITTONUM

http://legacy.fordham.edu/halsall/basis/nennius-full.asp

Edwin, son of Alla, reigned seventeen years, seized on Elmete, and Expelled Cerdic, its king. Eanfied, his daughter, received baptism, on the twelfth day after Pentecost, with all her followers, both men and women. The following Easter Edwin himself received baptism, and twelve thousand of his subjects with him. If any one wishes to know who baptized them, it was Rum Map Urbgen: he was engaged forty days in baptizing all classes of the Saxons, and by his preaching many believed on Christ.

64. Oswald son of Ethelfrid, reigned nine years; the same is Oswald Llauiguin; he slew Catgublaun (Cadwalla), king of Guenedot, in the battle of Catscaul, with much loss to his own army. Oswy, son of Ethelfrid, reigned twenty-eight years and six months. During his reign, there was a dreadful mortality among his subjects, when Catgualart (Cadwallader) was king among the Britons, succeeding his father, and he himself died amongst the rest. He slew Penda in the field of Gai, and now took place the slaughter of Gai Campi, and the kings of the Britons, who went out with Penda on the expedition as far as the city of Judeu, were slain.

65. Then Oswy restored all the wealth, which was with him in the city, to Penda; who distributed it among the kings of the Britons, that is, Atbert Judeu. But Catgabail alone, king of Guenedot, rising up in the night, escaped together with his army, wherefore he was called Catgabail Catguommed. Egfrid, son of Oswy, reigned nine years. In his time the holy bishop Cuthbert died in the island of Medcaut. It was he who made war against the Picts, and was by them slain.

Penda, son of Pybba, reigned ten years; he first separated the kingdom of Mercia from that of the North-men, and slew by treachery Anna, king of the East Anglians, and St. Oswald, king of the North-men. He fought the battle of Cocboy, in which fell Eawa, son of Pybba, his brother, king of the Mercians, and Oswald, king of the North-men, and he gained the victory by diabolical agency. He was not baptized, and never believed in God.

THE ANGLO-SAXON CHRONICLE

A.D. 642. This year Oswald, king of the Northumbrians, was slain by Penda, king of the Southumbrians, at Mirfield, on the fifth day of August; and his body was buried at Bardney. His holiness and miracles were afterwards displayed on manifold occasions

throughout this island; and his hands remain still uncorrupted at Barnburgh. The same year in which Oswald was slain, Oswy his brother succeeded to the government of the Northumbrians, and reigned two less than thirty years.

A.D. 643. This year Kenwal succeeded to the kingdom of the West-Saxons, and held it one and thirty winters. This Kenwal ordered the old church at Winchester to be built in the name of St.Peter. He was the son of Cynegils.

A.D. 644. This year died at Rochester, on the tenth of October, Paulinus, who was first Archbishop at York, and afterwards at Rochester. He was bishop nineteen winters, two months, and one and twenty days. This year the son of Oswy's uncle (Oswin), the son of Osric, assumed the government of Deira, and reigned seven winters.

A.D. 645. This year King Kenwal was driven from his dominion by King Penda.

A.D. 646. This year King Kenwal was baptized.

A.D. 648. This year Kenwal gave his relation Cuthred three thousand hides of land by Ashdown. Cuthred was the son of Cwichelm, Cwichelm of Cynegils.

A.D. 650. This year Egelbert, from Gaul, after Birinus the Romish bishop, obtained the bishopric of the West-Saxons.

((A.D. 650. This year Birinus the bishop died, and Agilbert the Frenchman was ordained.))

A.D. 651. This year King Oswin was slain, on the twentieth day of August; and within twelve nights afterwards died Bishop Aidan, on the thirty-first of August.

A.D. 652. This year Kenwal fought at Bradford by the Avon.

A.D. 653. This year, the Middle-Angles under alderman Paeda received the right belief.

A.D. 654. This year King Anna was slain, and Botolph began to build that minster at Icanhoe. This year also died Archbishop Honorius, on the thirtieth of September.

A.D. 655. This year Penda was slain at Wingfield, and thirty royal personages with him, some of whom were kings. One of them was Ethelhere, brother of Anna, king of the East-Angles. The Mercians after this became Christians. From the beginning of the

world had now elapsed five thousand eight hundred and fifty winters, when Paeda, the son of Penda, assumed the government of the Mercians.

OR PERHAPS IT HAPPENED LIKE THIS???? (HISTORICAL NOTES PART 2)

There is no way of knowing the events that transpired over 1400 years ago. The words of Bede are distant from events that he recorded (no matter how people try and argue that he might have known someone alive during the time of the events – go on, try remembering what you were doing five years ago, maybe ten.) And on top of that huge issue, another surrounds the survival of manuscripts and the manipulation that might have taken place since then. The victors write history, and, perhaps more importantly, is repeated by those who have the most to gain by reinforcing those viewpoints. The history of our surviving sources (manuscripts) is just as interesting as the history they purport to educate us about, and it shows us just how flimsy any of our carefully gleaned knowledge truly is. It was men with bias who wrote the history of this period, and even more men with bias who ensured the details were passed down through the fourteen centuries since then.

That said, I'll be honest and say that I've played around with events because it's only when I seriously started working through possible scenarios that many of them began to either make sense or not make sense. There's a huge difference between making scenarios string together when you add character traits to the dry words of those who write academic history. Motivation becomes much more important, and that motivation has to make 'sense'.

Modern historians of this period do very little but offer their own opinion, albeit wrapped up in very staid sentences and with a logic that seems to make us want to believe them, but to be honest, much of what they write could be as much fiction as my own interpretation.

As such it's believed by some that the attack of Bamburgh in 649/651 (or earlier – it depends on who you ask) actually resulted in a mutually agreeable treaty – this is where the marriages came from. Others believe that the marriages didn't occur at once, that Ecgfrith only became a hostage in 655 itself and that Æthelwald was raised by his uncle. Just these few facts would make my own story incorrect and more difficult to entangle.

It's also believed that the introduction of Christianity into the Middle Angles under Paeda, and Mercia as a whole (see D P Kirby for this theory) means that Mercia was conceding control to Bernicia. (I find this hard to believe. I can't see how allowing Christianity into Mercia made Penda weaker! If anything, as a pagan king, didn't it make him stronger, more tolerant than his neighbours?)

Whether Oswiu or Penda was the more dominant king during this period, it's difficult to say, but in terms of alliances and influence, Penda grew his kingdom, whereas Oswiu's contracted from the influence his brother had held. I think that's all that needs to be known. Oswiu is known for what he was able to accomplish after Penda's death and not before.

Reputations change, religion changes, but the past is always the past. It can't be easily rewritten unless, well, unless you've got a bevvy of monks secreted away on an island in the north sea with nothing to do but write what you tell them to, and your happy to let the passage of time do its own work as well.

ABOUT THE AUTHOR

I'm an author of historical fiction (Early English, Vikings and the British Isles as a whole before the Norman Conquest) and fantasy (Viking age/dragon-themed), born in the old Mercian kingdom at some point since AD1066. I like to write. You've been warned! Find me at mjporterauthor.com. mjporterauthor.blog and @coloursofunison on twitter. I have a monthly newsletter, which can be joined via my website. Once signed up, readers can opt into a weekly email reminder containing special offers.

facebook.com/mjporterauthor
twitter.com/coloursofunison
instagram.com/m_j_porterauthor

BOOKS BY M J PORTER (IN CHRONOLOGICAL ORDER)

Gods and Kings Series (seventh century Britain)

Pagan Warrior

Pagan King

Warrior King

The Eagle of Mercia Chronicles (from Boldwood Books)

Son of Mercia

Wolf of Mercia

Warrior of Mercia

Eagle of Mercia

Protector of Mercia

The Ninth Century

Coelwulf's Company, stories from before The Last King

The Last King

The Last Warrior

The Last Horse

The Last Enemy

The Last Sword

The Last Shield

The Last Seven

The Tenth Century

The Lady of Mercia's Daughter

A Conspiracy of Kings (the sequel to The Lady of Mercia's Daughter)

Kingmaker

The King's Daughter

The Brunanburh Series

King of Kings

Kings of War

The Mercian Brexit (can be read as a prequel to The First Queen of England)

The First Queen of England (The story of Lady Elfrida) (tenth century England)

The First Queen of England Part 2

The First Queen of England Part 3

The King's Mother (The continuing story of Lady Elfrida)

The Queen Dowager

Once A Queen

The Earls of Mercia

The Earl of Mercia's Father

The Danish King's Enemy

Swein: The Danish King (side story)

Northman Part 1

Northman Part 2

Cnut: The Conqueror (full-length side story)

Wulfstan: An Anglo-Saxon Thegn (side story)

The King's Earl

The Earl of Mercia

The English Earl

The Earl's King

Viking King

The English King

The King's Brother

Lady Estrid (a novel of eleventh-century Denmark)

Fantasy

The Dragon of Unison

Hidden Dragon

Dragon Gone

Dragon Alone

Dragon Ally

Dragon Lost

Dragon Bond

As JE Porter

The Innkeeper (standalone)

20th Century Mystery

The Custard Corpses – a delicious 1940s mystery (audio book now available)

The Automobile Assassination (sequel to The Custard Corpses)

Cragside – a 1930s murder mystery (standalone)

Printed in Great Britain
by Amazon